ALSO BY ROSE SANDY

The Calla Cress Thrillers Series

Book 1: The Decrypter Secret of the Lost Manuscript

Book 2: The Decrypter and the Mind Hacker

Book 3: The Decrypter: Digital Eyes Only

Book 4: The Decrypter: The Storm's Eye

Book 5: The Decrypter and the Pythagoras Clause

Book 6: The Decrypter and the Beale Ciphers

The Shadow Files Thrillers

Breaking the Code

The Kohinoor Conspiracy

JOIN THE ARMY OF FANS WHO LOVE THE CALLA CRESS SERIES BY ROSE SANDY...

What readers love about the Decrypter books

"**Takes you on a ride** and refuses to let you off until you reach the very end." *Marie*

"A brilliant read! I recommend this to anyone who enjoys mystery, suspense, thrillers, or action novels. The **detail is astounding**! The historic references, location descriptions, references to technology, cryptography....this author really knows her stuff." *Fran*

"An **action-packed adventure**, technothriller **across several continents** like a Jason Bourne or James Bond movie, but with an actual storyline!" *John*

"**Brilliantly written**. I loved the very descriptive side, which was a good way of visualizing and getting to terms with each new place, as the action takes place in several different countries." *Sean*

"The **description is so rich**, so immensely detailed that it just draws you in completely to its world." *Denise*

"There is **great tension and chemistry** between the two main characters, Calla and Nash, that has you begging for more." *Pam*

THE DECRYPTER AND THE ATLANTIS OF THE SANDS

A CALLA CRESS DECRYPTER THRILLER SERIES

ROSE SANDY

SILVER GRAVITY

For all those who are curious about our world,
its mysteries, history and the technology that runs it.

NOTE TO READERS

IF YOU'RE EMBARKING ON THE DECRYPTER SERIES FOR THE FIRST TIME...

Hold on tight and get ready for a wild ride through the world of espionage, cyber defense, and history like you've never seen it before!

Each novel in the series is a fast-paced, action-packed adventure that can be read on its own, but trust me, you'll want to dive in from the beginning to get the full experience. In a world where technology and science reign supreme, the series explores the forefront of human achievement and the threats that come with it.

Meet **Calla Cress**, the hero of our story and head of the International Security Task Force (ISTF). Her quest for answers to her mysterious past drives her to uncover her parents' secrets and ultimately leads her to embrace her unique talents as a codebreaker - earning her the title of the Decrypter.

But Calla's journey is far from easy. As she navigates the treacherous world of espionage and battles criminal organizations seeking to exploit new technologies, she is aided by two loyal companions: **Nash Shields**, a former military man and NSA advisor, and **Jack Kleve,** a successful tech entrepreneur with a passion for adventure and a soft spot for Calla.

Their latest mission takes them deep into the unknown history of the 'operatives,' a group of tech keepers protecting mankind from the dangers of unknown and powerful technologies. But when tragedy strikes and the stakes become even higher, Calla, Nash and Jack are forced to make tough choices and fight even harder to protect the world from those who seek to exploit its advancements.

So, buckle up and get ready to join Calla on her thrilling escapades through this digital age in the Decrypter Series!

CAST OF CHARACTERS

Allegra Driscoll: International Security Force (ISTF) board member and Foreign Affairs expert. Code name: *Gold Hyena*

Sheik Amir Salib: Oil tycoon who received military combat training from Nash Shields

Avo Schneider: ISTF Berlin agent

Calla Cress: British Museum curator and head of a secret, multi-government spy organization known as the International Security Taskforce (ISTF). Code name: *Red Fox*

Frau Fuhrman: Berliner Zeitung journalist based in Berlin with a strong desire to cover the activities of the spy agency ISTF

Ivan Schneider: Assassin for hire who is undercover at the University of Cambridge

Jack Kleve: Serial Technology Entrepreneur and Chief of Science and Technology at the International Security Taskforce. Technology Adviser. Code Name: *White Wolf*

Mason Laskfell: Former head of ISTF and chief of ISTF's research, signals intelligence, and linguistics divisions

Nash Shields: Former Marine currently employed by the National Security Agency (NSA) and attached to ISTF. Code name: *Silver Jaguar*

Octavia Steward: Archaeologist and professor at the University of Cambridge

Raimund Eichel: German intelligence with a keen eye on the International Security Force (ISTF)

Rowe Norkus: GCHQ intern who is later employed as an assistant to the Director General. *New Red Fox*

Stan Cress: Calla Cress's father and former MI6 agent

Taiven: Although undercover as a butler for Allegra Driscoll, Taiven is a mysterious operative working for a secret, multi-government spy organization known as the International Security Taskforce (ISTF)

PROLOGUE
TEN YEARS AGO

GCHQ Headquarters, Cheltenham
11:21 p.m.

SOME PART of her was already immune to authority. She needed to navigate the chaos she had plunged into by arriving at the fourteen-story concrete building on the far end of a motorway near the outskirts of southeast England. The aura of complacency and superiority was impossible to overlook.

She had never imagined she could be so fervent about the truth. This place had it and was Britain's most secure vault of secrets, the Government Communications Headquarters, or GCHQ.

Her breathing was heavy and unsteady. Every muscle tensed and strained, as if she were carrying a great burden. The taste of bile filled her mouth.

If they caught her... no, she couldn't afford to be seen.

Her heart thumped, and adrenaline rushed through her veins. She squeezed through the ventilation shafts and winced as she pulled her hoodie over her head upon emerging on the other side, surrounded by near darkness.

"Not yet," she thought as she focused on silently opening the grate at the end of the shaft.

Her fingers trembled as she fiddled with the bolts, but she pushed the grate aside making no noise. As she peered into the expansive room, she emerged from the ventilation shaft and into the enormous space. Splashes of light blue and pale yellow paint adorned the walls, and steel girders and fluorescent lights lined the high-ceilinged area. Several tables were covered with computer banks and servers, and the room was illuminated by the glow of monitors and screens. The air was dim and shrouded in shadows, with a distinct smell of ozone and electricity.

The sound of footsteps echoed through the room. Security guards chatted, laughed, and bumped into each other, completely unaware of her presence.

Heart racing, she took a few hesitant steps forward, her hands shaking with apprehension. The clack of her boots on the floor echoed through the space as she hurried to take refuge behind a desk. Steel bars, as wide as her thumb, lined the bottom of the desks, giving her the feeling of being trapped within a prison. The glass-topped tables seemed to close around her, increasing her sense of vulnerability.

Something stirred, and she swiveled around, on high alert.

Two security guards, their hands clasping what could have been weapons, and their eyes focused straight ahead, marched into her line of sight.

She waited three minutes, just like her contact had told her.

The guards moved on, and she breathed a sigh of relief. She pulled out her phone, which was on silent mode, and punched in the number for her contact.

"You in?" the voice asked.

"Yes," she replied. "I'm ready."

"We're outside the building now," her contact said. "What's your situation?"

"I'm crouching behind a desk," the woman said, patting her gun. "I heard footsteps in the room, and two guards were here." She checked her small tablet, which displayed the blueprint of the building she had downloaded from the dark web. The blueprints were two years old, but she hadn't had the time to find newer ones. "I have to go."

"Whatever you do, don't hurt them," her contact said.

She slipped out from behind the desk. "Seeing as you put me here, I know that."

She stood up as the surveillance guards disappeared around a corner. "I'm going to get the information. The hack on the security systems is active. Distract them."

"I've sent an alert to the system, diverting the guards upstairs. You have five minutes. Please do it now. From now on, use the earpiece. I've connected the reception to the getaway van," the voice continued.

The line clicked dead.

Taking a breath, she rounded the desk and dashed down the aisle, keeping her steps light and quick. Cat-like, she weaved between the nondescript computer workstations. Feet pounded against the concrete floors, echoing off the walls and the filing cabinets, and she covered her ears out of habit.

She ran to the other side. Keycard in hand, she swiped the card and punched in the access code.

She entered a long, abandoned hallway that stretched before her until she saw the GCHQ vault — a large steel door with a sophisticated security system blocking her way. There was no breaking into this. Her training didn't cover this kind of lock on the door.

She drew in a sharp breath, kneeled, and pushed her hair behind her ear to see her wristwatch. On the back were a dense surface sensor and a razor. A blue light faded, and a dim red light came on, but it didn't pick up anything.

A weight settled in her gut as she fished in her pocket for a microscopic spider camera. Then the red light on her watch grew brighter. It stopped and went out.

She counted the seconds. Then she snapped the wiring around the lock and tried not to swear. She leaned to the side and unscrewed the metal plate that covered it. How long would it take? What did they use, five thousand screws? Minute after minute ticked by, and she started feeling light-headed.

The lock pins slid apart with a metallic click. It broke. Screws free, she flung the plate aside and leaned in to grab the knob, cranking it to the right.

Click.

It was on the wrong setting.

She twisted again.

Click.

It opened.

She stepped through the door and hurried into the darkness, her palms moist. She had to be fast.

The thought of turning on the light terrified her. Her feet moved through papers and file cabinets as she navigated the shadows.

She glanced back. It had been almost too easy to break into the government compound and now into the GCHQ building vault. She had come too far to fail, to get the book.

Despite its age, the vault was a marvel of modern technology, with walls and floors made of an unusual metal. Papers were strewn around the floor in a haphazard mess, in varying colors of white, yellow, purple, and pink. She longed to stop and peruse the classified notes, but time was of the essence. She had to press on.

"Find anything?" her contact whispered through the earpiece.

The woman's heart skipped a beat. "Lower your voice. I don't want to get caught," she replied.

"Okay, okay. Do you have it?"

"I see it," she said, ignoring the other books and documents scattered around the vault.

The purpose of her mission became clearer to her. The ancient text she had once owned was within her grasp. It was there, behind the glass shelving.

With a swift elbow strike, the security door opened, and her eyes locked onto the book she sought.

She hesitated for a moment and then drew it out of the safe. The weight of the book felt like a burden, a great honor. Her fingertips brushed against the leather, and she felt power emanating from the volume. She marveled at the gold lettering embossed on the cover.

A ripple of electricity coursed through her veins. With trembling hands, she opened it and flipped through pages that felt like dead skin beneath her fingertips. Time had taken its toll on the ink, which had faded and smudged. If handled for too long, the contents of this ancient book could crumble to dust.

As she flipped through the yellowed pages, she noticed groups and rows of strange symbols. Lines of quirky characters littered the pages, covered in a perfect script that had faded over time but was written in a language fading from memory. It wasn't English or Latin, but something else entirely. No one knew what the letters meant.

Her hands shook as she opened the pages further. A musty smell ran through each page, like the insides of an empty house. Fragile, it was like new skin and weak bones. The market trader in Muscat who sold her the book didn't know what he had.

The first page had a date, the next was blank, and then six bare pages followed.

She left the room but couldn't resist peeking at the book

one more time before leaving. She slipped it into a slim backpack and looked around before heading back.

Footsteps sounded in the distance.

"I have it. Where are you?" she whispered into her earpiece. "The guards may be returning."

"Go back the way you came; we'll cover you," came the reply through the communication device in her ear.

When she reached the end of the hallway, she placed her hand against the cold slate door that opened under her touch to reveal the main room with the vent. In the pitch-black darkness of the ground floor, she searched around the dark area. A glance behind told her she wasn't being followed.

The woman moved toward the vent and peered through it. As she crept back through the dusty vent, she heard an unfamiliar shattering noise.

Crazy with fear, she crawled forward.

A strange cracking noise echoed beside her as she wriggled further through the vent, toward the scraping sound of someone stepping on the grounds outside.

She advanced, squeezed through the opening, and dropped into the tunnel below that lead off to the woods where the van waited.

She saw the figure of a man - Rowe Norkus, the GCHQ intern.

"Take this," he said.

Her hands shook as she snatched the access card from him. "Glad you left the vents open."

He gave her a slight nod.

She knew the drill. People like him had ambitions. For now, he was useful. She had put him here in this establishment. Rowe had initially been reluctant to take part in her plan but soon realized that he would benefit from following her instructions and acting as her primary contact. She recalled how Rowe had given her so much information. It was almost too easy. Rowe was no longer confined to the small cubicle of an office.

A once-forgotten internship became invaluable to her. After all, he interned for the Director of GCHQ.

"That should get you past the front gates and out of here," he said, smirking.

The woman squeezed the card in her hand, studied him, and gave a slight nod of acknowledgment as she slid into the black van that pulled up to the curb.

The driver glanced at her before turning on the engine.

Twenty minutes later, they were on the A40 Motorway, heading back to the capital. She was free from the clutches of a top-secret government organization and on her way to delivering the most important information in history.

As the van sped into London, she felt pride and satisfaction. After a successful heist, she was ready to move on to the next stage of her plan. But as she peered through the tinted windows at the bustling city, her stomach knotted, and her mouth went dry. She had to find a powerful computer.

The thought filled her with dread.

SEVERAL MILES AWAY

The Blackhorse Group Headquarters
II Temple Place, London
7:21 p.m.

Stan Cress gazed out the window to the River Thames before his attention shifted back to the room.

II Temple Place was a historical building, William Waldorf Astor's former private residence, in the heart of London along the banks of the Thames. The Blackhorse Group had been granted access to this secret location by Astor himself during his time as a core member of the group.

The English had a way with color. The room was lavishly decorated, with glittering black lacquer and mahogany furnishings, and the walls adorned with richly colored paintings of literary characters.

Stan was not alone; the other Blackhorse members and the twelve commanders had gathered to discuss the fate of one of history's secrets. The group was solemn, and the silence in the room was heavy.

Stan looked around the room and wondered how they had ended up here. The Blackhorse Group was a highly secretive and unknown organization, meeting every Thursday night. Only urgent business warranted meetings at this hour.

"We can't let her go alone," Stan said, showing the group the message on his phone with a single word:

Found

Stan studied Paxton Muldon, the man who had led and protected this clandestine meeting for the past six years.

Paxton breathed heavily and rubbed his forehead, then stared at the message again.

They had to decide, and fast. They needed to salvage the situation, but how? And who else was involved?

Paxton seemed oblivious to the gravity of the problem, the lies and secrets they had shared. Something had to give, and the Blackhorse Twelve knew they needed to get involved. But how much could Stan reveal about Atlantis of the Sands, and who else could they trust?

The men, dressed in black suits with white shirts and solid red ties, took seats around the large oak table in the library. The women wore white. They all looked more like a group of accountants than the resurrection of the Maltese St. John Knights, protectors of the Earth's deepest secrets for generations. The group had recently started accepting new members by invitation only, only those who served their causes.

"Friends," Paxton began, his voice echoing through the hall. "Let me remind you of the reason we are here. We are the Blackhorse Knights. We are the keepers of history. We are the ones who prepare the world for the future, and to do that, we must fund the investigation of Iram, the lost city of Pillars, the Atlantis of the Sands." He paused and looked around the room, meeting each of their eyes. "Some of you may doubt the existence of this city. You may wonder if we're chasing a fool's errand. But I ask you, imagine what we might learn, what we might see. The sands are a treasure trove of intelligence, and we must bring that knowledge back."

"But Paxton, it's been almost a century since the last expedition," a man named Richard said.

Paxton ignored the remark, not facing the man who had asked it.

"And if they didn't," Richard continued, "what makes you think anyone else could find it? What makes you think we can find it? There's nothing that doesn't have a price. And for us, the price is more than just money."

Paxton caught Richard's gaze. "There are possibilities in this world you cannot imagine, Richard. And some people would do anything to keep them secret. Anything. We're going to find the City of Sands."

Stan listened carefully. He was on the National Security Agency, the NSA's watchlist, and who knows where else. Unless he intervened, it wouldn't be long before the entire group was compromised.

As Paxton spoke, the room filled with wary discussion from the members. It seemed impossible to get them to agree on the number of resources needed, let alone accept that what they had feared had become a reality. Atlantis was becoming known to groups outside the circle.

Stan rubbed his goatee, waiting and observing each member's reaction to Paxton's words. He knew the professor had found the city and had been sworn to secrecy. While some in the group felt optimistic about the find, they were in the minority.

Paxton stood and moved to the far wall of the high-tech library. A digital world map was in the middle of the table, its lines of latitude and longitude like a grid pattern, and a projector with several monitors beside it.

"As you know, you are all sworn to secrecy," Paxton continued. "This is everything we have been working for since the inception of this group in 1826. We are closer to finding what happened at the Divide and why. After a meteorite's impact, historians can't explain it. The Divide caused by this meteorite is why we do what we do. The more we find out what happened, the better positioned we will be."

The conversation became a mumble, and Paxton had to wait for silence.

A few were still interested in what he was saying, but most

followed their own thoughts.

"The safest place for the information we have is here," Paxton added, glancing at the group. "We have the security and backup facility to handle the intelligence on Atlantis safely. We have the best computer experts, networking experts, and data managers that money can buy. This is exciting news. Professor Octavia Steward checked in with Stan Cress last night. She has unearthed the whereabouts of the lost city. Our Atlantis of the Sands."

"How do you propose we fund this?" one of the other men asked.

"Every person here should give generously to this cause, but I have made inquiries," Paxton replied. "And when I explained my plan to the board of Kronos, they agreed to fund it."

Stan raised an eyebrow. He had a better idea. Kronos Genetisys, the German company, had tried for years to find what lay beneath the sands. They had failed to understand the key to unlocking the city's secrets. It was too dangerous to involve them. He had to think fast. "We will appoint a group of Cambridge University students to travel with their Professor Octavia Steward to Ubar under the guise of a school trip. We will select the students based on their strong backgrounds in ancient civilizations and academic performance."

"I have already made a list of potential students," Paxton added, handing out a list to each of the men in the room.

Stan's heart dropped when he saw her name.

Calla Iris Cress.
Linguistics and History Undergraduate Studies.

Stan had always been a quiet man, but he'd learned to be more secretive after Calla was born. His daughter would be eighteen now. He'd only met her at birth for a few weeks, but he knew everything about her. He had not seen her since. Now a young woman at Cambridge University, as far as she was concerned, he'd died long ago. God knew what she thought, but giving her up had been the worst mistake of his life, and now it was here to haunt him.

Had he and her mother, Nicole, done the right thing? God only knew where Nicole was. She had left him after that, never to be heard from again. They'd left each other the day Calla was given up for foster care. Now he could never find her again, not even if he tried. This group would not make the connection between Calla and him. He could prevent it. They knew he had no family. It had been a strategic move to insist that Calla's adoptive parents keep her name, not to mention the trust fund he'd left in her name, to ensure someone looked after her well.

"This has to be handled with the utmost secrecy," Stan said. "Kronos can't be trusted."

"We shall see about that," Paxton replied.

"Once the archaeologists and students make it to Ubar, they will document the city with the latest 3D technology. And Professor Steward will be allowed to take whatever samples she needs to continue her research here in our laboratories," Paxton continued.

"How will they get there?" Richard asked.

Stan had been on a dig once in Ubar to uncover the lost city, but he never found it. Now was the time to act. He spoke with confidence. "We will construct an expedition tent and a full-blown expedition camp," Stan replied.

"But how will the expedition's infrastructure survive the harsh desert environment?" a woman added.

"That's why we need to throw money at this. In addition, an experienced fieldman will ensure a safe passage and lead and organize the expedition team," Paxton replied, turning to

Stan. "A man by the name of Ivan Schneider, Professor Steward, and her assistants will go, as well as ten students from Cambridge. I would like all of you to read the file. We will have to be very discreet about it."

"What do you propose we do if they find the city?" another woman asked.

"We want to silence any witnesses like we always do around these things. We need someone on the inside, and I can arrange for that to be Schneider. I can set him up as a professor's assistant at Cambridge University," Paxton said.

Stan's heart throbbed as he rose. "You want to send an assassin on this mission with young students?"

"Is it necessary?" another woman asked.

"Yes. The plan is for Octavia Steward to be kept in check by Schneider, in case she...."

"What if someone interferes?" Richard said.

"No one will, and Schneider will get the job done. It's only for ten days," Paxton said as he took the list from the desk and put it in his pocket.

Then he went to the bookshelf, searched for records with his finger, and took down a box. He set it on the table, unrolled the inside parchment, and placed it forward so everyone could see it. "I want each of you to write down what you're going to contribute. Keeping this secret will bring substantial rewards in the future. We must be prepared to keep the city's secrets, no matter what we find next week. Ivan is there to ensure that things run smoothly and follow my orders."

Paxton narrowed his eyes at Stan. "He will do significant work that will change history forever."

Stan stared at the parchment with the group's crest and the pledges of the other members. He hated this. It was his daughter, after all. He had to take action. He snatched the scroll out of Paxton's grip and took control of the group. "I'll cover all expenses for this mission," he said, "and I will coordinate everything." But even as he spoke these words, Stan's heart was filled with hesitation and an undeniable fear of what was to come.

"That's a lot of money, Stan," Paxton said. "Are you sure?"

"Yes. If it gets out that the group is up to something, the government will try to stop us. The students and staff must not know our connection to this, and I can pay for that kind of discretion."

The group nodded and set their seals on the new mission before departing.

Paxton approached Stan after everyone had left. "This has nothing to do with the fact that Ivan Schneider works in MI6 with you, does it?"

"My reasons are my own," Stan replied.

Pax's gaze was as penetrating as it was annoying by now. "Why did you join the Blackhorse Group?" Paxton asked.

"What do you mean?" Stan replied, putting on his coat.

"I mean, you, too, work for MI6. You could run many secret operations around the world. Why did you choose to dedicate yourself to this group?"

Stan clenched his fingers together. "My great-great-grandfather was a founding member of the Blackhorse Knights. My bloodline is tied to everything we do. Let's say I have my reasons."

Paxton smiled and joined his hands together. "You're a talented man, Stan Cress. Wealthy as hell and a spy, yet this cause interests you. It's intriguing."

"If you don't mind, I'd rather not discuss it," Stan said, rising.

Paxton nodded and glanced out the window. "I'll accept that as a 'no comment' for now, but that's not what I wanted to talk to you about. There's one more thing. If the city turns out to be what we think it is, some of them won't come back from that expedition in one piece."

RUINS OF KNOSSOS PALACE,
ISLAND OF CRETE

2:21 p.m.

THE ATTACK CAME FROM ABOVE, and Calla Cress quickly spun around, knowing all too well what it meant. He might have been twice her weight, but she wouldn't let him pass the ancient Minoan gate of Europe's oldest city.

Wiping blood from her lips with the back of her hand, Calla booted the lone attacker in the groin, catching him off guard. She followed up with a punch to the face, energy shooting through her as he stumbled backward.

His face twisted in anger before he sneered at her.

She lunged forward, her fists raised.

In one swift movement, the attacker leaped forward, his body a flurry of power and force. Before Calla could react, he caught her fist mid-swing and yanked her toward him, sending her tumbling to the ground.

Rolling up onto her feet, Calla turned to face him and sent a punch to his gut, followed by a boot to the chest.

He stumbled backward, away from her and the sanctuaries

of Minoan civilization. She had never felt so empowered, so angry.

He grabbed her leg and drove her back to the ground, but Calla refused to give up. Just as he was about to overpower her, a gunshot rang out, and she took her chance to thump him in the pelvis.

He collapsed to the ground, unconscious.

Ground commander Nash Shields rushed to her side. "Are you okay?"

Calla smiled at his handsome face. He could do it for her anytime with that look: strong frame, toned abs, deep gray eyes, and a clean-shaven face. Nash was a fine specimen of Earth males. He had her heart when she first met him, and he still had it. His Marine background intrigued her, and his intelligence didn't stop in the field. Right now, his awareness of the Minoan culture, heritage, and languages won her over.

She didn't know how he did it, but then again, he had been working with the International Security Taskforce, ISTF, an espionage agency linked to five government agency arms, for a few years. He had even assisted with the newly formed Alpha Force, which she had been asking him about.

Looking around at the ancient Palace of Knossos, Calla said, "Yeah, we're done here. I think he was the last one."

The grounds of the palace stood in silence. A few birds called out above the crumbling ruins, their chirps echoing off marble walls and clay buildings. A gentle breeze wafted through the ruins, accompanying Calla, Nash, and their dependable head of technology and science at ISTF, Jack Kleve, as they paced past temples, courtyards, and statues, all still in one piece thanks to the efforts of the Greek Knossos Foundation, which had poured money into the site to preserve it. Knossos was the capital of the Minoan civilization, and the concept of a palace made legendary by a king was fascinating, especially when that king was said to have created an infamous maze as a deathtrap.

They had limited time to find the three bombs that Jack had traced to the site. Calla wondered how Jack figured these things out. Like Nash, he could handle himself and track any abnormalities in physics, such as those recent UAPs or unidentified aerial phenomena. This was because Jack had an excellent working knowledge of technology and science, and had a background in espionage, just like Nash. She only wished she had a fraction of Jack's curiosity about how the world worked.

Trained in the field more than most, both men could fight back any assailant. They each had an amiable smile, although Nash's was more of a half-smile, and they were both as sweet as apple pie. Like now, they were both playing gentlemen, as always.

Calla wasn't too bad in the field herself, though not by choice, and had a few scrapes and bruises, just like they did. She was so lucky to have them. Together, they made a formidable team. She smiled her thanks at Nash and touched Jack's shoulder.

Nash radioed the Greek ground forces at the site's entrance through his earpiece. "We've cleared the south entrance. You can pick this last one up before we go in."

Only minutes ago, they had arrived at the gates of Knossos. Calla had not known what to expect as she took the small team through the north entrance. Someone did not want them there. Someone had made this threat personal to her by bringing the fight to Knossos. After all, she preserved history at the British Museum in London when not working for ISTF. This was mostly so she could understand her past and her future.

"I'll search the north side of the palace," Calla said, pointing to the left. "You and Jack can search the right." She held up her tablet to show them the schematic. "You should stick close to the walls. The hacker's cipher from Jack's interception shows the three bombs are close. If I find the first one, I'll radio you."

Calla's muscles strained as she walked.

Three minutes later, they regrouped, but without a bomb in sight, time was running out. If she didn't disarm the bombs in time, the entire site would be destroyed.

"Who's doing this?" Jack asked.

Nash spoke first. "I'm not sure, but they're trying to send a message. This hacker has struck before, in Malta."

Calla stopped and swung around. She knew what Nash meant but couldn't think about it now.

"Three explosive points," Jack added. "According to the phishing emails sent to Greek Intelligence."

Calla groaned as Jack stopped in his tracks. "I have four minutes on the clock if I'm right, and we should be close to the first one," he said, his eyes glued to his mini tablet. "My tracker is picking up heat."

"Okay," Calla said. "It doesn't help that each of the three bombs is coded with an ancient cipher of some sort. That information was useful, Jack."

Nash scanned the area for explosives with his equipment. "Then I'm glad we have you, the Decrypter."

She gave him a gentle punch to the shoulder. "Hilarious."

"It won't be if we don't wrap this first one up in three minutes and seven seconds," Jack chimed in, studying his datapad.

They proceeded into a marble room, crunching white sand under their boots. Frescoed walls were painted with colorful Greek gods and goddesses greeted them, some of which were still bright, while others had faded after many years. They hurried through an archway into a small, circular room covered in ancient pottery shards. When they reached the far wall, they saw it.

It was a strange device attached to a touchscreen that transmitted coded language with a light beam on a terrace wall, displaying a grandiose fresco.

Calla studied the code. A beeping sound came from the explosive, the size of a football and covered with a thick layer of dust. She had never seen anything like it. Its black cylindrical cables and wires were connected to a laptop. The screen showed different numbers changing constantly.

Bombs were the ultimate weapon, and to Calla, this one reeked of disaster. It was one of the worst smells she had ever encountered, with its pungent odor of melted insulation. The stench of dead electronics and sulfur nearly overwhelmed them. Then they heard a calming hum, a quiet hiss, and a whir of electricity. A faint ticking of a clock and a soft ping of metal cooling were all they had to go on for now. Hearing a soft, steady beep, she inspected the device.

Calla studied the cipher again, drawn to the fourth row from the top with a star in the middle. A series of dots and circles were etched into the base of the Minoan text. She translated and read aloud, "The female goddess, the blessed mistress of the underworld, keeper of secrets and wisdom, who weighs the souls of the dead and decides where they go, who cuts the thread of life at the end of time, who gives life and substance to the world, and whose name is spoken only once in a day, who blesses man and beast, who sees all and knows all, who blesses the beginning of all things, and endures to the end of all things."

Her fingers flew across the keyboard attached to the bomb in front of her, decoding the message. "I think I can get us out of this." She glanced back at Nash. His face was uneasy and tight, but she saw relief on it as she typed the last word.

They were going to be okay. The bomber was playing riddles with her and had explicitly chosen puzzles to arm the bombs. Why?

The bomber had also pointedly called for the Decrypter. It had taken Greek Intelligence several tries before they understood and reached out to GCHQ, who connected them with ISTF.

The beeping quickened.

Calla could see cold sweat breaking out on Jack's forehead. She was determined to get them out of there. The thought of perishing in a bomb explosion wasn't something she was ready for yet. She had too much life to live. Her heart throbbed as she punched more symbols on the keyboard. "Besides Minoan mythology, it's based on the Albert Disk," she said, moving her fingers over the letters and signs on the keyboard.

The familiar shapes and curves of the disk were etched in Calla's mind, perhaps because of her natural knack for code breaking. She immediately recognized the functions as she recalled the disk in her mind. It comprised two concentric rings: the outer ring was engraved with a standard alphabet, and the inner circle was inscribed with letters written out of order. By rotating the inner ring, a coder could use one set of letters to represent another and vice versa, rather than simply using a one-to-one substitution such as 'A' for 'B.' The engravings within the Albert Disk were of the alphabet written in reverse, with one symbol for each letter in the alphabet.

"Thirty seconds, Cal," Jack called out.

"I need to imagine rotating the inner ring of the Albert Disk," Calla said, her voice trembling as she looked at the computer screen, which displayed symbols that matched the characters on the Albert Disk. Then the gibberish transformed into new symbols, which corresponded to the inner ring of the Disk.

Nash took a sharp breath.

The computer screen displayed a line of code as the beeping grew faster.

Jack's voice was strained. "Fifteen seconds."

CHAPTER
TWO

JACK'S VOICE wasn't helping Calla concentrate.

When she read the last symbol, a wave of excitement washed over her. The characters were coordinates for a star system. She spun the Disk around in her mind repeatedly, reading it from different angles of light and shadow until she felt she had memorized it all over again.

Then she searched through her pocket for her communication device, brought up a 3D map of the local region, and plugged the coordinates into it. When she saw the name of the closest planet to them, she grinned. "There!"

She punched the last keys, and they took a deep breath as the light on the explosive went out altogether.

"That's my girl; you get it each time," Nash said.

"Right," Jack said. "We have two more, and it's coming from about thirty feet from here."

They shuffled through the entrance and entered an ancient, decrepit chamber.

Calla had heard of this, something not known to many scholars, the secret maze in the Knossos Palace, filled with archaic ridges based on ancient architecture.

She put her hand into a hole in the wall and pulled at what her hands uncovered. Dirt and rock scraped her fingers, and the hole tore at her skin. She kept pulling, and the hole burst wider as she felt for a latch under the surface and found one. There was a click, and the wall crumbled.

She had not wanted to do that to the wall, but then again, it was the only way in, and the bomber had known that.

"Quick," Calla said. "Let's go."

"Now, why didn't I think of that?" Jack said.

Calla shot him a smirk as they inched through to the dark room. "It's in here somewhere," Jack said. "The ticking is this way," he said, pointing to their left.

"Okay," Nash said, lighting a flashlight on his combat gear and leading them to an opening in the corner of the room.

They walked in silence, their footsteps echoing in the empty ancient hallways.

The ground beneath their feet vibrated, then convulsed.

They looked around, then up.

A loud, metallic clanking resounded high above them.

The sound bounced through the cavern and off the walls.

They turned to an opening on their right, dimly lit by sun rays. It was deep, dark, and foreboding.

The clanking sounded again, powerful and closer. Then, iron grating against stone echoed through the room.

"Let's continue," Calla said.

They moved into the darkness. The clanking sound grew louder as a strong and sharp gust rushed toward them from an old mechanical wheel turning on the floor. The wheel was attached to a long metal rod that ran up the wall and into the ceiling.

"Look," Nash said, pointing to a small metal box on the wall.

It had three buttons, each with a picture of an animal: a lion, a snake, and an eagle.

"They look like Egyptian hieroglyphs," Jack said. "What do they mean?"

Calla scrutinized each animal carefully. "The lion represents strength, the snake represents cunning, and the eagle represents wisdom," she said.

"So, what do we do?" Jack asked. "Do we push a button or something?"

They glanced down at the base of the wall. Like the first explosive, the bomber had attached the second one to a laptop.

"It's an ancient language," Calla said, approaching and studying the symbols on the bomb's laptop. "I've seen nothing like it before."

"Do you have any idea what it means?" Nash asked.

She nodded. "I have an inkling."

"That's why we need you," Nash said. "You're the best codebreaker of ancient ciphers and languages."

"I think I've got it," Calla said.

The men studied her.

"It's in archaic Latin," she said. "I'm going to change the keyboard settings from Greek to Latin."

Calla began working on the keyboard. "This one's trickier, though. It's not just stamped on the keyboard. It's mixed in with the computer program."

The symbols on the keyboard flashed a soft red light, and the characters on the box changed. Each one flickered through a unique symbol, text Calla recognized from a language she knew well.

The patterns shifted back and forth in a dance of alien beauty, and the characters remained burned into her mind. Symbol after symbol filled her vision from the box on the wall until nothing was left but clarity.

"It's definitely Latin merged with computer code," Calla said. "This one is based on Vigenère Square," she said.

"What does it say?" Nash asked.

Calla scrutinized it. "No time to find out. We need to hurry," she said. "Because it's going to blow in twenty-seven seconds," she said.

Jack advanced. "What?"

The light on the bomb was blinking rapidly.

"How do you know that?" Jack asked.

"Because it's set on this timer underneath the keyboard," she said, showing them. "The Latin twenty-seven just emerged, and it's counting down fast," Calla said.

"You sure you can't defuse it?" Jack asked.

"Give me a few seconds to figure it out," Calla said. Her mind raced as she tried to figure out what the bomber had intended. Sweat poured down her forehead, and her throat was parched. "Okay," she said finally. "Here's what we have. The timer is running out faster than it should because the dial is stuck."

"Stuck?" Jack asked.

Calla pointed to a strand of wire sticking out of the back of the dial. "It's stuck between zero and twenty-seven and keeps moving forward too fast."

"So you can't turn it off?" Jack asked.

"If you're right, we only have about twenty seconds now," Nash said.

Calla took a deep breath, concentrated on the scramble of letters again, and tried to make sense of the cipher. She closed her eyes and felt the tension in her body release. Counting the seconds and thinking simultaneously, this was how she could break codes so quickly. While it had been a long time since she'd worked with a polyalphabetic cipher of this type, it all came back to her in a flash.

Calla's eyes were still closed, and she was breathing deeply, venting the anxiety from her system so that she could concentrate. She remembered studying the sequences during her first year of cryptology at Cambridge University. The sixteenth-century cipher used a simple keyword to generate differently shifted messages in the same series. While the decoding process was easy to figure out, it had resisted all attempts to break it for over 300 years, earning it the nickname 'the undecipherable cipher,' *le Chiffre indéchiffrable.* That's when she remembered. "Of course!"

The men's anxious faces watched her as she almost laughed out loud now that she knew where the keyword had come from. She just needed to figure out how many cycles they had used.

The seconds ticked.

It took her a few moments to recognize where she had seen the cycle before—the game of Hangman. "Zero," she said.

Jack looked at her with a puzzled expression.

"The code is zero. That's the keyword we must type in to stop it," she explained.

"Don't you think the bomber is trying to trick us?" Jack asked.

Calla locked eyes with him, nodded, and he froze.

"You're the boss," Jack said.

She worked quickly, her fingers flying over the keyboard. 'Here we go,' Calla said, punching the zero key. She then pulled a thin electrical wire from the explosive and held it in her hand. "We're good."

"What did you do?" Nash asked her.

She turned, holding the wire. "I figured it would cancel out whatever was supposed to happen. Okay, one more to go. The bomber has timed them in sequence, and I doubt we have more than half an hour between each bomb. Jack, can you find it on your tracker?"

Jack smiled with relief and placed his device in front of him. He looked at the screen, then turned it around. "It's below us."

"Underground?" asked Calla.

Jack nodded.

They stepped back.

Jack braced himself and kicked the ground.

The floor creaked, then suddenly caved in, sending them plummeting to unknown depths below.

With a deafening thud, they landed on a narrow walkway illuminated by a sliver of light shining through the small round opening high above them. The light shone onto a magnificent room of pillars and stone walls, and in the center of it, a giant chrome device rested, resembling a machine from the future.

It had a circular frame with wires protruding at chaotic angles and an oval-shaped display screen with a tiny holographic beam with symbols floating on the surface. Attached to it were a bomb and a timer, steadily counting down to zero.

"Oh God," Calla said.

"How much time do we have?" Nash asked.

Jack took in a sharp breath. "Twenty-two minutes and thirty-seven seconds."

When Calla saw the emblems on the bomb's keyboard, she hit the enter key.

She froze.

It wasn't in any language that Calla recognized, but it was something she had seen before.

CHAPTER
THREE

CALLA STOOD THERE, staring at the code, trying to make sense of it, but she couldn't. A series of numbers and symbols that made little sense to her plagued her mind.

There was no way she could disarm this bomb. She couldn't force herself to go back to that dark place she had been ten years ago when she had seen the same code.

Calla felt her heart sinking. She turned to Nash and Jack. "I'm sorry," she said. "I can't do it."

Nash advanced. "It's okay," he said. "We'll figure it out."

Jack nodded.

"Come on. We have less than twenty minutes now," Nash said. "Cal, try to read it. You can do this. We can help."

Calla remained still. Her knees shook.

Nash and Jack studied the bomb, looking for anything that might give them a clue on how to disarm it, as Calla remained frozen.

"I'm not giving up," Nash said, stepping forward. He laid his hand on the wall behind the bomb. "We can do this," he said, looking into her eyes.

He always gave Calla strength, but not this time.

"Believe in yourself," said Jack. "You can do this."

"Push yourself beyond your fears," Nash said. "What's happening to you, Cal?"

As Calla stared at the cipher, her eyes burned, and she felt sweat drip down her forehead.

She remembered. It was a long time ago, but she recalled it vividly.

She was on an archaeological trip in the Rub'al Khali desert. It was the middle of the night, and she was alone, straining to decode an ancient text under a single light bulb. She had been awake for hours. Calla and the rest of the team were investigating a site rumored to have ancient artifacts. But as they excavated, they realized that the sand was quicksand, and they were sinking. They could not get out. She had survived that terrifying ordeal in the desert; but in doing so, she had unknowingly trapped herself inside her own fear.

Calla felt her body tense as she leaned in to read the code. Her hands shook, her eyes watered, and her mind went blank. She tried to take a deep breath, but panic was slowly taking over. She wanted to push through her fear and solve this code, but no matter how hard she tried, she couldn't bring herself to do it.

Calla had seen this same enigmatic code before on a chrome-colored gate in the desert, but like the last time, the code left her challenged.

Nash planted a quick encouraging kiss on her lips. "Cal, all you have to do is read it, and we will punch in the numbers."

She couldn't do it.

"It's okay," Nash said, sensing her fear. "We'll do it together."

He put his arm around her, and she leaned into him, drawing strength from his presence. Together, they studied the bomb.

"Guys," Jack said. "We have little time left."

Nash held her stiff hand. "I have an idea. Trust me. Stand back," he said.

Jack and Calla watched as Nash approached the bomb.

NASH THREW himself on his belly and considered how he could move the bomb without detonating it.

Slowly sliding his hand beneath it, his fingers felt along the sides, and he noticed a slight indentation. Breathing heavily, he stood up, squinted at the mound of wires and cables, and wondered how he would get it out of there.

The bomb was the size of a small suitcase. He just needed the explosive part. The wires had to go. He could get rid of the cube and many of the wires. Then, he would remove the cube and take the strands attached to it by their naked ends. He would twist them together, and that would remove the whole thing.

He looked back at Jack and Calla. "I want you two to get as far away from here as possible."

Calla said something, but Nash cut her off. "There's no time. I'm going to have to get rid of it."

"What are you going to do?" Calla asked.

"I don't know yet."

Jack intervened. "Nash, I must warn you, it's too dangerous…"

"I know. All I can do is hope I'll be far enough away."

Twin red lights on the bomb flashed.

"Nash, time is ticking," Jack said, his eyes fixed on the bomb.

Nash raised an eyebrow and got to work. "Cal..."

She placed her finger on his lips and kissed them. "Shh. You're going to make it."

Nash gritted his teeth and planted his hands below the bomb. His fingers dug into the sides, and he pulled himself up with one swift movement.

The bomb stuck to his chest as he struggled through the door and up some stairs to the top level they had fallen through.

Outside, Nash's fingers shook as he balanced the bomb between them. He squinted into the sunlight and spotted a police motorcycle further down to the site entrance, where two Greek agents stood talking on their phones.

Nash marched toward them, veering off to the side so the bomb wouldn't have to take any unnecessary bumps.

The agent in charge cut him off mid-stride, dropping his phone as he saw what Nash was carrying.

"I need rope!" Nash yelled, sweat dripping down his forehead.

The agent looked uncertainly at one of his men before turning back to Nash. "I don't think we have any here...," he stammered.

Nash ripped off his shirt under his bulletproof vest, wrapped it around the back of the motorcycle, and cinched it around the bomb. He pulled it as tight as he could.

The agents stood and stared.

"I'm going to have to go slow enough to keep it steady but fast enough to make time," Nash said. "There's not a lot of grip on this road. Let's keep our eyes peeled for distractions along the way, and I need an escort," he told the agent.

"We'll follow you and give you cover. But what do you plan to do?" the agent asked.

Nash didn't reply; he merely nodded and revved up the engines. He swung his leg over the bike, settling onto the leather seat.

With practiced ease, he weaved between traffic, expertly avoiding any potential accidents or injury to himself or others.

Wind rushed past him as he took off, like a force of nature propelling him closer to his destination. His hands clasped both handlebars as the bike raced down the highway.

Sweat formed on his forehead from the effort of controlling the two powerful engines. The deafening sound of their combined roar filled the air as he left the city in a blur of speed toward Heraklion and the Mediterranean Sea.

He knew the beach would be his only hope.

Nash darted his eyes from left to right as he zipped down the road, with the agents following attentively behind. He had to be crazy, but he had lived through worse.

Eyes focused on the road, he checked to see if the bomb was securely balanced behind him. Once he was confident of its balance, he sped up.

He slammed his foot on the gas, and the bike shot forward.

The engine noise roared from the cycle as he revved the engines, but they seemed to be on the verge of breaking down with the power he was demanding of them.

Nash didn't know how long the bomb timer had left. He had to concentrate and spoke in his earpiece. "How much time, Jack?"

"Sixteen minutes," Jack responded. "We're following with the cops behind. You're possibly one of the craziest and bravest men I know."

"Back at you."

"Where are you going?" Jack asked over the radio.

"The sea. I don't know how big the explosion will be, but if

I can use the sea as a backstop, I might get lucky and stop the explosion from going off altogether."

Finally, Heraklion beach was in sight, a stretch away from the main city center.

Nash sped off to the side motorway as the road turned into a dirt trail that led to the water.

He had about twelve minutes and was driving faster, but the explosive still weighed a lot, and he was having difficulty keeping the bike steady.

Nash peered back at the bomb for a brief second.

The bomb was rocking back and forth from his fast driving. He had no time to stabilize it. He read the sign to Ammoudara Beach, which was just ahead. The engines roared louder when he pressed harder on the accelerator.

The bomb seemed to sway.

More sweat dripped into his eyes, and Nash's grip on the handgrips loosened. "Jack, I don't want to go too fast, but I'm having to," he said.

"Understood."

He twisted the handlebars of the motorbike to the left and yanked the brake, sending a shower of sand up from beneath the spinning tires.

The bike skidded to a stop in the middle of the trail, and Nash could feel a warmth coming off the still-rumbling engines.

He unstrapped the bomb from the back of the bike and jumped off, carefully cradling it in his arms. As he rushed down the beach, Nash glanced at his watch; there were ten minutes left on the bomb's timer.

Nash approached a dock where tourists awaited their excursion boats. He splashed into the water and approached a man with a speedboat. "Five hundred euros for your boat," Nash said in Greek, his voice urgent.

The man gave him a startled look, his eyes imploring, and

his body tense. The man's eyes widened, but he stepped aside to let Nash board the boat.

Nash carefully balanced himself as he stepped in. Before seating himself, he nestled his bomb securely in the middle of the boat.

The man looked at his boat and threw the keys over to Nash. "And the fuel," he yelled.

"Don't worry," Nash said, "it's on me."

Nash eased out of the harbor, missing the tour boats by centimeters. He looked behind him at the island and twisted the throttle to full speed, and the boat jumped forward.

"Two minutes," Jack said in his earpiece.

Nash brushed a bead of sweat from his forehead, took a deep breath, and exhaled slowly. He just needed to get it out to sea, far away from boats and people. He took another deep breath in the spring heat.

"Nash, now!" Jack shouted.

Nash glanced back at the explosive and quickly realized what to do.

The bomb shuddered as the boat turned and sped up. Like the crack of lightning before the storm, everything slowed down.

He thought fast and reached for a loose wooden plank in the back of the boat and ripped it from the seat.

The bomb rocked harder as Nash threw the plank over the side of the boat and vaulted over after it. He seized it as the boat sped away.

Sea water churned with white crescents of foam on its surface, and the horizon was just a speck. He opened his mouth as the boat left him and took one last gasp of air.

The boat got smaller.

Nash waited underwater for the explosive to detonate.

Nothing.

Nothing.

Nothing.

Then he felt the force of the explosion, but he stayed afloat. His chest heaved, and he kicked hard when he saw an immense ball of fire in the middle of the water.

The blast grew into a giant wave. Its force and pressure knocked him over, but that was all he felt as he flipped underwater.

Nash swam up to a tide coming in that rammed him under again, then threw him up into another wave that scooped him up again and spat him out.

The boat was in pieces, floating.

A black smoke cloud rose from where the bomb had detonated, but the explosion hadn't spread beyond the sea.

He clambered back onto the plank as he lost sight of the wreckage.

CHAPTER
FIVE

Berlin, RTL Television Studio
8:01 p.m.

"WHAT DO you think it all means?" Manfred Bierman, the German TV channel RTL broadcast interviewer, asked.

"I don't know," Octavia Steward replied. "But it's something big. We've never seen anything like it before."

"And it's all happening in our backyard, with materials from our museum. Are you saying artifacts from the Pergamon Museum have helped us find this lost civilization?" Bierman said. "It's like a movie."

On the TV studio stage was a vast expanse of gray canvas. Stage lights above her were as bright as the sun, washing out every detail. The studio was quiet, with only the sound of camera shutters breaking the silence. Voices were hushed and distorted by the equipment surrounding her.

Octavia tasted dryness in her mouth. Her eyes moved to the camera labeled *"Camera One,"* studying it intently, trying to take in every detail of her surroundings.

She felt a chill run down her spine. The only way to get

what she needed was to press forward, despite the weakness entering her knees. A crushing wave of shame and self-doubt washed over her, even though there weren't many people around at the exclusive secret interview. Only a handful of camera people and crew had gathered in the spacious room.

"Yes," she said. "The city was an outpost of the sunken ancient civilization," Octavia said, her voice low and intense. "Or a tribute by its survivors or descendants to something even more dangerous. NASA sightings in the eighties explained it as a lost race, although we still do not know who they were."

Octavia could see the disbelief in the eyes of the studio crew. "It's true," she insisted. "I've seen the evidence. I've studied the writings, but something stopped us. That's why I can't tell you where this evidence is."

"Do you have any idea what you're suggesting?" Bierman asked. "If you're right, it would be the biggest discovery in history."

Octavia took a deep breath. "I know," she said.

She was doing well in the interview, better than she had expected, but the questions were trickier than she thought they would be. And she needed this money. She needed the grant if she was going to find him, the man from Muscat, so they could return. She couldn't let them know that. She had to act like she didn't need it.

Octavia smiled. "I feel like I'm in the middle of it all."

Bierman gave her an intense look. "Hope you're not in any danger."

Octavia laughed. "No, no. I'm perfectly safe."

"I hope so," he said. "We've seen a lot of unusual things here in Berlin, but I think you've got the story of the year. Who would have known that artifacts in the Pergamon Museum vaults would have helped discover a lost civilization?"

"I hope so, too," Octavia said. "Iram, or Atlantis of the Sands, as it's known, has mystified us for years."

"So, have you learned anything new about the artifacts? They've been sitting in the Pergamon vaults for decades," Bierman asked.

"We can now determine more precisely what century the artifacts came from, but we've found out little about why they were in the city or what they did," she said, showing him an artifact she had thought about and hadn't been able to figure out for days.

She raised another. A thin piece of polished basalt carved into the shape of a somewhat stylized head. On the left side, a small hole appeared to be a keyhole. Carved into the right side at its widest point was a crisscross pattern that reminded her of an abstract illustration. The narrow hole seemed to glow like an ember in a campfire. It was a momentary thing. Then the hole was dark again.

Every time she took her eyes off it and then looked back, it seemed to glow again, faintly, as if someone had triggered an electric switch. Who?

She had thought she was tired and possibly dreaming when she had discovered it in the Pergamon vaults, but she was sure now.

"It's carved in basalt?" Bierman said, looking at the first artifact. "Any theories about its true purpose?"

"That's what my research intends to find out. I'm not sure what to think about it yet."

"And the origin of the other artifacts here?" Bierman asked.

"Some look like intelligent beings made them, but others look like a child made them. It's quite puzzling, yet fascinating," she replied.

"Can you tell us more about the city, Atlantis of the Sands?" Bierman said.

"Well," Octavia said, "I'm not sure where to start. It's a fantastic story, stranger than fiction, but it's true."

"Truth is stranger than fiction," Bierman agreed.

"That's what I'm finding out," Octavia replied. "Perhaps an earthquake or a meteorite annihilated the city in the desert around 1000 BC. But many believe it was prosperous, with unparalleled gold, silver, and gems. It's been mentioned in many Arabian Nights. The people who lived there were extremely powerful and highly successful beyond anyone in comparison. Its extensive buildings and the entire city were built on eight pillars. The wealth was enormous and pre-dated many prosperous cities, but somehow it collapsed underground. Some believe the wealth of the Queen of Sheba that she brought to King Solomon may have originated there. Many cannot find its exact location today, although science has recently helped spot it. Even with superior technology, it has not been easy to find. Those who have tried have come back empty-handed."

Bierman leaned in. "Except for these artifacts found in the fifties, here in Berlin."

"Correct."

"How did you learn about the Atlantis of the Sands?" Bierman asked.

"Well," Octavia said, "I've been excavating in the area for about fifteen years and have a lot of local knowledge, including awareness of the nearby Bedouin tribes. They're very helpful, but also very superstitious. I've learned to take their beliefs and turn them to my advantage."

"How do they help?" Bierman asked.

"They respect and fear the desert and its mysteries, so they often tell me stories they believe are true, but I know are mostly legends. You can use their legends to your advantage if you listen carefully."

"What do you mean?" Bierman asked.

"For example, one legend I heard from a Bedouin on a trip told of a fabled city of gold supposedly in the northern part of an oasis in the sands of southern Saudi Arabia. The Bedouin believed it was a city of gold, but I knew it couldn't be because the geology of the area doesn't allow for the existence of gold. It's just sand."

Bierman, a tall man with thick limbs and a wide chest, ran his fingers through his salt-and-pepper hair. "What did you do?"

"Well, we drove up to the northern part of the oasis and started looking for it, but we couldn't find the city."

"That's very interesting," Bierman added. "Do you think this is a warning from history?"

"It's hard to say," Octavia answered. "But the artifacts are unusual."

He stared into the distance with his deep aqua-blue eyes before turning back to Octavia. "You're writing a book on this? You've almost completed it... Why are there seven blank pages?"

She couldn't tell him.

The words were in a safe, seven pages of code written in a language that, until a few weeks ago, had been thought dead for fifteen hundred years. It was precisely why she was there. She needed to raise money. Her hand shook as she adjusted the silver and green scarf around her neck.

Movement behind Bierman caught her eye.

A crash near the entrance made her stop.

Her heart leaped to her throat.

She quickly glanced around the room, her mind racing with possibilities of who could cause the commotion.

The unmistakable sound of breaking glass filled the air, and the studio door was suddenly thrown open.

Octavia felt a rush of air, heard shouted orders, and then the sound of chairs being moved as people scrambled.

A woman's voice rose in a wail, and the bright television lights went out.

In the momentary darkness, a single spotlight illuminated the center stage where Octavia was seated with Bierman on the interview couch. She saw two men dressed all in black, their faces concealed behind night-vision goggles, perched like birds of prey at each corner of the room. It was then that she realized snipers had come down from the roof.

Bright flashes filled the room as a man dressed in dark gray moved toward them, his face concealed by a mask that resembled a knight's helmet. The visor was smooth, thin, and light gray, made of high-tech chain mail with no identifiable features.

He approached Octavia holding a handgun while his followers, men dressed in gray business suits with silencers, took positions on either side of the studio. Two of them flanked Octavia.

She felt her skin turn to ice.

More bright lights illuminated the room, making everything look artificial. Those in the studio who saw the masked man were paralyzed by fear as snipers followed behind.

A beam of light shone across the man's masked face. "I'll buy your manuscript," he said in a voice altered by a voice changer.

Octavia stared at him. "What manuscript?"

"You know the one I mean."

"It's not for sale."

The man pulled out a phone with Octavia's account information. "How much do you want?"

Octavia hesitated. She needed grant money to continue her research and go back to the dig site, but she couldn't sell her manuscript. The man repeated, "How much do you want?"

The entire room seemed to wait for her answer, and Octavia's heart pounded in her chest.

Even with the face mask, she could still feel the intensity of the man's scrutiny. "I don't want your money," she said, her voice shaking.

Bierman, who she had almost forgotten was there, spoke up. "Who are you? What...?"

Octavia shot a glance at Bierman, then at the man, and then back at Bierman.

The man spoke again, seeming taller now. "I'll buy it for one million euros."

"That's a lot of money," Octavia said, standing up and wiping her hands on the front of her skirt. "I haven't finished the book. Besides, it's an academic thesis, not even a book."

"Then I'll buy your research."

Octavia shook her head. "I'm not selling anything here."

"Yet you took an exclusive. That can only mean the want of money by one of ancient Arabia's greatest scholars and archaeologists, a Professor of Cambridge and a guest curator for the Pergamon Museum's great Arabian collections."

The man hesitated. "Going to play this the hard way, Octavia?" He leaned over her, pulled out a wad of five hundred euro notes, peeled off a few bills, and placed them on the table. "I'm not gonna ask again."

She was tempted to take the money to pay off her credit card bills and return to Cambridge, but she knew she couldn't. Octavia's eyes met his masked face. "Please don't. Because my answer will be the same."

The man raised his arm as if to strike, but then he stopped and looked at her again.

Rage swelled within her, and her hands clenched tightly as the skin on her lower lip quivered. She breathed deeply, focusing on her body to control the anger inside her. The anger felt like an inferno about to explode, but she had to stay strong. Who was this man? Finding Calla Cress, the woman who could translate the seven pages of code she could not read, was all that mattered.

The code on those pages could be the key to unlocking the secrets of Atlantis.

Octavia had put up with enough, so she took another deep breath. But before she could say anything, a blow to the head knocked her to her knees.

CHAPTER
SIX

The Scorpion Tide Yacht
Off the Coast of Crete
11:27 p.m.

THE SCORPION TIDE glided toward the dock in Heraklion, its smooth mahogany hull reflecting the bright Greek moonlight. Its electronic sails were furled gracefully, and the state-of-the-art navigation systems flashed brilliantly.

A gentle Mediterranean breeze swept across the deck as they approached the harbor, and the sleek lines of the yacht made it look like it was soaring on air. Moonlight glinted off the small waves of the sea, creating a peaceful atmosphere.

Calla breathed in the salty air and the aroma of fresh seafood coming from nearby restaurants. She dragged her feet heavily on the yacht's deck as she approached the jacuzzi. Stepping in, she felt the hot water wash over her tired body. It was almost too hot to bear, but she let out a sigh as the warmth relaxed her tight muscles. Her eyelids drooped with exhaustion, but she felt her spirit lighten as she sank deeper into the hot, bubbling water.

She tried to shake off her thoughts and relax, but it didn't work, weighed down by the day's events. Memories of their journey to the desert city gates kept flashing back to her.

With painful clarity, she recalled the terror that had overwhelmed her as they approached the gates all those years ago, and how her limbs had suddenly gone limp. She could see the other students and archaeologists around her reacting with disbelief, but she was too stunned to do anything but stand there, unsure of what was happening or why. As they left Cambridge afterward, she felt particularly isolated at being the only one who couldn't remember what had happened at the gates.

Her fingers fumbled as she pulled her phone from the side table. She took a deep breath, and saw an email from Professor Octavia in the inbox. Memories of their shared expedition to the southern Arabian Peninsula flooded back, bringing a wave of apprehension. She hadn't seen the professor in years, yet here was an email sent two days ago. Its tone was urgent yet direct, asking her for something she didn't understand.

Professor Octavia had left Cambridge shortly after their expedition, and it seemed like a lifetime since she'd last heard from her. Calla wondered what Octavia was like now, and if she would still be the same person she remembered.

She heard a noise behind her.

Jack placed a tray of champagne and flutes on the side table, then settled into the steaming water of the jacuzzi, bobbing as he flashed a boyish grin. "What's wrong?" he asked. "We just defused three bombs today. Come on, no reason to be feeling down."

Calla gave him a small, knowing smile. "What makes you think something's wrong?" she said.

"I can always tell when something's bothering you. You've been pacing and muttering on the deck for the past hour," he added. "I know you well enough to tell when something is bothering you."

"You do? Do you?"

"Yes, now tell me what it is before I guess."

Calla took a deep breath and looked into his encouraging eyes. "What Nash did today was so brave. You too. I don't know what I would do without you two and what I would do if I lost you."

"You won't. Nash and I are here with you. Cal, long ago, we decided we would always be a team—you, Nash, and I. When you and Nash got married, I worried it would change things between us. But that was one of the best days of my life, seeing my best friends get hitched." He laughed. "Somehow, we stick together. That hasn't changed."

Calla stretched her leg to relieve a cramp. "I was so worried I'd lose you both. I froze when I couldn't read those symbols, almost hypnotized."

He put his arm around her as the water continued to relieve her muscles, and he looked straight at her. "Nash loves you, and what he did today would have been calculated with you in mind. Always. That man is crazy about you."

"You always know what to say to make me feel better," she said.

"I try," he said, moving back to a position against the nozzles.

Before they met, they were both loners, feeling out of place with others, but when he introduced her to Nash, the circle was complete. As ISTF agents, they faced danger every day, but as long as they had each other, that was all that counted. They always had each other's backs.

"I love Nash," she said. "And you are just as much a part of me. I can't live without either."

"I know," he said. "We're family."

"I worry about something happening to him and you because of me."

"Why? You shouldn't. Nash is a brave man, and you can count on me too. Stop worrying about us."

She smiled sadly and leaned back. Taking a deep breath, she tried to suppress her roller coaster of emotions. Though she couldn't shake the feeling that something was missing from her life, something that could change everything, she couldn't remember what it was. Her mind wandered back to the ancient ruins of Arabia and the strange secrets they held.

"Now, drink something and stop worrying about everything," he said, reaching for a flute of champagne. "We deserve it."

"Did I hear my name?" a voice said.

They turned to see Nash standing in the doorway wearing a thick white robe and clutching a blue towel to his chest.

"Just in time to celebrate," Jack chuckled, motioning to an empty spot in the jacuzzi.

Nash smiled and let the robe slide off his shoulders as he stepped toward the water. He wore nothing but a pair of tight, black boxers that clung to his lean body as he submerged himself in the water.

Calla and Jack watched in awe as Nash resurfaced and spun around, pressing his palms against the sides of the jacuzzi.

"Couldn't sleep either," Jack asked, leaning back against the edge of the jacuzzi.

"Guess we are three peas in a pod," Nash said with a wide grin. "Just glad we made it out alive."

They sat in the jacuzzi. The silence was punctuated only by

the bubbling of the water and champagne as Jack poured each of them a flute.

Calla cradled her glass, never taking her eyes off Nash. His skin radiated with a golden light, and his eyes twinkled with life. She felt her chest tighten and her heart flutter as her eyes swept over his muscular frame. His temples were high, his jaw was firm and chiseled, and his body fit and trim.

"Hey," he said, placing the glass down, taking her in his arms, and kissing her on the mouth, his lips soft and warm. Nash's voice was deep, like the steady and soothing sound of distant thunder. He raised an eyebrow. "It's okay. We work as a team. Now, what's wrong?" he asked.

"I asked her the same thing," Jack said, smiling.

Nash was trying to keep the worry out of his voice.

"I just couldn't do it," she said, trembling. "I'm sorry."

Nash frowned. "Don't worry about it. Something bothered you back there. Something I've never seen you do." He reached down and brushed a strand of hair away from her face. "Okay, beautiful."

She blushed and looked away.

"Should I leave?" Jack joked.

Calla pulled away from Nash's embrace and turned to face Jack. Her voice trembled as she spoke. "I received an email from an old professor from Cambridge, Professor Octavia Steward."

Jack's eyebrows furrowed, clearly puzzled at her distress. "And what did it say?"

Calla wrung her hands and looked down at the water, debating how much information to divulge. "I didn't open it."

Nash moved closer, his voice soothing and gentle. "Why not? What's so scary about an email sent by an old professor from Cambridge?"

Calla bit her lip. What would happen if they knew the truth? "I'm afraid to know what it says."

Jack drew back, his mouth agape. "What?"

"My life is in danger," she added. "When Octavia left Cambridge in a hurry ten years ago, she told me she would never communicate with me again because it was too dangerous for us, especially after what happened in Rub'al Khali, the desert in Arabia."

Nash was silent for a moment. "I don't know if you should be afraid."

"It's not a straightforward email," she said. "It's strange."

"In what way?" Jack asked.

"Jack, you should have seen the look on her face as she was packing in a hurry. I know it was ten years ago, but that's a look you don't forget. She was afraid of something and protecting me, but I don't know what from."

Nash massaged her shoulder. "Maybe you should wait until I'm with you when you open it. That way, whatever it is, we can deal with it together."

Her body tensed as the reality of the situation sunk in. She wanted to tell them what was happening, but was too afraid. She wanted to cry, but she knew that wouldn't solve anything. Calla knew what she had to do, but didn't know if she could bring herself to do it. She leaned into Nash's embrace as if it would protect her from the truth of the email that had arrived out of the blue.

Calla,

I'm sorry to have to contact you this way, but I don't know who else to turn to. I hope you still work on deciphering the language I taught you. I've found an entire notebook written in it. This could be the key to understanding its origins. But I can't keep it here. It's too dangerous. If they find it, they'll kill me. Could you take it and keep it safe? Please, Calla, don't let my work go to waste. The old notebook has seven pages I can't read. But I know you can. If you can read them, this whole thing will go away.

Octavia Steward.

Calla felt sick inside. Seven pages Octavia couldn't read. How could she read text she couldn't see? Blank pages.

"Calla?" Nash said.

She forced herself to hold Nash's gaze. "It's nothing."

He ran his hand through his hair. "Is it...?"

She swallowed. "No."

Jack shrugged. "You need to let me look at it, at least the server it came from and all that. It's possible she did not send it."

Calla sighed. "Yes, I've thought of that. But it's just an email from a woman I haven't seen or heard from in a long time. Octavia Steward was a professor from Cambridge on the archaeological dig in Rub'al Khali."

"You've read the email, haven't you?" Nash said, raising an eyebrow. "What does she say?"

She nodded and looked at them both. "That she needs my help with something. Reading an ancient text related to what happened today. Whoever set up those bombs in Knossos is connected to me ten years ago. And I'm frustrated because I don't know who it is. Very few people, and I mean a handful, have ever seen that language from the lost city of Iram. Heck, many scholars contest it was an actual city. And that text from the third bomb, those symbols, come from Iram."

"Really?" Nash asked.

"I don't want to help her," she added.

"Why not?" Jack asked.

"It's a hard subject for me to go back to."

Jack breathed hard. "Maybe you should tell us what it is. You know we'll listen. So you don't want to talk about it? Is that why you froze in the Knossos Palace today?"

She bit her lip. "Yes."

Nash's eyes were encouraging. "You have to, Cal. You can only conquer your demons if you face them."

Calla drew in a sharp breath and recalled the moment as the bubbles oozing became the only sound between them. "The accident happened on the last day of our expedition. We had been searching for seven days, combing the southern area of Rub'al Khali for any sign of the remains of the lost city. But we found nothing. Then on the eighth day, we found something - an entrance, we thought, hidden in the sands leading underground.

"We were all excited as we entered the ominous tunnels. I was hesitant, but Octavia insisted I come with them. She said I could help with what she believed were ancient lithoglyphs. Guys, I was only eighteen and barely knew what I could do, let alone understand my code-reading ability. I felt so much pressure, and things went wrong as we went further into the caves. The floor broke beneath our feet."

She was shuddering now.

Nash pulled her close. "What happened next?"

"I hit my head on something and blacked out. When I woke up, I was alone in the darkness. I couldn't see or hear anything. I was completely disoriented and didn't know which way was up or down."

"Did you call for help?" Jack asked.

"I panicked, and only then did I realize my foot was caught in something. I tried to move, but I couldn't. Then I heard someone calling my name. A man."

Nash leaned in. "Someone you knew?"

"I'd never seen him in my life. He was running toward me, but I saw fear in his eyes as he got closer. I saw the look of horror on his face and realized something was not right. He then got stuck in the quicksand. He begged me to help, saying only I could stop the sand, but I had to open the gate by reading the lithoglyphs. I thought he was mad. There were no lithographs or text in sight. I must've fainted. It was a miracle we survived, and somehow, I made it back to Cambridge. I'll never forget the face of that man. Nor do I know who he was. But he certainly knew who I was." She paused. "Later, I was told he was our security on the trip. A German man by the name of Ivan Schneider. He never made it back, and it was because of me. I had to read the blank text, and now Octavia has a book, an artifact from the city I understand, with seven empty pages that need reading. It sounds like she's in danger and is about to do something… foolish even."

"And this has haunted you since that day," Nash added.

She couldn't forget the dread she felt when trapped under the sand, the sound of the man screaming, screaming for her to read the code that would stop the quicksand. The fear of being buried alive. She just couldn't.

Octavia had taught her about Iram, but even she had been skeptical. The characters were not like anything else from similar civilizations. Symbols that Octavia now needed her to recall and unravel, and if today was anything to go by, she couldn't do it. She just wouldn't. No, she would not go there.

"Cal?" Nash said. "You're scaring me. That was a long time ago. We're here now and can help."

She snapped back to the present, trembling.

Nash held her, studying her closely.

Jack had jumped out to retrieve a towel.

"It's nothing," she blurted. "I'm just tired."

"Are you sure?" Nash asked. "Because you look like you've seen a ghost."

"Yes," Calla said, trying to sound more convincing than she felt. "I'm just tired, that's all."

Nash didn't look convinced, but he let it go. "Okay," he said. "If you're sure."

"I am," Calla said. "Octavia taught me all about Iram and

its unique language and form, but honestly, I found it hard to believe it was an actual place until we got there. But..."

Nash leaned in. "What?"

"A few days ago, my father told me a package arrived for me on the same day I received Octavia's email. It was sent to my father's Cotswolds cottage, an ancient book bound in leather. And here's a freaky thing. It was wrapped in GCHQ-branded film wrap. Someone had also included a printed translation, about 200 pages. The book seems to be a historical account of the city."

Jack raised an eyebrow. "GCHQ?"

"Yes," Calla replied. "How did they get the book and why? As her email showed, some of the book's pages were blank. Seven, to be exact. The other pages were filled with patterns. This wasn't just some ancient text - it could be a map. A map that leads to something dangerous hidden beneath the city. A city still alive with something."

"Cal," Nash said. "You're an incredible codebreaker, and I don't want you to forget that. Whether it's encoded in technology or an ancient language, you figure it out and don't let today distract you. It was just a bad day."

"Thanks, Nash, but how can a cryptanalyst read code that's not even written? Code that's not visible to the naked eye? If I had read what I couldn't see back then, maybe that man would be alive today."

CHAPTER
SEVEN

Manhattan, New York
6:33 p.m.

A PRESENCE SEEMED to fill the halls. Kronos Corporation's US headquarters in Manhattan loomed like a fortress, with its curved, mirrored facade reflecting the clouds above.

Avo Schneider walked into the building, passing through the security checkpoint and taking the elevator up to the sixty-third floor. She was impeccably dressed in a white blouse, thin black tie, and black slacks that hugged her hips.

Mason Laskfell strolled next to Avo, and she looked up. He was an intimidating figure—tall and broad-shouldered, his dark blue suit crisply pressed and his eyes sharp with purpose. As the former head of ISTF, he was involved in countless covert operations. Rumors had spread that he handled ISTF's counterintelligence and was now one of their most wanted fugitives. She had heard stories about him but had never actually met him before.

Avo always had wondered at Laskfell's ruthless tactics. He

had also heard that he had been willing to sacrifice his own team members to get the job done. His methods led to many victims over the years, and thus, many considered him a ruthless man.

"You're not to contact or meet with anyone on our deal. Don't leave this building until the bankers agree with you," he said in a serious tone.

Avo didn't know why he was telling her this. She knew her mission. He had worked with her father, on God knew what, yet she couldn't help but feel a strange sense of betrayal. Laskfell had all the information to make the Iram mission successful.

Trying to stay composed, she spoke to him in a clipped voice. "I'll get it done."

"You're to listen to my every instruction. Understand?" he said.

Avo watched as his eyes seemed to darken, and he pressed his lips together. "Let me do my job," she continued, her words filled with an emotion she couldn't name.

"For Kronos's sake and the memory of your father."

The reminder of her father caused her heart to clench, but she tried to push away the memories.

Laskfell smirked. "Ivan Schneider was greedy. He should have listened to me when it came to the Cress girl," he continued, taking a step toward her. "And now you have paid with blood."

Forcing herself not to react, Avo turned away and continued her march toward the meeting room, leaving him behind, watching as she moved away.

Her heels echoed against the fluorescent-lit corridors as she walked down the hall. She entered a long, narrow conference room where four men in suits and three women waited for her at the head of the table, their faces expectant.

Avo swung her briefcase onto an empty seat and smiled.

"Good afternoon," she said, her voice warm and her accent thick as honey. "I have what you want."

The men examined her with dissatisfied glares. "I've found the Lost City of Iram," she continued. "I have found what lies beneath it, and I'm willing to show you and give you your share."

"And what do you want in return?" a man with a nasal voice asked.

Avo approached the front of the room. "I want money," she said. "I want to be paid for what I know and can give you."

The bankers looked at each other. "What will you show us?" a bald man with round glasses and a shiny face asked.

Avo took a deep breath, her throat tight. She had considered how she would convince them to believe her, but the words wouldn't come out now that the time had come.

The more she struggled, the more panic set in, as if the Lost City of Iram was speaking through her, calling her a liar, telling her to keep it hidden, never to reveal its existence.

"I'll take you to the city. You can experience the wonders of our project yourselves," she said.

The bankers looked at each other again, greed in their eyes. They were going to agree. She could feel it.

Avo began her story by describing the scorching sun, the howling sandstorms, and the possibility of a forbidden city hidden beneath the desert. Despite her apprehension, she pushed forward, telling them about the mysteries of the ancient civilization. She described the entrance to the lost city, exploring its secret chambers, and the awe and dread she felt at its long-forgotten engineering feats.

The bankers leaned in closer, their eyes widening with eagerness as she spoke. They asked questions about the size, layout, and what it was like inside.

She could see their excitement growing with each answer

she gave as if they were already thinking of ways to make the most of this new opportunity.

Avo ran out of things to say as the bankers sat silently, digesting what they had heard.

"This is an incredible story," the bald man said.

She smiled.

The bankers had believed her story and were already wiring money into Kronos's account.

Avo would claim it without giving them what they needed.

CHAPTER
EIGHT

Scorpion Tide
11:41 p.m.

CALLA TOOK a deep breath and leaned back in the hot tub as the jets pulsed around her. She felt Nash's arm wrap around her, and his lips pressed into her neck. It was both comforting and exciting. Her body melted under his touch, but she was uneasy—unable to open up to him fully.

He mumbled something in her ear, making her laugh.

Nash had been a constant source of support for her through the good times and bad. He had been there for her when she was happy and when she was facing challenges, but despite all this, Calla couldn't shake off the feeling of unease within her.

She ran her fingers through his hair and looked him in the eyes with a smile. "You're such a good man," she said before pulling away.

Calla watched him. After completing an impossible mission, she longed for his kiss and waited patiently as she tried to relax and pushed the painful memories away.

"Still in pain?" he asked, stroking her shoulders.

"I think it's almost healed," she responded softly.

"Good," he replied, his fingers caressing her arm as he looked down at her.

"I wouldn't be here if it weren't for you. Thank you," she whispered.

"I'm trying to be the best husband I can be. We've been through a lot," he answered, his voice sincere. "Cal," he said. "Do you understand why I'm so concerned about you? I can't bear the thought of losing someone I'm trying to protect. I know I come off as overprotective, which can be annoying, but I care so much about you."

Her heart filled with understanding. "I know you're trying to keep me safe, and I appreciate it. Nash," she said, stroking his ear. "I know what happened with the hostage situation a few years ago. I know you blame yourself for not being able to save the person that you were trying to protect all those years ago at KJ-20 Ops training. But you have to know that you're a good man and an amazing agent. You've saved my life many times."

Nash paused, looking down at her, possibly trying to process the overwhelming emotions he felt. He had been so focused on protecting others; he hadn't stopped to consider that he might need to protect himself.

"And you're a brilliant husband," she said, wrapping her arms around his neck and meeting his gaze. She leaned in, brushing her lips against his before pulling back and smirking at him. "I love you, Nash."

He stared at her for a moment before leaning down to capture her lips with his own.

She felt the power of his love with every kiss, every touch, every caress. She couldn't explain it, but it was exactly what she needed, an escape from the darkness of Iram and an embrace from the one person who truly understood her pain.

He pulled back, one hand cupping her chin. "You're the most amazing woman I've ever known," he said. "You're stronger than you think."

Though the dangers of Iram threatened her existence, Nash was one part of her sanity she wouldn't compromise.

CHAPTER
NINE

Jack's Cabin, Scorpion Tide
11:59 p.m.

JACK CURSED under his breath as his phone's alarm went off when he returned to his cabin.

His energy conservation project was almost complete, and he had hoped for one more night of peace before unveiling it to the ISTF. He had spent months on the project and cursed himself for not having a better security system; whoever infiltrated his organization was highly skilled.

He hurried over to his laptop and started investigating. The first thing he noticed was a reference to a project known as Project Mercury.

He had never heard of it before, but he knew it was important. Jack opened the file and saw that someone, using the name 'The Orchid, had hacked it. They had left the file open and unprotected, and 'Orchid' was not an ISTF code name. Jack couldn't understand who this person was.

Jack shook his head, unable to fathom how someone had breached his system without leaving any trace.

He had taken great lengths to ensure the security of his work and had even taken precautions to protect the project from third-party interference. Yet here he was, facing a breach with no idea how or why it had been made.

For a moment, Jack wanted to ignore it and move on, but he knew better. If this was related to government-level espionage, he had to take it seriously and had to act fast to understand it.

It was his research, and artificial intelligence could protect energy reserves, or if weaponized draw them from any corner of the world.

Jack took a moment to collect and organize his thoughts, deciding that visiting the ISTF archives was the best course of action. He had been at the forefront of research, development, and implementation of advanced science and technology around the world for years, so there had to be a trail of Project Mercury somewhere.

He hoped the ISTF archives would provide him with some answers.

Jack grabbed a glass of water from the kitchenette, returned to his desk, took his jacket, and opened the door, stepping out into the night.

He took a deep breath of the cool night air. He was about to embark on something that promised to be full of danger and mystery. He would uncover the truth behind this project and protect his creation.

As he was about to leave, his phone rang.

"Yes?" he answered.

"Jack Kleve?"

"Yes?"

"It's the Foreign Secretary's Office. He needs to see you about something urgent."

CHAPTER
TEN

Day 2
The Scorpion Tide Yacht
1:56 a.m.

LOSING the baby was a devastating blow but also a wake-up call.

Nash realized he could not keep living as he had been. He glanced at the clock.

Calla was fast asleep in their bed. He pulled up his email account on his phone. A message was in his inbox.

Nash clicked the link in the email and read the contents. He then slipped out of the bedroom, not wanting to disturb Calla's sleep.

He closed the office door behind him, turned on the desk lamp, and used his laptop to access a website he had been following for months called 'Two-Way Mirror'.

Nash had created a secret account a few months ago just in case, although he didn't know why, but he felt he would need it someday. And now, it seemed, that day had come.

He clicked on the folder marked "Projects". Inside were a

series of files, each with its unique password. Nash entered the first password and opened the file.

The source's information was there, just as he had been promised. He scrolled through it. Everything was there - the truth about what had happened to Calla and their baby.

The source had used the NSA's highest powers to determine who ordered the termination of Calla's pregnancy a few months ago - his baby.

He couldn't wrap his head around Calla's pregnancy; an enemy had ordered the ambush months ago, which forced a miscarriage. The source returned with a full report on the pregnancy, complete with photos and videos of the developing fetus. He'd even been able to find out the sex of the baby before Calla had found out herself - a girl.

He studied the ultrasound photo of his child, a fetus aborted by high-tech science and now being preserved in a test tube, paid handsomely for his daughter's fate was sealed. He had done the same thing that had been done to Calla... failed his daughter.

Calla's father, Stan, had failed Calla too.

He closed the account and sat back in his chair, letting the information sink in. For months he had suspected something was wrong, that the official story had been covered up, but he had never proved it. Now he could. Someone in the NSA had betrayed him and fed information to sinister operatives. That's how they found them in Malta a few months ago. It had been one of his own. Someone who once spoke to a man named Ivan Schneider.

Their baby was gone. He hadn't even known the child yet felt an overwhelming sense of loss swarmed. Deep down, the idea of being a father and raising his child had been something he had been looking forward to, but he had never let himself think too much about it.

He wanted to fill the part of her that was missing, but he

had put Calla through more pain again. He had tried to do the right thing for her, but maybe he had made things worse.

Nash stared at the photo again. He had never held a baby in his arms and didn't know what it was like to feel the connection to a child, but damn right, he wanted to. He would uncover the truth and bring those responsible to justice. Until he avenged his child and wife, he wouldn't rest.

Nash slowly stood up from the chair, torn between the two paths before him.

He wanted to seek justice for his family, but it meant risking his own life and the safety of others. Aching to know the truth and find those responsible for his wife's forced abortion, he could not act without more information.

Ivan Schneider.

Did he hold the key to unlocking everything?

Nash stepped out of the office. No matter what he chose, it would be a hard journey ahead.

With every step he took, no matter the cost, he had to do what was right.

CHAPTER
ELEVEN

Day 3
GCHQ, Cheltenham, UK
3:01 p.m.

JACK ENTERED Michael Compton's office, Senior Director of Cyber Intelligence at GCHQ, and was immediately struck by the walls lined with books and screens.

A desk was in the center of the room, and Compton was sitting at it, looking up as Jack approached.

Having never met Compton before, Jack didn't know what to expect.

He rubbed the back of his neck. The quick four-hour flight back to London had taken its toll on all of them.

"Glad you could come, Jack," The Director said, rising from his seat.

"What can I do for you?" Jack asked.

Compton motioned him to a chair. "Please take a seat."

Once Jack was seated, Compton fixed him with a steady

gaze. He was amiable enough, yet Jack couldn't shake the feeling of being closely watched.

"Jack, you're an incredibly talented agent. ISTF tells us you're the best in all things engineering and technology. How much do you know about Project Neanderthal?"

Jack hadn't heard of it, but something told him it had to do with an old code. They would only name it that way if it were important. "I'm looking forward to hearing about it," Jack answered, trying to keep his tone neutral.

Compton cleared his throat. "In 1942, the British military searched for a better way to communicate with its soldiers in the field. They used Morse code, but they encountered several obstacles. First, it was slow and had a high error rate. Second, it could not traverse vast distances. The military searched for ways to send audio across enormous distances using radio waves to fix these problems. They wanted to send voice messages across enemy territory covertly and avoid detection. The British military codenamed this project: *Neanderthal.*"

Jack leaned forward, placing his elbows on his knees.

Compton continued. "The military looked at all technological possibilities. One of those was a music-based code. One day in Rub'al Khali, some men came across a Bedouin tribe that had an interesting way of talking to each other.

"They spoke to each other in music. We brought in a team of specialists in music, cultures, and languages, and they tried to decipher the Bedouin language being used to send messages through coded music. As our men investigated, it became clear they were using a special code to communicate with each other across the desert, and they transcribed much of what they spoke in a book, an ancient book. A book that had been written for centuries.

"Our military purchased the book from them, but on the way back, it went missing, possibly in Muscat. Several years later, the book was found in the Cambridge University Library, and we brought it here for safekeeping and study, full of undecipherable code. We hoped our code breakers could decipher the language and create new communication methods. As the team worked, they soon discovered the book was much more than coded music language."

Jack's mind raced with possibilities. He was being drawn into something big and dangerous and was determined to uncover the truth behind Project Neanderthal. "Tell me about the book," Jack said.

"It detailed a vast mathematical and physical theory, and was kept in the vaults of this building," Compton replied.

"Was?" Jack pressed.

"Yes, it was. The book was stolen from us a decade ago. Despite many attempts, we could never locate it. We think someone who knows what they're doing and has deciphered the language and the physical theory took it. We need to know how it was done," Compton added, his tone serious.

"What else was in the book?" Jack asked.

"Some of it also had Arabic poetry, possibly written 3000 years ago or at the inception of the Iram civilization. They wrote it in code too, and for hundreds of years, no one knew what it was. Most of the book was a prophecy about the future. We could decode almost all of it. Except for seven blank pages," Compton said.

CHAPTER
TWELVE

London, UK
3:15 p.m.

NASH SLAMMED the keys on the desk as he stormed into their two-floor apartment, feeling familiar walls closing in on him.

The black and white furniture was a mute reminder of the life he and Calla had only enjoyed for a few fleeting months before their dreams of happily ever after came crashing down.

He collapsed in front of his laptop, letting out an anguished cry as he felt his heart nearly bursting out of his chest and his mind racing out of control.

Nash closed his eyes and desperately tried to take slow, deep breaths to find an ounce of clarity in the chaos.

What had happened to Calla at Cambridge? He still didn't have an answer.

Nash's eyes opened, and he went downstairs to make himself a cup of green tea. He needed to calm down, to think.

As he stalked toward the window, a wave of heat surge

through his veins. His eyes searched the London skyline from the towering apartment close to the River Thames.

"She has her own demons she's struggling with," Nash said out loud. "How can I help her?"

He knew he couldn't give Calla any peace of mind, not when she had been put into a fight with Europe's most dangerous criminal organization.

Nash went into the kitchen, pulled the green tea bags out of the drawer, and set them in the teapot. He filled the teapot with water and placed it on the hot plate, then went over to the counter and pulled out a chair as he waited for the tea to brew.

When he pictured the fear in Calla's eyes on the Scorpion Tide yacht, the terror in her body, the pain and the trauma in her face, it was more than he could bear. She was struggling with her decision to leave the post of head of ISTF; it was for the better. As a field agent, he had to do more. He had to gain control of their lives and not let those that would want to harm them do so.

When he returned to his desk, a calmness came over him. He had to go to Cambridge. Maybe he could find the professor, Octavia Steward's past records. Someone had to know something. He needed more information on the archaeological dig in Rub'al Khali that had taken place ten years ago and pair that with data from NASA on sightings of a lost city in Arabia.

Nash checked the NSA files to see what he could find. A few minutes later, he had a list of people at Cambridge who went on Calla's trip to Arabia. Were any of them still at Cambridge now?

He typed in the name of one listed professor.

A few seconds later, he had an address in Cambridge and knew precisely where it was.

He had been there before.

Nash wiped the sweat from his brow as chills ran up and down his spine in all the places that had skin and nerves.

This was it.

He put on a jacket and grabbed his keys.

Moments later, he jumped into his Jaguar.

CHAPTER
THIRTEEN

Cheltenham, GCHQ
3:32 p.m.

"THAT'S IMPOSSIBLE," Jack said, his mind struggling to comprehend the implications. "There's no way to predict the future."

"The book doesn't predict specific events," Compton replied. "But it predicts the consequences of certain actions. Actions we believe we can interfere with right now. I forgot to tell you that the men were in the desert because they believed something in there would change the world."

"The butterfly effect," Jack said, understanding dawning. "Big changes can come from negligible differences."

Compton nodded. "That's true, but I'm sure you know the book is much older than the butterfly effect. We decoded one chapter about using the butterfly effect to change the past. You, of all people, know it rests on two basic premises. One: big changes can come from small causes. Two: the world is deeply interconnected, such that the fate of one small niche can influence a wide range of phenomena affecting the entire world."

Jack shook his head. "How?" he asked.

"The book's main pages talk about altering history by passing through a time window. A window that requires an abundance of energy and resources," Compton explained. "Time is a dimension like space, and our timeline is very similar to the timeline of any parallel timeline. It says that certain points in history are fixed and that events before those points must have happened the same way in every timeline. Otherwise, the timeline would not exist. The book says that time windows occur when the past is altered and happens simultaneously in all timelines."

Some of this sounded very much like something. The operatives he'd worked with would tell him. Jack sat back in his chair, trying to process the information. "If that's true, then a lot of what you're saying makes little sense. A time window can't alter the future. If you alter only the past, the future will remain the same. In addition, if the timeline is converted into energy, then that timeline disappears. Plus, if there is a one-time window per timeline, then I don't understand how it can open on 'every parallel timeline."

Compton looked at Jack, his expression unreadable. "That's why we need you, Jack. We hope you can help us find the book, decipher the rest of the code, and understand what happened in the desert all those years ago, from a scientific perspective so that we can verify this. We believe the answers to all our questions are within those blank pages. And we need you to help us understand how to use the knowledge in the book to protect our future."

Compton circled his desk, thinking. "The book says that the time window opens in every parallel timeline, only altering the past. Those who lived through it keep their memories, while those in other timelines never experienced it.

The energy created by the time window applies a change to all subsequent timelines, creating variations of each person."

It was all very puzzling, but Jack would investigate it later. Somehow, Compton seemed more interested in impressing him with the decoding than telling him why he had called him there. "What happened to the book? How was the book taken?"

"Stolen from its vault a decade ago," Compton replied, his voice grave. "We have a video of the theft and have been working on it since then, but no faces are visible."

"How big was the book?" Jack asked, his mind already turning to the logistics of the heist.

"Just over a foot square and three inches thick, made from camel leather, older than science," Compton replied.

"And you think they stole it using future technology?" Jack pressed.

Compton nodded. "The vault is impervious to all known forms of entry. We used some of our new technology to check for any extant forms of video or sound recording, and we found a small wire-like camera with a very tiny lens embedded in the bookshelf of the vault. A security measure was taken, but the camera dropped out, and we found it on the floor."

"So they stole the book while recording themselves?" Jack asked, disbelief creeping into his voice.

Compton found another file. A large screen was in the room, and he called up a video from his laptop. "Take a look at this," he said.

The video was black and white and looked like it was shot at night, with a thin layer of fog obscuring the view. There was no illumination, which made the image more ominous. The camera pointed at an old book displayed on a table. It zoomed in to get a closer look, and there was a light on the book. The light grew brighter and brighter until the screen was completely white for thirty seconds and then faded to black.

Jack waited, but the video didn't continue.

"Is there more?" he asked.

"It was recorded ten years ago and was sent to us yesterday. There's no more to the video as far as I can see," Compton replied, his voice heavy with disappointment.

"What is it you want me to do with the video, exactly?" Jack asked.

"Trace the video, see who sent it to us, and see if you can find out what happened to the book," Compton said, his eyes boring into Jack's.

Jack thought for a minute. "Tell me about the seven empty pages."

"No one has been able to read them," Compton said, his voice tight with frustration. "They appear to have been written by a right-handed person, but the left side of the pages are identical. We think the pages are maps, but we don't know what the maps represent."

"How many people have seen the book?" Jack asked.

"Only a few people at GCHQ," Compton replied, his voice low and guarded. "And fewer people have seen pictures of it."

"And you want me to find out why it was stolen and what's going on with the seven pages?" Jack added.

"Correct."

"Okay," Jack said. "I'll need permission to use some of my contacts for this."

"Of course, Jack," Compton said, nodding. "And you'll have access to GCHQ's database. Especially if you want to find out who sent the video to us."

"I'll have to go to my office in London to work on it," Jack said, rising from his seat.

"I'll have the video sent to your systems, but you can use my office now if you want to start."

Jack took the opportunity and began working in the Director's office with an interactive console.

Jack moved to the desk and drew his laptop from his bag. He pulled up the database for GCHQ staff and searched through employee records. He then called up the database for ISTF to make comparisons. There was one name he wished to find: the former Director of the Kronos Empire, Ivan Schneider, a name Nash had given him that day after Calla's story in the desert, just yesterday.

Jack glanced down at his screen and waited a minute. He couldn't shake off the feeling something was off.

CHAPTER
FOURTEEN

Cambridge, UK
5:11 p.m.

AS NASH ENTERED CAMBRIDGE, a feeling of unease crept over him.

The city's intellectual prowess was undeniable, with world-famous academics having studied within the same ancient brick buildings that now housed thousands of students from around the world.

The University of Cambridge was a labyrinth of ivy-covered structures, with rows of Tudor houses lining the cobbled streets. Colleges established long before the university were nestled in historic green spaces surrounded by ancient trees. Each exuded a sense of tradition and warmth, boasting its own chapel, library, and dining hall. They were the best in England, attracting the brightest and the best of each generation.

Nash studied the address and spotted the building—the Department of Archaeology. Moments later, he stepped into the lobby and scanned the directory of names, and spoke to the doorman.

He found the right office and knocked.

"Come in," a voice said.

Nash strode through the door and was met by a man who appeared to be in his late thirties or early forties.

He extended his hand. "Hello, I'm Nash Shields from the US Embassy."

It wasn't a lie. Nash was still very much a security adviser at the Embassy in London, though ISTF and the NSA took most of his time.

The man shook his hand. "I see. Come in. We rarely get US Embassy folks here. Make yourself comfortable."

He sank into a leather couch and looked around. "Nice office," he said when his gaze set on a painting on the wall.

"Thanks," the man said. "I like it. My name is Professor Dre Garrett. But, seeing as you're not a student, we can skip the formalities, and you can just call me Dre."

Dre raised an eyebrow and turned to where Nash's eyes were looking. "Ah, that's just an oil portrait of a local man who was one of the prominent figures at the university. He's often called the founder of the British Archaeological tradition."

"I'm looking for information," Nash said, choosing his words carefully. "Can you help me? About ten years ago, there was an archaeological dig that I'm trying to find out more about. It was a dig of a supposed lost city in Arabia, possibly in the Rub'al Khali desert. Does that ring a bell with you?"

"Yes," Dre replied. "I'm aware of what you're talking about. I know people who were involved in that expedition. Why are you interested in it?"

"There's a woman who might be in danger because of that trip, and I feel that the information of the dig is somehow connected to whatever is happening to her," Nash replied.

"What do you know about the expedition?" Dre asked.

"Not much. There were a few archaeologists and students involved. Some of them were from Cambridge, I believe. I'm not sure if any still work here, though," Dre said. "I can help you. I'm affiliated with the Cambridge University Historical Society and can get you some information. You said you were from the Embassy. Is the woman American?" he asked, reaching for a phone.

"She's married to one," Nash replied, the weight of the situation heavy on his shoulders as he prepared to dive deeper.

CHAPTER
FIFTEEN

Off the East Coast of England
4:17 p.m.

WINDS WHIPPED through the underground caverns, making the air feel colder than it was. Rain and sleet fell on the head engineer, who hurried through his job so he could stay. The caverns had been drained of their water, but the in-house geologists and solution reserve engineers monitoring the dimming danger levels of the caverns couldn't figure out why. After twenty years of solution mining to create a repository facility, their work was now at risk because of an unexpected development that had occurred six hours ago.

The engineer reviewed the data but couldn't understand what caused the change. They mainly used the caverns as storage units. In-house geologists and solution mining colleagues monitored changes in pressure levels and wondered how they could keep their projects running smoothly.

Sweat rolled down the engineer's face, and the veins in his neck bulged as he reached for the phone.

Engineers jotted notes furiously, but the man stood still, staring at the floor, and counted to ten as he waited for a pickup.

Compton was meeting with a group of ministers when the phone rang.

He excused himself from the group and answered the phone.

"Sir, this is urgent," the engineer reported. "There's a severe breach heading toward a catastrophic scenario that will lead to the depletion of our oil and gas reserves. We've seen nothing like this before. We need help. You told me to alert GCHQ if anything got worse."

The Director General's eyes grew wide.

"We're losing gas and oil at a distressing rate, and we don't know why. The storage caverns are being emptied at an alarming rate," he spat the words out. "The computer models show a depletion of our inventories. I've been in charge of this facility for ten years. We've had a few anomalous readings, but this is severe. Some sort of anomaly that's causing our reserves to dwindle. The depletion is not normal," he said.

Compton twisted his lips. "Halt all oil and gas extraction immediately until we know what's going on. We're losing too much of it, and the threat is increasing. I'm afraid it's a hack, a global one." the head of GCHQ said.

"The reduction is happening inside the storage facility, not outside, threatening our country's supply. Deficiency is severe, and someone is taking over the maintenance."

Compton hung up and returned to the session. "I'm sorry, gentlemen. I have to respond to an emergency. We'll finish this meeting at another time."

CHAPTER
SIXTEEN

Cambridge
5:40 p.m.

"HELLO," Dre said into the phone, his voice tinged with urgency. "Is Emily there?" He shot a glance at Nash. "Can you get me information on Professor Ivan Schneider? He worked with this institution ten years ago in archaeology. I think he was German."

Nash watched him closely.

"Emily," Dre continued. "I have a question. Do you have any information you can give me on an archaeological dig that took place ten years ago and Ivan Schneider's involvement, possibly others?... Yes. It was a dig for a lost city in the Middle East, possibly the so-called City of Pillars or the Atlantis of the Sands. The one that Lawrence of Arabia went looking for. Would you mind checking?"

Nash listened intently, assuming Emily was searching for the information.

"Yes," Dre said. "Thank you very much." He hung up the phone, turning to Nash with a grave expression. "OK," he said. "Emily has just pinged over the information to my computer."

He quickly logged onto his laptop and studied the notes on the screen. "Ivan Schneider never returned from the dig, nor to Cambridge, but he was employed here, according to some of my diggings from an informant. A former student's father."

Nash felt a lump form in his throat. What was an assassin doing, posing as a professor? He remained calm as Dre read out more information.

"Says here, our professor Ivan was the only one not to return to Cambridge, but also one of the key organizers. The lead professor, Octavia Steward, also failed to return to Cambridge, though we know she survived the trip. I believe she may have been, shall we say, fired? A handwritten note here suggests she and one student could have been responsible for the man's death. The police never investigated, and it went to British Intelligence Services. Strangely, they also asked a man named Rion Loman, of Irish origin, with little to his academic record, to accompany the group. Rion returned with an amputated arm." Dre looked up at Nash for a second and narrowed his eyes. "What sort of expedition was this?"

"Not sure," Nash said, his mind racing. "What about the students? Any information on them?"

"I'm afraid I can't give you that information. We're bound by privacy protection."

"Fair enough," Nash said, his mind already turning to other likely sources. Calla, a key witness in their investigation, had been on that trip, but the bodies were stacking up, and somebody must have been behind this whole thing. Who? And why? The trip had caused a memory gap for Calla, almost as if the trauma had pushed parts of the trip from her brain. "And Ivan? How long was he with the university?"

"I don't know," Dre replied. "There was never a body found according to this. I have his last address here."

Nash lifted his chin. "My information tells me they only hired him for that expedition, and he was not with the university long before he was assigned. How could he have gone on an archaeological dig in Arabia with students?"

"I assume he must've been with the government. Perhaps for protection, as our department was quite new then, and going to some parts of the world required it," Dre answered. "I assume he was on loan, but from where, it's not clear."

"Okay," Nash added. "Anything else?"

"One more thing," Dre said. "Says here, on the day before the dig began, there was an enormous sandstorm in Arabia. They canceled all flights to and from Salalah in Iram, Oman. The expedition had to wait three days before anyone could get to the area."

"I see."

Dre continued. "I remember reading an article about a set of DNA found in the expedition area. They were of an unknown genealogical type. MI6 seized that information before we could investigate. That's where the trail ends, I'm afraid. I find it strange our files don't have any logical records on this expedition, which is not normal. We usually have excellent records, but I have no more for you."

"That's very helpful. Glad to get the confirmation about Schneider," Nash said. "Thank you very much."

Dre lifted an eyebrow. "No problem. But if you don't mind me asking, what's your interest in Ivan Schneider?"

"I have a colleague I think was close to him," Nash replied.

"I have the names of some student archaeologists on the expedition," Dre said. "If you can wait a day or two, I might get the clearance to give out more information on them. I have pictures of them, and I have the name of a current professor who works in Cambridge now and often goes to Berlin to Humboldt University for research. Would you want this information as well?"

"Yes, please," Nash said.

It was strange to be intrigued about something that might have no obvious benefit to his investigation, but he couldn't deny that this was what he needed. Perhaps he'd even find more to it, but he was getting ahead of himself.

"Great," Dre said. He wrote a few notes on a piece of paper and handed them to Nash.

"I don't know what this is all about," Dre said. "But if you think it is important, I hope you find what you are looking for."

Nash gave him a nod. "Thanks. You've been a big help. Here's my number for when you get clearance to release the files and if you think of anything else."

He shook Dre's hand and left.

The professor had undoubtedly unearthed what Nash needed. Ivan Schneider was a mock professor at Cambridge University, somehow connected to the government and possibly ISTF. How? Nash would have to work that out. Ivan had never returned from the expedition. Octavia Steward led it all, and a certain amputee, Rion, possibly a former Irish Army officer from the Defense Forces of Ireland, was also involved. There was also a debate about who was responsible for Ivan's death.

His phone beeped. Somehow, he must have warmed to Dre. A series of photos and notes began popping up on his phone. Nash studied the pictures of the archaeologists. There was Calla, beautiful at eighteen, even as she was now.

Dre's information also had an address of an archaeologist who also had been a scholar at Cambridge University and moved to Berlin three years ago, a certain Ralf Urs. He had been noted for his work in South America.

Nash studied the paper, trying to remember if he had heard the name before. He couldn't quite put his finger on it.

Hands on the steering wheel, he thought hard, then turned

on the engine. At this time of day, he hoped it would only be an hour to his next destination.

As the car sped, Nash decided he wouldn't mention what he was learning about the expedition and the people involved until he had proof—something to back up his claims.

But what would he tell Calla?

Ivan Schneider had been on the NSA watchlist for twenty years. Nash had contacted Stan in Crete. Calla's father knew much more than he sometimes shared. Schneider had at some point been tipped off to lead the Kronos Genetysis Empire and was also the man who had been paid to target his and Calla's unborn baby many months ago and caused her miscarriage.

CHAPTER
SEVENTEEN

Schloss Engel, Schleswig-Holstein
Northern Germany
8:13 p.m.

THERE WAS nothing colorful about the castle. It didn't even have a flag on the roof. Schloss Engel was an ominous ancient stone fortress that overlooked the valley. Windswept, barren mountains were too far away to see in the dark, though here and there, a glint of light hinted at their presence. The structure sparkled like diamonds, not as a metaphor, but as a technological feat.

Snow swirled around the fortress, and the wind howled as it blew through the high open windows. The castle's foundation of turreted walls was made of white marble. A maze of intersecting staircases adorned the exterior, some with spiral ramps of iron that led to the peak next to wide concrete walls. Built into the side of a mountain, the exterior of the building was steel, as smooth as a mirror, with large tinted windows.

A window flashed with lightning as a pair of lone security

guards stood at the fortress's peak, watching the storm through the many windows. Kronos Genetysis Engineering headquarters was nestled within the fortress, a modern structure that contradicted the old castle foundations.

Octavia stirred and opened her eyes, feeling disoriented by the darkness that surrounded her. Not a single beam of sunlight or glimmer of moonlight made it in. She tried to take in her surroundings, seeing the walls were a grimy shade of gray that could make any heart sink.

There was a bed to one side with nothing but an old, tattered blanket and a toilet and sink.

Octavia reached for her head, feeling the bandage wrapped around it. Her nose filled with the smell of nothingness. She wanted to get out of there but was unsure what new danger awaited her outside.

She remembered being in the middle of a crucial interview with renowned journalist Manfred Bierman of RTL TV when an intruder barged into the studio out of nowhere.

On the one hand, the prospect of having her manuscript bought had excited her; on the other, she was terrified by the unknowns.

As her mind started racing with questions, a feeling of dread overcame her, and she felt herself fading into darkness. Her throat was dry, her mouth dryer. She shuffled to the door and pressed her face against the small rectangular window above the doorknob.

Two men stood outside, one on either side of the door. It was like staring into a wax museum. Their expressions were blank, their eyes wide, and they stood utterly still.

She tried the door, but it was locked from the outside, the deadbolt firmly in place, and it looked like it had been newly installed.

"Hey!" she called out. "What's going on here?"

When there was no answer, she pounded on the door with

her fists until she thought the bones in her hands would break.

The door opened with a hiss, and a man with a prosthetic arm entered the room, his broad shoulders stiff with irritation.

He yanked her arm, grabbing her elbow so tightly that she grimaced. The man looked familiar; she was almost sure she had seen him before, but she couldn't quite place where. It was too dark to see properly.

His face bore the scars of a burn. "Enough of this," he said.

She could barely taste the blood from her bitten tongue. Octavia's hands were slick with sweat as she tried to keep her voice steady. "Who are you?" she asked. "What is this place?"

"Get back," he said. "You're still weak."

"No," she replied. "I want answers to my questions."

"Get some rest."

That sounded like he cared.

"Look," Octavia said, "I don't know who you think you are or what you think is going on here..."

He studied her. "You don't remember me, do you?"

She saw him clearly for the first time. A boxy man, rectangular as a piece of paper, his bulky body was packed into thick clothes. He had a skull tattoo on the back of his neck and the letter "R" on the back of his left hand. "Maybe you're better off not knowing," he said.

She squinted an eye.

He then walked out and slammed the door shut behind him.

Octavia listened to him trudge down the hallway and round the corner. Hearing those sounds brought back a sense of reality. The memories rushed back: someone had kidnapped her, and she did not know why. She didn't know how long she would be there or how to escape. For now, Octavia tried to focus on what kind of place this was.

She needed to know if any of her friends would hurt her and had to accept that.

Suffolk, UK
8:27 p.m.

NASH DROVE DOWN THE A-14, passing through Witchford, Oakington, and Chippenham villages. The spring sun beamed down on him, providing no reprieve from the increasing traffic. Every turnoff seemed to bring more obstacles in his way. He gritted his teeth as he maneuvered around the ever-increasing number of vehicles, dreading his arrival at Bury St. Edmunds.

Several minutes later, he parked his Jaguar outside a concrete building.

A beige slab was in front of a white, unmarked building. Other than the bleached letters of the National Security Agency carved into the glass doors, there was no sign of what lay inside. The building was located just a mile from the Royal Air Force Base Mildenhall in West Suffolk, home to the United States Air Force and other American Special Forces units.

Nash stepped into the NSA section of the building.

He opened the door to a room that almost felt like a

mausoleum, with a silence more tangible than the peeling gray walls.

Old boxes were scattered across the mottled floor, casting eerie shadows in the dim light.

Stan was hunched over his desk, pecking away at his keyboard.

As Nash entered, Stan looked up and greeted him.

It wasn't a place Nash wanted to be, and he forced a skeleton grin. 'I'm not late, am I?' he asked, already knowing the answer might be worse than he feared.

Stan shook his head with a lopsided grin. "No, you're not late," he replied. "Come on over and look at this."

Stan was staring intently at a laptop, but only glanced at Nash as he sat down, then turned back to the screen.

"What have we got?" Nash asked.

Stan turned to look at him, and for a moment, there was a flicker of humor in his eyes. Then it was gone, and he was all business again. "I was just about to tell you when you walked in the door. This was sent to Rodney Cook recently. The operatives found it in the Arabian Sea area. I think it might interest you."

Nash did not want to discuss Rodney Cook, his former NSA boss who had gone AWOL and was now considered a traitor. Since Cook's disappearance and betrayal, he had been rumored to be in the Middle East. Nobody talked about him anymore.

Nash raised an eyebrow. "The Arabian Sea?"

Stan pointed to the screen, and the light illuminated his face as he stared at a rock in his open palm and a gadget technology in the plastic box he had placed on the desk.

Nash's jaw clenched as he tried to hold back any emotion. 'Did you have any trouble getting in?' Nash asked.

"Nope," Stan said, looking up from the table. "I used your

credentials as you instructed. I thought you wouldn't show up."

"I almost didn't," Nash said. "This place gives me the creeps."

Stan nodded. "I know what you mean. It's like being in a mortuary that's been abandoned for years. I keep expecting to see a ghost or two."

Nash laughed. "Yeah, a couple of ghosts wouldn't be that bad. Maybe they can tell us what this technology is. That thing you picked up looks like it's from another world."

Stan nodded. "It is."

Nash walked over and picked up the rock.

"The technology is a key, and the rock is the lock. It came from Rub'al Khali, perhaps the only thing I got from my investment from the Cambridge archaeological trip."

"Why did you pay for that trip?" Nash asked.

Stan looked at him squarely. "I don't think I need to answer that. It was to save Calla. With me in charge, I could monitor my daughter and make sure she returned safely."

Nash examined the rock and thought he saw a slight indentation on one side. "What do you think?"

"Think you have it right," Stan said, handing Nash the rock. "This thing feels like it's charged with unusual energy from another world. It's the thing I've never understood about the operatives. I think it might be theirs. It was found in the Lost City of Iram, a city I'm increasingly thinking deals with the beginnings of the operatives' lives in history and an event we codenamed at MI6—the Divide. It's strange. I never knew when I joined MI6 that I would chase criminals from other nations whose connections we strongly tie to history. The kind of history we don't understand that affects terrorism worldwide today."

Nash studied the rock again but couldn't see any more indentations. "Do these pieces go together?"

"That's what I'm hoping," Stan answered. "They might tell us more about the NSA's investigation and findings around companies that have invested in Rub'al Khali."

Nash laid the pieces on the table. "If I'm to protect Calla, I must figure this out."

"Don't give yourself such a hard time, Nash. You're everything she needs. Sometimes your love will be enough."

"And others?"

"Do what I couldn't do for Calla; and her mother, Nicole. Give her an existence in this world by keeping the ways of the operatives subservient to her and not the other way around. Calla, like her mother, is an operative, which is a strength, not a weakness," Stan added.

Nash picked up the rock again and slipped it into the indentation in the piece of technology. The two parts locked together, and then the piece glowed. His eyes widened, his curiosity aroused. "How did this thing get here?"

"The Blackhorse Group has many secrets. Some good, some of them not so much," Stan replied. "But they're on our side, and I'm part of them, like my father and great-grandfather before me. He helped the operatives when he first knew of their existence and helped them from the moment he learned of the Divide."

Nash mused. "I suppose that's why it was easy for you to understand Calla's mother."

"I must admit I pursued her when at MI6. I was fascinated and knew she was an operative. Nicole is the best of them. Strong, stubborn, but a damn good operative. We just made one minor mistake. We had Calla. But in my eyes, that's the best thing that ever happened to me, but we must not let whatever happened in Rub'al Khali ruin that for us. I want you and Calla to have the best life you can, and if it involves children, I want that for you and will protect that right. I want you to have what I gave up by loving an operative." He paused and stared at the rock. "I've seen what dark matter does to people. But there's a way to change things."

Nash studied him. "You saying we're dealing with dark matter here?"

Stan drew in a sharp breath. "Possibly. But we won't know until someone returns to Iram."

CHAPTER
NINETEEN

London
9:32 p.m.

CALLA'S PHONE RANG, and she answered, "Allegra?"

"The Foreign Secretary is in the ISTF building waiting for you. He's been briefed," Allegra said.

"At this hour. What does he want?"

"My guess is he's looking to protect his party's chances in the next election and wants to be on top of anything that could endanger British politics in the future," Allegra explained. "Just hear him out. He's harmless."

Despite her reservations, Calla's curiosity got the better of her, so she took her Maserati with Jack and Nash, after consulting them, to the ISTF building in London.

The Foreign Secretary's piercing gaze locked onto Calla as they settled into their seats in a large office. His dark hair was slicked back but not quite neat enough to hide the hint of unkemptness. A trace of stubble adorned his jaw and cheeks, adding a rough edge to his otherwise polished appearance. He was dressed in a crisp shirt and tailored jacket, but the creases in his clothing suggested he had been in them for some time. He stood tall but not as imposing as she remembered.

It had only been a day since ISTF had revealed to her the chaos in Berlin, Octavia's disappearance, and the mess that the British government and ISTF were left to clean up. Calla couldn't shake the feeling that something sinister was brewing.

The Foreign Secretary could see the questions in her eyes. "Octavia used to work for the British government and went undercover for us in Berlin about three years ago. She recovered an ancient book with answers to the City of Sands. GCHQ took the book to study it, but it went missing about ten years ago."

Calla considered the possibilities. Octavia must've had the book when they went on the expedition all those years ago.

She peered at Jack and Nash and thought about the book, safely tucked away on Scorpion Tide, which her father had sent on to her.

The Foreign Secretary continued, "Octavia's mission was to work secretly as an adviser to the Pergamon Museum in Berlin. Within some of Berlin's archives from the museum, they found artifacts that supposedly came from the Lost City of Sands 2000 years ago. We need to know a great deal more, and we don't have access to any of Octavia's work. I need you to find those artifacts and confiscate them."

Things hadn't ended well the last time Calla had been to the City of Sands. And now, every time the thought of it crossed her mind, it felt like a weight pressing down on her.

The ciphers she had seen in the Knossos Temple in Crete had triggered memories she wished she could forget, a weakness in her deciphering abilities.

The Foreign Secretary leaned forward, his voice low and

urgent. "Confiscate all remaining artifacts from Mesopotamia and Arabia at the Pergamon Museum. Destroy any evidence of her having worked there. No one is to find her or her secret project. She was a plant, Agent Cress. And we need you to find her before anyone else does. Do you understand?"

Calla met his gaze, a hint of skepticism creeping into her eyes.

Nash and Jack exchanged a glance.

The Foreign Secretary leaned in closer, his voice barely above a whisper. "The ancient book was broken out of GCHQ. Octavia's mission was to find out who else would want it. But now it seems like she had other ideas and has gone missing.

"This is a matter of the utmost importance," the Foreign Secretary said in a low, intense voice. "Octavia's kidnapping must be kept under wraps at all costs. The public cannot know about any of this. Octavia was sent to Berlin, undercover at the Pergamon Museum, to secure the secrets of the Lost City of the Atlantis of the Sands. She was to be sent back to the desert with the right team and equipment. That's why I'm calling you now. We need to find out who else would want the book and what they might do to get it."

"What's in the book?" Calla asked.

"I don't know," the Foreign Secretary replied, his expression grave. "I only know what Allegra told me in the briefing. Allegra Driscoll was only her handler for a brief time."

The pause hung heavy in the air as the Foreign Secretary scratched his head. "I think it was more than that. Octavia was always very secretive about her missions."

Calla could sense the urgency in Jack and Nash's silence as they waited to hear what he would say next. Her mind raced as she tried to piece together all the information she had. "So if Octavia was trying to find out who else would want the book, why did she give an exclusive interview to the German press?" she asked.

The answer was complicated and not one that any of them wanted to hear.

The Foreign Secretary drew in a deep breath. "We believe it was to raise funds for her expedition. It's all very personal to her, and we don't know why."

"Octavia had been in Berlin for two years and had made little headway," he added. "We believe she went off the grid. She reasoned that the only way to secure immediate funding was to make a splash in the media. I had turned down her request for more funds. My guess is she intended to go back to Atlantis. She had some grants, and she needed more."

"My understanding," Calla said, "was that the first expedition was funded privately and had nothing to do with the government. Why should the government expect to be involved now?"

The Foreign Secretary cleared his throat and dropped a series of photographs on the mahogany table.

Calla knew what she would see before he could finish what he was saying. The photographs were of the expedition, and their university group was at the gates of Atlantis of the Sands. There was a code. The same code that had hardly slipped her mind for years. The same code that a hacker had used in Crete.

"Because of this," the Foreign Secretary continued, tapping a finger on one photograph. "It's the same cipher GCHQ has been trying to decipher for years, and it resembles the text in the stolen book. We need you to find out who might want it."

Nash reached for the photos, sharing them with Jack. "We'll look at these and let you know," he said.

Calla couldn't help but feel a sense of dread at the thought of approaching the Pergamon Museum again. The last time she had tried to break in, she had nearly been killed. Despite her fears, she knew she had to do it. If this book was truly valuable, the wrong people might try to get their hands on it before the ISTF did.

"Do whatever you need to do," the Foreign Secretary said, steeling himself away from them.

CHAPTER
TWENTY

Central London

9:47 p.m.

TAIVEN LEANED against the table at the back of the club and scanned the room. He had to see Calla immediately and had no time to waste.

He rose and pushed past the crowd to his private table, away from prying eyes. The news about the Book of Iram had to have been terrible for Calla to hear. Stan had called him urgently after she had left with it.

Taiven rose and went to take a seat at the bar so he wouldn't miss her. He complimented the bartender on their artistry and ordered a glass of whiskey with a pineapple slice and a lime twist. The combination of flavors delighted him, and he thought it was worth the cost, despite the price.

A few weeks had passed since Taiven had last seen Calla. They hadn't been in touch, and Calla was uncertain about delving into the past and potentially unearthing deeply buried memories. The possibility of being unable to decode the language of the ancient Iram culture weighed on her, despite her exceptional skills in analyzing ancient texts and ciphers.

Taiven knew Calla was trying to forget something, and he feared that her talent for deciphering ancient languages might have been lost in a web of emotions. Taiven needed to help her break through barriers.

He sat at the bar, waiting for her to arrive. When she did, she looked tired. She was wearing a black dress, and her face showed no signs that she had traveled far, but her eyes gave away the weariness that had settled in the wake of the late hour.

The hostess asked if she was meeting someone, and Calla smiled and waved at Taiven.

The hostess nodded and gestured to where Taiven was sitting.

Taiven rose and moved over to Calla. He looked her in the eyes and smiled. "I'm glad you're here," he said.

"I'm here now," Calla replied, returning his smile.

"Didn't think you'd come," Taiven said. "Thought you'd been avoiding me."

Calla grinned. "Now, why would I do that? No," she said. "Taiven, even though we only met officially about eighteen months ago, something tells me you've known me all my life. No one knows more about me than you do, Taiven. I just went through a rough patch."

Taiven studied her face, then led her back to the private table, and they ordered.

"So," Taiven said. "Do you want to talk about Crete?"

Calla recoiled. "Nothing concerning the operatives is easy to explain. My dreams are bothering me. In Knossos, it was the first time my enemies used a real-life threat. Somebody desperately wants me back in Rub'al Khali. I froze. When I was in the Minoan ruins, I was suddenly back in the desert.

The ciphers were so frightening. I'm losing sleep and finding it hard to concentrate."

Taiven placed a warm hand over hers. "I'm here to help you remember and protect you as much as possible. It was the second time we knew this had happened to you. I believe that whatever was done to you in that hospital in high school was triggered when you went on the trip to Rub'al Khali. Remember, you're a powerful operative. If Mason Laskfell, the only man who has come close to killing you, continues to stop you wherever he is, it's only because you're more powerful. You've got to believe that. Laskfell continues to operate in the shadows and uses more powerful people. All he wants is to consume you; if he can use others to do it, he will. I won't let that happen, and I never thought I'd say this, but I don't think Nash or Jack will let that happen, either."

She leaned in. "Taiven, I fear I'm losing my mind. You and higher-standing operatives didn't want me with Nash. You thought it threatened the operatives."

Taiven listened intently, not wanting to interrupt her as she spoke, but he needed her to know. "We saw what happened to your mother and your father. We were wrong. Somehow being with Nash strengthens you and the operative genes in you, a person of the Divide. We underestimated how much separating you from your parents would create bonds to others that are deeper than family and more profound than operative genetics. As you know, the first time we ever saw this was when we learned if you and Nash ever had a child, it would be something we have not seen. Those who wanted you harmed feared that."

When Calla had finished eating, he leaned back in his chair and looked at her. "Calla," he whispered. "These dreams... they're not real."

Calla grimaced. "What do you mean?"

"I mean," Taiven said. "They're just echoes of the past."

Calla shook her head. "No," she said. "They can't be. Why won't they leave me alone? A man died."

"I believe I know what caused the dreams."

"What?" Calla said.

"That first year at Cambridge, the expedition took you to a place where you had to use a skill you hadn't mastered, and it played with your mind. It doesn't mean that you can't. We need to get you to a place where you can master it and take control of it. When you were in that desert cave chamber surrounded by sinking sand, you froze then, too, just like you did in Knossos."

"What should I do, Taiven?"

"That's not the question you should be asking. You need to ask what point in your memory do you need to visit to unlock what happened back then," he responded. "I think you saw something in that chamber you weren't meant to see."

"What do you mean?" Calla said, her voice barely above a whisper.

"I think," Taiven said slowly, "you saw something that triggered a memory. A memory of something that happened even when you weren't conscious."

Calla shook her head. "No," she said. "That's not right." Her brain was shielding a part of her memory, and she was in denial.

"Open your mind to remember," Taiven said.

"You mean hypnosis? How? I don't want to."

"You've got to try something. Otherwise, the nightmares will never stop."

Taiven was right, but it still scared Calla she might remember everything. Things her brain had made sure she forgot for a reason.

"Your coding skills are innate and deeply rooted in genetics and heritage gifted to you. It's the same with your fighting power and strength. It's also connected to how you react to gravity."

Taiven watched as Calla's eyes glazed over. "I'm ready to help you remember when you are," he said.

"Here?" she said, looking around.

He nodded. "I've paid handsomely for this private space. No one will disturb us."

"All right." She closed her eyes, and he waited for her breathing to calm before she began. "There was a high wall and a door made of solid sand," she whispered.

"What else?" said Taiven gently.

CHAPTER
TWENTY-ONE

Day 4
Valetta Palace, Malta
8:15 p.m.

THOUSANDS OF LIGHTS on dozens of yachts bobbed in the harbor, casting a shimmering pattern on the water's surface. Malta glimmered like a shining city of light, with its harbor as the most luminous point.

The Valetta Palace was a masterpiece from a bygone era, a smooth and modest fortress that served as a single, unique mold for the metropolis, exuding an elegance, grandeur, and luxury that spoke of a time when a man's house was his castle. A mighty fortress of light, the beacon of the city, it rendered all other lights insignificant.

Calla remembered the court surrounded by fanciful statues and portraits of old, forgotten leaders, boasting architecture that was a mix of beaux-arts, Baroque, Rococo, and neoclassical styles.

She wore a burgundy and gold gown with a corset waist adorned with large beads, and a hemline trimmed in gold lace.

Her hair was elegantly styled in a French twist, and diamond earrings sparkled on her ears.

Jack and Nash donned formal black tuxedos.

Security and secrecy were of the utmost importance. Without a pass, no one could enter or leave.

They entered a foyer, an impressive sight with the main staircase in front of them. To their left were two wings of the palace, and to their right was the eastern wing.

An organization of security guards closely scrutinized everyone who stepped through the palace doors.

Calla looked to her right and saw a row of sleek, high-tech scanners and metal detectors that hummed and beeped as people passed through them.

At every entrance, security personnel stood watch, their eyes scanning the crowds for any sign of trouble.

Calla smoothed her dress, and Nash complimented how she looked.

She felt uneasy, but Nash told her she looked damn good. That was enough for her. Calla tugged at her dress. One thing she had to admit, the men looked splendid.

Calla, Jack, and Nash ascended the grand staircase and entered the palace's second-floor ballroom. Elegant iron chandeliers sparkled, and white marble floors gleamed from the light reflecting from the mirrors on the walls. Paintings of the palace, musicians, trees, and birds and horses—scenes familiar for hundreds of years—hung on the walls. Persian rugs spread across the floor, adding to the luxurious atmosphere. Classical statues—frozen in time—made the place majestic. Paintings of Maltese landscapes and elaborate marble trim decorated more walls, and the harbor was visible through a wall of glass to the north.

Calla was awestruck by its sheer opulence and grandeur as they walked deeper into the palace.

Even though she had only been inside for a few minutes, Calla felt like she had stepped into another world entirely.

Kronos had gone to great lengths to ensure that the best archaeologists, scientists, and historians were in attendance. They wanted the best minds working on their project.

The gala was in full swing, with the aroma of champagne and lavish food filling the air. White-coated staff brought out trays with glasses, filling them as quickly as they were drained.

The tinkling of the drinks and murmur of voices echoed in the marble halls of the grand ballroom.

At the center of the room, a quartet played a Beethoven piece. Guests moved around them, sipping drinks and admiring ancient artifacts.

"Yes, there's a good contingent of the Blackhorse Group. Kumar, the billionaire, Samuel Riche, Salib. We bumped into them not too long ago," Nash said, checking his GPS watch, something he rarely left home without these days. "But notice there's no sign of the CEO of Kronos. He or she has no name and goes by a pseudonym, Kronos 1."

"Yup," Jack replied. "They'll spend money to uncover the Earth's secrets and more."

The room hushed as the lights dimmed and focused on a large stage for what seemed like a grand presentation, with two people standing on the platform: a man and a woman.

The man towered over his co-presenter. His dark hair was slicked back from his face, and he wore an elegant, dark tuxedo.

The woman stood half a step behind him, her shoulders thrown back and her head held high. Her long black hair framed a heart-shaped face, and red sequins adorned the length of her dress that shimmered under the lights.

The crowd fell silent as the curtains opened, revealing a

blue light sweeping across the stage, accompanied by the thrumming of an acoustic guitar.

A few spotlights illuminated the back of the platform, which was out of view for most. The rest of the stage was bathed in an eerie blue glow. In all its glory, a hologram of the reimagined Lost City of Iram emerged before them.

The blue light flickered across the stage, illuminating only the back. The holographic image was an accurate representation of the city. Tall obelisks, lush with greenery, stood high above the city. However, the hologram flickered and wavered from the obelisks as if something was interfering with the signal.

The presenters cleared their throats and unleashed a small chorus of coughs as they found their places on the podium.

As the small crowd waited expectantly, the curtains swung open behind the speakers, revealing an enormous wall encased in glass.

The female archaeologist who was first to speak gestured to the large model behind the glass. "This 3D projection is based on our data from the Lost City of Iram, also known as the Atlantis of the Sands. Fabled to have been destroyed in the great flood of the second millennium BC, the citadel was lost to the Persian Gulf sands during the opening years of the Bronze Age and was thought to be a myth by science until now."

She smiled as she addressed the audience. "This 3D projection is the result of a decade-long collaboration between scientists and archaeologists. We're still working to verify the data, and we'll likely have some revisions and perhaps even new findings to report in the coming months. But for now, we proudly present the molecular model of the Lost City of Iram. A city that some believed never existed."

The woman held a stack of papers in one hand and a rolled-up map in the other. "Ladies and gentlemen, we will begin. Prepare to be amazed by what the world conceals. As you know," she continued, "we have unveiled several artifacts from the Lost City. They are a remarkable discovery, but we have no information about the city's whereabouts. However, we will soon. If you wish to be part of this adventure, you can. Tonight is about celebration and contribution."

"At least now we have a clue where to start," the man interjected.

She walked to a table covered in papers and unrolled a map and documents. One piece of paper slipped off as she aligned the edges of the papers to cover the table. She stooped down to retrieve it and put it back in place. Holding one end of the map, she picked up an object from another stack of papers. "This is one of the objects we found. We believe it's a map of the city, and we think the next clue is in these pages." She unfolded the pages. "They're pages from the diary of a sailor who sailed to where the city is believed to be. He was on a ship called *The Eleven Prow*."

The crowd gasped.

Calla examined the diary, a famous artifact that had never been seen in public before.

The woman pointed to the top of the map. "The Blackhorse Group. This is from your very midst and your heritage. The Group has existed for millennia. You and others have tried to find the city in the 16th century. It may seem like a strange coincidence," she continued, "but we believe that this sailor may have discovered the city."

"The artifacts show evidence of advanced technology, far beyond our own. Therefore, we believe the city could have even more advanced technology. To be part of history, we will contact you about your interest in involvement, and we expect deep pockets," the man added.

After the presentation, Calla, Nash, and Jack made their way back to their table. A live Latin music band boomed, causing Calla's ears to vibrate. She sat down and lifted her arm off Jack's chair.

Nash pushed through the crowd and took Calla's hand, leading her to the dance floor. He pulled her close, his hands on her waist, and looked around the room carefully.

Calla felt like a delicate flower in his arms as he twirled her around the floor.

The music slowed like a candlelit flamenco, and she closed her eyes, trying to commit the moment to memory. More music echoed in the air, their faces close together, and his breath warm on her cheek.

"Is this how we do undercover work from now on?" she asked.

"Best to blend in," Nash said, looking at her. "So these are artifacts they have found but do not know how they came upon this information? My money is on Ivan Schneider, the double agent who worked for Kronos and the British government," Nash added.

"Seems like such a far-fetched idea. And yet, some people are convinced that this lost city holds advanced technology that could change the world as we know it," Calla said. "At Cambridge, we were never sure we even set foot on the ruins of this ancient city. We only got to the gates, I believe."

Nash raised an eyebrow. "These artifacts blend high tech and ancient science?"

"I suppose. What if we're not looking for a city in ruins? that city holds something else. A dark secret." Calla said. "You and I know anything is possible in our line of work."

"The presenter who showed the map insists on artifacts. Do you suppose they want to raise money from the treasure hunters in the room?" Nash asked.

"I realize," she said, "if this city exists, and if it has the technology we think it does. Could be dangerous."

Nash jolted his head. "But what technology? Why are they

being cryptic? You always make me see things differently, but it all seems impossible."

"And yet, some people would risk everything to find this lost city," Nash added. "Plus, the British government wants us to confiscate anything, Octavia was working on. Which only means Kronos knows more than they are sharing."

Calla had seen the look in the eyes of such people. They would die for a cause or money. She felt an itch between her shoulder blades as she noticed the other people in the room. "Let's stop dancing."

"What is it?" Nash asked.

"Him."

CHAPTER
TWENTY-TWO

Valetta Palace, Kronos Briefing Room
9:34 p.m.

SOMEONE HAD to pay for the past, and she had to finish her father's work. Avo stood in the doorway of the briefing room, peering through the crack at the ballroom.

Calla weaved through the crowd, her dark hair bouncing off her shoulders, and a glint in her eye.

Avo's left hand tightened around her pocketbook containing an ultrasound photograph.

Memories of pain flooded back to her of her father's death in the desert of Iram and losing her child, taken too soon. Panic welled up in her chest as she realized she had to stop Calla from going to Iram.

Calla's presence would foil Kronos' plans, and Avo couldn't let that happen.

Ivan, Avo's father, had gone to Iram to secure a critical resource for Kronos, and if Calla hadn't abandoned him, they would already have the information they needed.

The trauma of those events caused a panic attack, resulting

in her child's premature birth. The baby had been far too young to survive outside the womb, but Avo had survived the ordeal.

As an operative mother, Avo had been trained to keep her emotions in check, no matter the situation. But watching the woman responsible for taking everything she held dear was almost too much to bear.

Avo moved back to her chair and gripped the hard plastic armrest tightly, grinding her teeth as Rowe Norkus, head of ISTF, and the new Red Fox began explaining the mission and its importance.

Her toes curled inside her shoes, and she felt a little sick to her stomach. Despite proving herself in fieldwork over the last five years, ISTF leaders had never allowed her to lead an operation. Avo had just finished a long-term assignment in South Africa, but ISTF assigned the next project to another agent.

Rowe had assigned Calla and her team, including NSA specialist Nash Shields and tech expert Jack Kleve, on a code or artifact retrieval mission.

Avo had graduated at the top of ISTF's training academy, had field experience, and was a skilled pilot. She couldn't understand why they didn't think she could handle this mission. Avo had never been on a mission like this before, but she was determined to prove herself. Her mind wandered as Rowe continued discussing the boring details of the back office mission.

Feeling like a child again, watching her mother walk away without noticing her, Avo had the urge to grab Rowe by his jacket and demand that he look at her. Instead, she took a deep breath and reminded herself that this was only the beginning. She was going to prove her worth on Iram, one way or another.

"I'm ready," she said, making her way to the door.

Rowe looked down at his datapad. "You're pushing your luck, Schneider. Look at that gap in your code-breaking record...." He shook his head and tsked his tongue. "I didn't forget about you when making my selections for this mission. I need people I can depend on."

"I can do the job," Avo insisted.

"I'm sorry, but there's no room for you on this team."

Avo felt her face flush. She hung her head for a moment before raising it to look at Rowe. "One of these days, you'll realize your mistake," she told him before turning on her heel and leaving the room.

CHAPTER
TWENTY-THREE

Valetta Palace

9:43 p.m.

NASH RAISED AN EYEBROW. "HIM WHO?"

A thousand ants seemed to crawl over Calla's skin. "Rowe Norkus. He's here."

Nash followed Calla's gaze to a slender man in a tuxedo. He wore a suit so crisp it might have just been purchased, a white dress shirt, a black bow tie, and black dress shoes.

Rowe stood by the bar observing the room, arms crossed over his chest and captivated by a wide-beamed chandelier hanging above him.

When he saw Calla, he paused and ordered a whiskey. His face became a stone mask as he stared at her, and his eyes pierced into her being.

A smile broke out on his face as he took a sip of whiskey and nodded, then he made his way to her side and tried not to look uncomfortable.

"I'll get us drinks," Nash said. "Be right back. Don't let him bully you."

"Never."

Nash smiled. "I know you can break him in two."

"Dance with me," Rowe said, approaching and taking her hand as Nash left for the bar.

She hoped it would be a brief dance. Calla tried to pull away, but he held her close.

"I didn't mean to make you uncomfortable," he said. "I need a favor."

Rowe had something else he wanted. Calla had never forgotten her encounter with Rowe at Beacon Academy, although she had tried to push it to the back of her mind.

She admired his ambition and drive. Rowe had grown up in London and was of Lithuanian descent, his grandparents having emigrated and established one of the largest tech corporations in Europe. But she didn't know he worked for GCHQ until they met again at a technology summit.

"A favor?" Calla asked, then frowned. "What's the favor?"

"Be careful out there."

"Sounds like you care, but you have caused a lot of trouble over the years when you were at GCHQ. Not the least interfering with my missions."

"I know the Foreign Secretary has already alerted you to the mission, but be careful because it's dangerous," Rowe said. "You just heard here tonight. Whatever Octavia Steward was working on, it's not meant for human eyes. The Foreign Secretary is on my back."

"You get intimidated by authority?" she asked, smirking.

He ignored her sarcasm. "Steward was working on a book a few months ago, a thesis. It's too dangerous."

"To stop the spread of gossip."

Calla didn't believe him.

He moved closer. "Even the artifacts and the so-called map showcased here tonight are to impress treasure hunters and those who think there's more to this than meets the eye.

Nothing but trouble has ever come from that place, I hear. Octavia Steward was just another believer in the Atlantis of the Sands. It's a noble cause."

Calla held back a bitter word. "Octavia is an accomplished archaeologist, spy, and historian. We need to give her the benefit of the doubt."

His eyes pierced into hers. "She knows something, and we need to know what."

Calla felt a growing sense of unease as the conversation turned to the fateful expedition. The government should not have approved it, especially since a university organized it.

Calla was stuck between her duty to her country, and her gut feeling that something darker and more sinister was at play.

Rowe swung her round, her back now to Nash and Jack. "I know it won't be easy," he said. "But we can't take the risk that what she was working on falls into the wrong hands. We need to make sure that it's destroyed."

He leaned in close and whispered. "Calla, I need you."

Rowe had always been a snake with wandering eyes. She kneed him in the groin, and he reverted. "Okay," she said. "But on my terms."

He scuffled backward, holding his middle.

She shook her head, her lengthy hair spilling over her shoulders out from where it had been in place. It was too personal, but she had to admit Rowe was right. Whatever Octavia knew had to be contained. It was too close to the darkness she had tried so hard to leave behind in Iram.

Rowe straightened his tux. "We need to know who is behind her disappearance and why. Your duty as an ISTF intelligence officer is to help us resolve this situation as soon as possible. This is a matter of national security."

Calla narrowed her gaze and clenched her jaw. "I'll decide my fate," she said through gritted teeth.

She wanted to disagree—not to accept the burden of a mission that had already caused her so much pain. But if she didn't take action, the consequences of the evil spreading through Iram could bring more destruction than anyone had ever imagined.

She reluctantly agreed.

10:10 p.m

AVO SAT in the shadows of the ballroom, watching as Calla was given her assignment. She would work with a new team, and they were to rendezvous with a contact in Berlin. As if she felt eyes on her, Calla faced Avo and approached her.

"Do I know you?" Calla said.

"I'm Avo," Avo said, extending her hand. "I work for ISTF in Germany. I heard you're going to Berlin to destroy whatever Octavia Steward was working on."

Calla frowned. "Do you always eavesdrop on other people's conversations?"

"I only know because my assignment mirrors yours. Like you, I'm here to understand what we have in the presentation of Atlantis. I've been brought in as back office from the German side."

Calla narrowed her eyes. "I recognize you from some of the ISTF meetings. Weren't you in London not too long ago? You were at the briefing for Hadrian's Manuscript?"

"You should remember me from further back than that. I

want to come with you," Avo said. "I can help. I'm a native of Berlin, and I've been following your work for a long time."

"Why would you want to help me?" Calla asked.

"Because I know what it's like to lose someone you care about to a secret project," Avo said. "Someone close to me was killed working on something similar."

Nash walked over to Calla. He looked at Avo. "I'm sorry. What was your name?"

"Avo," the woman said. "Avo Schneider."

"You don't have to worry," Avo said. "I'm not a threat to Calla."

"I'm not worried," he said.

Calla looked down as Avo gripped her hand.

"You must understand. I can help," Avo pleaded.

"Thank you for your offer, Avo, but I think it's best if you don't," Calla replied. "I appreciate your help, but I need to do this."

Avo frowned. "You sure?" she asked. "I think I could help with the German authorities."

"I'm sure," Calla said. "But thank you."

"You have always been the one, Calla," Avo said, her voice icy. "You were always the best in our class at Beacon Academy. All the professors were eating from your hand. Always been the one who went on all the trips, wrote all the great papers, and made all the discoveries."

Calla didn't respond.

"You can't deny it's not at least partially true. Yes, you were an exceptional student, had always gotten the best grades, and were offered a lot of digs from prestigious universities. You received much attention from professors and other interested parties at school. That you'd been super young and naïve about how the world worked didn't change the facts: you have an innate talent for codes and history."

Calla tried her best to stay calm, but the way Avo reacted to her insecurities pushed her buttons.

"Yes, it is true," Avo said.

"Incidentally," Calla said. "I've never understood why you care so much about what I do."

"You're always looking for your spotlight."

"My spotlight?" Calla said.

"Yes, your spotlight," Avo replied. "Make a discovery, write an important paper, get a promotion, become the best agent. That is what you have always wanted."

Calla shrugged. "In case you have forgotten, I no longer run ISTF."

"I'm sure the British government still wants you to. They'd feel safe in cyberspace and beyond," Avo said. "I've always been in the shadows."

"If you don't mind, I'd like to return to my evening. Thank you for the offer, but I don't think we need more help."

Calla put her arm in Nash's, turned, and walked away, leaving Avo alone.

Berlin?

Again?

Berlin was never good news.

CHAPTER
TWENTY-FIVE

TWO HOURS LATER, Avo arrived in the basement of a small brick building, an antique shop on the waterfront in Valetta.

She paused in front of the keypad by the door and entered the code she had been given.

After slipping inside, she stumbled through the darkness until she found the final doorway. She stepped inside and felt a blast of cool air.

Feeling along the wall, she found the light switch and flicked it on with her thumb. She stepped into the Kronos Corporation's temporary workstation.

Vaughn Artemis, the lead tech adviser at Kronos, leaned against the doorway of his office and craned his neck. "Bad night, huh?" he said, cradling a mug of coffee.

Her fists curled with suppressed fury.

Vaughn, the leader of the ground team, turned away from her.

"Don't start," she warned, pacing across the room and breathing deeply to keep herself from yelling.

"I've heard that Cress's getting the mission to Berlin. It won't stop what we need to do." Vaughn set his coffee down on the table beside her. "She's been working harder than anyone else at ISTF for months."

Avo glowered at him, her eyes narrowed. "This is a crazy decision," she spat. "I'm the most qualified person for this mission. Why did they select her over me?"

Vaughn shrugged. "They always do. Unlike you, she can break codes, ancient or cyber. She finds hackers who don't want to be found."

Avo stepped closer to Vaughn. "I'm a superior agent."

Vaughn smirked. "Don't I know it? You're always asking me to supply you with new technology." Vaughn shook his head. "No, she won't fail. She's one of the best agents we have. There are plenty of other agents that want your job. Maybe you need to raise your game. Calla Cress has never spent a day in training at ISTF, yet I hear no one can beat her at a fight or code-breaking, which is what this mission needs. Serious code-breaking of things never seen."

"I have experience. That woman doesn't have any field experience to speak of," Avo hissed and took a sip of a drink from the small bar in the corner.

Vaughn nodded approvingly. "Yet she gets it done every time and in a way no one expects. I don't know what your problem is with Cress. She's one of the best agents ISTF has. Leave it at that. She has worked hard to get where she is and won't fail this mission. She's going to succeed."

Avo narrowed her eyes. "Remember who's paying you."

"Yes, boss. I suppose none of them will ever see what will happen next," he said, smirking. "Let's see how much code-breaking can take care of this, he said, angling his laptop at her."

Avo shook her head. "No, she will fail. I know. I'll make

sure of that. There's got to be something that holds her back. For one, why stop being the head of ISTF?"

Avo looked down at the laptop and crossed her arms over her chest. She knew what Vaughn was saying was true, but she couldn't help but want to go to the Atlantis of the Sands herself, a desert city that had cost her everything.

CHAPTER
TWENTY-SIX

Day 5
Off the Coast of the North Sea
10:12 a.m.

THE ENGINEER WALKED down the long metal catwalk, his steps echoing in the silence. He reached the end and looked down at the cavern below. The storage caverns were almost empty.

He walked to the control room from the catwalk, saw the geologist in charge, and went over to her. "I think we have a problem."

The geologist looked at him. "I know we have a problem. I've been trying to tell you that."

"No, I think we have a bigger problem."

"What?" the geologist said.

"I think we have a hacker."

"What do you mean?"

The engineer's face was a mask of concern. "Someone hacked into our systems. The reserves are dropping fast. We're using more than we're getting, and I don't know why," the engineer said.

The geologist stared at him skeptically. "That's ridiculous."

"I've been monitoring the caverns since before you came in this morning. There's a deep depletion that shouldn't be happening."

"I've been monitoring the caverns for three years," the geologist said. "You've only been doing this for a few months, and you think you can tell me what's wrong?"

"I'm telling you, there's something wrong. The reserves are being depleted faster than we're getting them out of the ground."

The geologist shook her head. "No, that's not possible. We've done rigorous analysis on this site, and there's no way the reserves are being depleted faster than they are removed."

"There's nothing you can do to check my findings?" the engineer asked.

The geologist scratched her head, let out a brief cough, and continued to stare at the computer monitors in front of her. She clapped her hands together and let them explode apart in disbelief, then paced around the small office, running her hands through her hair.

The engineer shook his head.

On the wall behind the geologist were graphs and charts of gas supplies and reserves. The engineer stood before one chart showing the depletion, a slow downward slope. He pointed at the chart. "But it's impossible. We have one of the largest storage facilities in the world here."

Then they heard it.

An explosion.

Moments later, they rushed to the site and saw the devastation.

The pipes had exploded, and the reserve was depleted. She

slammed the phone down and pressed the emergency alarm. "Help, I need help," the geologist said.

A colleague responded. "What happened?"

"The pipes exploded!" she said.

"Are you alright?" he asked.

"Yes, I'm fine."

"Why did they explode?"

"I don't know why."

"Okay, stay calm. I'll get the emergency teams. You must have records of the pressure in the pipes. Where can we get those?"

"In the office," she said.

"Call me when you find the data."

The geologist rushed to her office and called her colleague. "I found the data."

She listened as the man spoke.

"I can't be sure."

"Then we need to get everyone out of here now."

In another part of the facility, the engineer shot through the twisting underground tunnels.

Ahead of him, the loud pounding and clanging grew louder.

He was one turn away from the elevators when he slowed down, cursing that his cracked ribs hadn't healed right since the last explosion he had been in.

The attacks were a shock, but the news of depleting gas and oil reserves was cataclysmic.

He ran to the server room and found his computer. He had little time but would try to send out a warning. The attack was sophisticated and intelligent, but also primitive. It was only a precursor to something much larger, and he had to warn his global colleagues.

The United Kingdom and the European Union entirely depended on energy imports, and now they had none. The gas storage facility outside of Oxford was the second-largest in the UK, and the largest one in Wales wasn't being used to its full potential. The rest of the UK's oil reserves were in the North Sea, off the coasts of Scotland and England.

Hours had gone by, and the engineer sat frowning at the data pad. The UK wasn't the only target of the assault, the US had also lost several oil rigs in the Gulf of Mexico. The same predicament now faced many countries.

The US depended on oil imports for about fifty percent of its total consumption, and several oil rigs were in the Gulf of Mexico. Oil prices would shoot up, and gas prices would increase by over thirty percent. The UK's economy was going to face an immediate decline, as would every other country that depended on imports for energy.

Workers shuffled out of the facility, spilling outside, evacuating.

The geologist led the workers, and the engineers deferred to her, knowing she was the only one who could decide what to do about the gas reserves.

"What more can you tell us?" the engineer said, catching up with her.

"Hackers have compromised the computer systems controlling energy production and distribution, causing the oil and gas reserves to vanish. We may see the UK go from being a major superpower to a third-world country in one week. The United States says a single person operating undercover had compromised its energy infrastructure for decades, leaving the United States reeling from the attack," added the geologist.

"Do you think they'll go public with this information?" the engineer asked.

The geologist rubbed her forehead. "Soon, they won't have to. The United States government has taken some initial measures to secure critical infrastructure. These measures are working well, but only if they meet the initial response to the attack with a counterattack. The three most critical measures to secure the infrastructure are Physical Security, Logical Security, and Network Security. Unfortunately, these measures are still being implemented, and we're all still vulnerable to a determined cyber-attack."

CHAPTER
TWENTY-SEVEN

Kronos Headquarters
Northern Germany
11:07 a.m.

RION PACED THE HALLWAYS, his loose white sleeves draping over his hands. The dry air felt like a blanket over his body, and though he wanted to turn around, he couldn't bring himself to do it.

For two years, he had worked for Kronos and had never thought to question it. He was well provided for and could barely fathom ever leaving its security. But now, at thirty-five, there was a ticking time bomb of debt putting him in a bind. Avo had her hooks in him deep, and he felt the noose around his neck getting tighter.

He rubbed the back of his neck, desperation settling in. Could this last job do it? Could this be his way out? Rion wasn't sure if his body could survive much longer, but it was necessary to keep going. The future couldn't be predicted, but he knew his actions would change the course of history he was trying to destroy.

He flexed his muscles, trying to hold on, but his body was failing him. Rion thought about his field operative work for Kronos. His former SAS training would come in handy now. He had been given a mission to go to Berlin and find an artifact handler that the shadow organization was after.

His boss, Avo Schneider, had been deceiving them the whole time. The curator Octavia Steward was easy to find. It wasn't like Iram was an ancient myth that inspired the origin story of this ancient organization.

Why was Avo keeping Octavia prisoner? Possibly because Octavia knew about the artifacts, the city, and its secrets, and would eventually tell someone.

Rion found his office and pulled out his phone. As he was making the call, Avo threw herself into the room and slammed the door behind her, a fire in her eyes.

Rion rose from the chair as she stared at him.

Avo was not as flattering as she thought in a charcoal gray pinstriped suit with a pale pink paisley tie. A small scar above her left eyebrow seemed to detract from the overall attractiveness of her face, framed by curly black hair. "I don't like your attitude," she said.

"Attitude? You're the one who tried to cheat me. I'm the one who made you rich," Rion replied.

"You turning against us?" she said. "Are you trying to take our secrets? I know of your history in Iram."

Sweat trickled down Rion's forehead, and he had to resist the urge to wipe it away as he looked into Avo's eerie green eyes. He wanted to look away but felt unable to do so.

He cleared his throat. "Why Octavia Steward, and what do you plan to do with her?"

She moved with speed, faster than he would have thought her capable of.

She shoved him against the wall, his back hitting hard and causing him to grunt in pain. "We're going to use her knowledge to advance our plan," she said. "Then we're going to sell the results to the highest bidder. I've already got them lined up."

"So, as you typically do, you're going to make yourself rich on the backs of others," Rion said.

She narrowed an eye. "Watch it. That's what Kronos does. We're aiming for a breakthrough and are going to make history. And those who make history write the future."

Rion didn't reply as Avo turned and left the room.

He paced back and forth, his low boots against the cold concrete floor echoing off the walls. Years ago, he had been on a job for Kronos and lost his arm. Avo had found him in a hospital and convinced him that robbing others of their technology and science was all he could do.

Kronos agreed to give him a new prosthetic arm and promised they might advance it when it was finished. More like a deadly supercomputer than an artificial limb. The steel fingers were icy to the touch, not the cold of ice or winter, but of the cold of space. They were sharp and filed to a point — a weapon to be feared.

Rion stared at his prosthetic arm and ran his hand over the smooth, polished steel that made up the framework of the limb. A few small black wires ran from a computer screen embedded into the small of his elbow. When his thumb touched the screen, a mini laser shot out and burned a hole through the door. It could even cut through a steel door. A soft magnetic hum filled the small room as the arm interface booted up, and the screens and wires glowed red. The metal was cold, and the joints were tight. Though they felt like they were moving, they were completely still. This was what he had now.

Rion felt like a rat in a cage, pacing back and forth in the narrow room. Working for Kronos Corporation was a miserable option, but Avo's blackmail had given him no choice.

Working for Avo required deft multitasking, and Rion constantly juggled two or three projects simultaneously. He'd move around products and technology but didn't know what they were, so he often snuck through her office, staying long after everyone else had gone home, and tried to piece together what she was developing. Avo always returned in the early morning, her heels clicking on the tile floor, and she was never the wiser that he had been snooping around.

A phone on a nearby table buzzed.

He picked it up. "Headquarters," he said. "Send a message to the gate." He paused and listened for a moment. "I'm ready."

He'd been told to keep Octavia quiet and alive long enough to tell them where the ancient book was.

Rion had a feeling that things were not that transparent. He knew they had one woman, but the woman they needed to get to was Calla Cress.

Why?

What did she know?

Rion felt he'd known Octavia forever. It was as if they had been fated to meet each other. Why would Mason Laskfell, former ISTF head, want to use Avo to kill her?

None of it made sense to Rion.

He'd gotten so close to Cress ten years ago that he could smell the scent of her hair and feel the warmth radiating from under her olive skin before a team of hunters, whom he'd heard they called operatives, had come in and saved her.

That's why he had stayed around.

Rion gripped a gun in his palms. Why would they risk their lives for a girl no one knew?

What was so special about Calla Cress?

CHAPTER
TWENTY-EIGHT

Richmond, London
5:27 p.m.

IN THE DISTANCE, thunder crashed, deep and rumbling.

Calla exchanged a nervous glance with Nash. Her father had recently bought a Georgian house in Richmond so that he could stay closer to her, but she hadn't heard from him in a couple of days after leaving messages.

Nash seized the doorknob and twisted, but the door wouldn't budge.

Calla didn't want to break the door down, so she walked around to the back.

It was pitch black, but she wandered around the side of the house.

Glass insets in the door revealed heavy drapes on the other side, looking as if they were covering boarded-up windows. They had to be hiding something important if they were covered.

The house had two stories, was white with light blue

shutters, and the grass in the front yard was green and freshly trimmed.

She ran her hands over the garage door as she passed it, then returned to the front door.

Nash was still at the doorknob and tried again. This time, it turned, and she stepped inside her father's new home.

"Dad!"

There was no answer.

She shuffled through the house, calling his name.

There was nothing to show he had been there recently.

The lights were off, and there were no clothes lying around. There was no food in the refrigerator.

Calla circled back to the living room and stopped short. "Where do you think he is?"

Nash shook his head. "Not sure, and it's not like an ex-MI6 agent to just leave his phone behind," he said, picking up Stan's phone from the kitchen table.

Calla looked around. "There's no sign of a break-in."

She stood and watched the rain pelt the window, obscuring her view of the street below. A smudge of dirt marked the bottom corner of the pane. Calla stared at it. It looked like a handprint like someone had pressed their palm against the glass.

She moved closer to the window and looked out at the street.

A feeling of dread seized Calla. Her father had been here. He must have been looking out that window when something happened to him.

Something terrible.

She approached the glass and observed the deep fissures scattered across it. Someone had desperately pushed against it, trying to break it open and enter.

She paced down the hallway, up the stairs, and found herself standing outside her father's office.

Taking a deep breath, she pushed open the door and was met with intense light from the streetlamps below, which illuminated her father's office through its tall glass windows. Despite the room's brilliance, she couldn't shake off a feeling of dread that was slowly enveloping her.

A large desk sat in the center of the room, and a bookshelf lined one wall.

Calla walked over to the bookshelf and scanned the titles. Most of them were history books or biographies, but she found a row of books with titles like *The History of the Knights Templar* and *The Knights Templar in the Holy Land* at the back of the shelf.

Calla pulled one book from the shelf and flipped through it, hoping to find a picture of her great-great-grandfather. But what she found instead was a large black-and-white photo of an old man standing in front of some pyramids with a caption.

Sir Newton Cress poses in front of the Great Pyramid of Giza, Egypt, in 1677—the Blackhorse Knights.

Could it be a relative? When Calla looked up, she saw a photograph just above the desk of her father standing with a woman. It had been taken long ago. Her father was younger, and his hair was shorter. He was smiling and seemed happy, but he didn't look like the man Calla knew today.

As Calla was about to put the book back on the shelf, a piece of paper fell from between the pages.

She picked it up and saw that it was a handwritten letter dated ten years ago. At the top of the page, someone had written:

Cambridge Excursion to Rub'al Khali

Calla's mouth fell open. She scanned the first few lines and saw that it was a letter. She skimmed down the page, eager to find out what it said.

"I'm writing to you today to tell you I am leaving Oxford. The Blackhorse expedition will leave on an important journey.

We will travel to the East, the desert coast of the Holy Land, in search of the Lost City of the Atlantis of the Sands. I will share with you in my next letter, which I pray reaches you before I do, all I know of this most fascinating and mysterious place. I will be vigilant and report anything I find."

The letter ended there.

Calla stared down at the page.

This was why her father had a copy of *The History of the Knights Templar and the Brotherhood* on his bookshelf. It was a book about the Blackhorse expedition in the Holy Land and Arabia years ago. Her father seemed interested in historical excursions to the Middle East and beyond. Long before she ever went.

There was one more thing Calla needed to do.

She returned to the bookshelf and scanned the spines of the other books to find one with an author's name.

She finally found one. It was called *The New Arabia*, and Octavia Steward had written it.

Did her father know Octavia well?

How?

Octavia.

Calla stared at the name. She couldn't speak. Her heart climbed into her throat, and she could not breathe. It was impossible, but was it?

The name of the woman who had lectured on the Knights Templar, unknown history, secret societies, and her old professor at Cambridge? Was it a coincidence that her professor was the same as her father's old friend?

Or could it be that her father and Octavia Steward had something to do with each other?

Her father's disappearance while working for MI6 and then her mother's, a thought which tumbled out of the box of memories like a package she had never opened.

At that moment, her father's mysterious spy life felt like it all linked back to Octavia Steward, the woman she had known at university but now questioned desperately.

Calla stared at the name, her eyes hot and dry.

There was no doubt. Octavia Steward had been her father's old friend.

She looked away. It wasn't a coincidence that her professor was the same woman. Calla had learned never to believe in coincidences.

Calla quickly pulled out the book and flipped through it. She returned to the letter and looked at the signature at the bottom. She read the name:

Ivan Schneider

Next to the name was another name:

Avo Wiesz-Schneider

It all made sense now. Avo had been at Cambridge and was now part of ISTF, but somehow, their lives were more connected than Calla wanted to know.

She remembered Ivan. They told the excavation team he was sent to protect them on the trip. Not for a second did Calla ever feel safe around him. And now her fears resurfaced.

Calla recalled the moment Ivan fell beneath the sand in Arabia.

His body was never found.

She remembered standing by as he sank, unable to save

him because she couldn't read that code at the city gate. She remembered his face.

Calla blamed herself.

Ivan was someone special Avo had lost on that expedition. Why had she not put two and two together?

He was Avo's father.

Why had her father funded the entire expedition?

She was holding two pieces of a puzzle that fit together. But how?

Calla had to find out. And the answers began in Berlin.

CHAPTER
TWENTY-NINE

Day 6
Central Berlin,
11:00. a.m.

CALLA, Jack, and Nash reclined in the back of a British Airways flight from London to Templehof Airport in Berlin.

Upon landing, a driver met them in front of the terminal and opened the doors of a black Mercedes, and they climbed into the back. The driver, a short man in his fifties, had a solid, gentle face that reminded her of a farmer.

They drove on the Autobahn, passing a stream of orange traffic cones and white lines on either side, until the city rose like a white wall before them.

The Mercedes crawled down Dorotheenstrasse and soon pulled up in front of the Berliner Zeitung Offices, where their meeting was scheduled.

Frau Fuhrman was an older woman with kind eyes and a sympathetic face. She welcomed Calla, Jack, and Nash into her office and offered them tea. "I'm so sorry about what happened to Octavia Steward," she said. "I was in the audience that day. I'm not sure if I can help, but I'll tell you everything I saw."

"That would be great," Calla said.

"Your offices say I get an exclusive. Should we come to an agreement?"

Calla raised an eyebrow. "We'll see about that. We're interviewing as many witnesses as possible. You are one of seven."

"What I remember most is how brave Octavia was," Frau Fuhrman said. "She was in the middle of an interview with RTL's Bierman."

The investigative journalist took a sip of her tea and leaned back in her chair. "Though I was in the audience that day, I can't identify the people who ambushed the studio. They were masked."

She took a file out of her desk drawer and handed it to Calla.

Calla leafed through the file. Fuhrman had been thorough. There were pictures of the men from the security tapes. An audio file had recorded an interview with the cameraman who had taken the photos.

Fuhrman continued. "I saw three men, one in a suit, one in some custom military uniform, and one in a jacket with a prosthetic arm. They rushed in and grabbed her. One held her while the other two did something to her. They looked like they had injected something. The one in the jacket, who I think was holding her, looked right at me through his mask when they did it."

Calla glanced up from the file and saw Jack and Nash leaning against the doorframe. She peered at Fuhrman. "I don't think you are telling us everything?"

Fuhrman shrugged. "I don't know what you mean, but I can give you an address." She pouted. "It's a residential building in Charlottenburg. That's where Octavia lived for the last several months. The Pergamon Museum, where she was working, set her up in that place. I was going to meet her there for an interview the following day."

She handed Calla a slip of paper with an address on it.

Calla read it out loud to Jack and Nash: "Sonnenalle 18."

"Okay," Jack said. "That's not far."

Calla chewed her lip. "Frau Fuhrman, what exactly had Octavia been working on?"

There was silence in the room.

Nash and Jack waited as Frau Fuhrman poured tea from the carafe on her desk and sipped it. When she finally looked up, her eyes were bright. "She was working on a book about a lost city, an empire, I think. I'm sure you have seen the artifacts in the press. They are from an unknown empire recorded in history. It was her passion. Steward found something. She was going to tell me about it when we were to meet for coffee."

"So this meeting was going to happen…?" Jack said. "At her home. At Charlottenburg, on the Sonnenalle. Number 18."

Fuhrman nodded. "That's all I have."

Several moments later, Fuhrman watched them from her office window a few minutes later, her lips pursed behind a lit pipe as they left.

She picked up the phone and dialed a number, sweat beading on her forehead.

THEY LEFT Frau Fuhrman's office, hailed a taxi, and gave the driver extra money to hurry.

The cab zigzagged through traffic and screeched to a halt at the given address.

"Not sure we're getting close to what Octavia was up to," Nash said.

"I'm not sure," Calla said. "But we'll find out soon."

They located the house and rang the doorbell.

A disheveled-looking woman answered the door with a baby in her arms and a toddler clinging to her leg.

"*Guten Tag*. Hello. We're looking for Octavia Steward's apartment?" Calla said in German to avoid scaring the family.

The woman shook her head and said in broken English, "She no longer lives here. She moved two months ago."

Calla thanked her, and as they were leaving, the woman called out to them. "Wait! I have an address."

She dug through a drawer and produced a piece of paper. "Here," she said, handing it to Calla.

Calla studied the address on the paper, which was in Prenzlauer Berg.

They took another taxi to the location.

The street was lined with low brick buildings of varying heights, and they took in the tranquil neighborhood as the cab stopped by a young tree outside the building.

After surveying the area, they crossed the street and entered the cool, dim hallway of the old building.

The apartment was on the first floor, and a green door opened into a small hallway.

A battered mailbox was screwed into the wall, and the name on it was illegible. With no name on the door, the number 1 was written in green. They peered through the crack in the door.

"This is the place," Jack said.

"Doesn't look like anyone's home," Nash said, pacing.

Calla shrugged.

They approached the door and knocked.

No one answered, so they entered the cramped hallway of the apartment.

There was only one doorway in the room with a small window at eye level, and they could see a tiny kitchen with creamy yellow walls and a dark wood floor. A small table with a vase of flowers on it was next to the door.

The next room was a small sitting room, with two armchairs and a small sofa with blue and red velvet covers. At one end of the room, an entertainment center housed a TV and a stereo system, and a row of built-in bookshelves lined the wall.

"This is where Octavia lived?" Jack asked.

"I guess so," Calla replied.

There was another door.

Calla opened it and discovered the bedroom with a single bed, a black and white checkered coverlet in the center of the space, a matching dresser, a small closet, and a chest of drawers. Two lamps on the bedside tables matched the fixtures and light switches with a white porcelain finish.

"I recognize her style. It feels familiar somehow," Calla said.

"Why did she give Fuhrman her old address?" Nash asked.

"I think she thought Fuhrman was a nosy journalist," Calla said.

Nash and Jack looked around the room. "It's so small," Nash said.

"I know," Calla said. "But it's cozy."

She went to the closet and opened the door, revealing a laptop. "Jack, can you hack this?" she asked, handing him the computer.

"I'll try," he said.

He sat at the laptop and began typing furiously, his fingers flying over the keyboard. The sound of keys clicking and rattling filled the air. He was soon lost in his work, consumed by the process, his face lighting up with a smile.

Calla observed Jack as he worked on the old laptop, which had a yellowing screen and a dirty keyboard covered in white residue.

A blue mouse was plugged into the front, and the laptop whirred and clicked like a propane tank about to run out.

Jack spent a few minutes hacking into it and started going through Octavia's files. "What are we looking for?" he asked.

"Anything that might help us understand why she was taken and how," Nash replied.

After going through several files, Jack said, "There's nothing here."

"Wait," Nash said. "What's this?"

He pointed at a folder labeled "Project J."

"I don't know," Jack replied.

"Open it."

Inside the folder were several documents, including notes and research materials.

"It looks like she was working on some kind of project on Middle East history, and it's right next to calculations related to global energy pipes," Calla said.

"What kind of project could that be?" Nash asked.

"Not sure," Calla said. "But looks like she was onto something."

As they were reading through the files, they heard a noise and hid.

A man entered the room.

"What's this? A break-in?" he asked.

Nash, Calla, and Jack peeked out and saw the man wasn't a threat, so they approached him.

The man appeared to be in his twenties and had dark brown hair and a serious expression. He was wearing jeans, a wrinkled t-shirt, and had an open laptop in one hand and a backpack slung over his shoulder. "*Wer sind Sie?* Who are you?" he said.

"Friends," Calla replied. "We're looking for Octavia Steward. Do you know where she is?"

The man shook his head. "That's why I'm here. I'm her assistant, Ralf. Are you the police? Interpol has already been here, and German Intelligence. A man by the name of Raimund Eichel."

CHAPTER
THIRTY-ONE

Northern Germany
11:26 a.m.

OCTAVIA STOOD STILL, her back pressed against the wall by the door.

She strained to hear the men downstairs, but they were too far away to be heard.

She crept to the door and tried the handle.

Above her, the light flickered off and on, on, off.

If they were trying to disorient her, it was working.

She closed her eyes, stilled her breath, and waited. She was trapped.

She returned to the bed and collapsed, feeling hopelessness overcome her.

She'd never get out of here, not without help. This all felt like a dream, but it was so real, so visceral. They'd brought her to this place, Rion.

How could Rion be part of this?

Was it really Rion Loman?

He'd followed her to Cambridge after a brief affair in Beirut.

Octavia could still remember the first time she had laid eyes on Rion, standing at the back of the lecture hall, his blond hair cropped short, and his muscular frame encased in a dark suit. Something about him immediately piqued her curiosity, and she found herself lingering after class to ask him a question. He turned out to be an SAS soldier, recently returning from a mission to Beirut. She wasn't sure what his connection to Cambridge was.

Flushed by the thrill of talking to this intriguing man, Octavia invited Rion to her office for coffee. He had accepted.

Their conversation was electric, and they soon found themselves wrapped up in each other's arms. Over the following weeks and months, they continued to meet secretly, stealing moments of pleasure together whenever they could.

But their affair was always tinged with tension and fear, for they knew the authorities could easily discover their trysts. And indeed, one day, their longing for each other proved too much, and a group of fellow professors caught them in a passionate embrace.

Octavia licked her lips, recalling the memory of Rion's lips on hers, how he held her in his arms, and how their bodies moved in perfect sync. Later, Rion accompanied them to Arabia for the dig in search of Iram. But the affair had ended in disaster, and she had always felt it was her fault.

Even now, she could not help but long for Rion, haunted by the memory of his touch. But she was now his prisoner, and judging from what she'd heard about some SAS men, Rion would have no mercy.

During the last few hours, she had overheard her captors' radio conversations whispered in dark corners. They had to be criminals or something.

As she crept to the door once more, Octavia paused,

knowing that guards were nearby. She glanced around cautiously, wondering if they were watching her or monitoring the estate's perimeter. She didn't know what security measures they had put in place or whether the guards were armed. The uncertainty made her anxious.

Octavia didn't know how many kidnappers there were, but she knew they were there, and she could get away if she could make it past them.

She listened at the door, wondering if she should wait for them to go or try to slip out.

The inaudible murmur of masculine conversations filtered through the floorboards, informing her that the guards were still deep in conversation downstairs. They sounded like they were in their thirties, though it was hard to tell over the faint nasal drawl that spoke of alcohol and ignorant inflections.

Octavia waited nervously for a few minutes. She slipped her hand underneath the fabric of her shirt to tease out one of the wire clasps from her bra. Holding it between her fingers, she slowly reached forward and inserted the wire into the keyhole with trembling hands.

After a few moments of fiddling, there was a satisfying click, and the door opened a crack.

She stood still for a moment, straining to hear any sound coming from outside. When everything remained silent, she let out a timid sigh of relief.

Octavia's heart beat wildly in her chest as she tiptoed into the hallway. Her palms were slick with sweat, and her breathing was shallow as she navigated the stairs, one trembling foot at a time.

After successfully reaching the bottom without making a sound, she paused to listen for any sign of disturbance before continuing to creep across a living room, pausing once more before finally reaching the front door.

Rays of sunshine filtered through the windows, a reassuring sight that gave her a sliver of courage.

Octavia stared at the guard outside, her body tensing.

She had been expecting one, but now she had to decide. If she attacked him, it might give her a chance to escape. But she did not know if there were other guards or what might come next. Even if she got away, she was still in an unfamiliar area, far from home.

Taking a deep breath, she steeled herself and tried to figure out her next move.

CHAPTER
THIRTY-TWO

Berlin

11:35 a.m.

CALLA WATCHED RALF CAREFULLY, trying to gauge his reaction. There was more to his story than he was letting on.

"I work for Frau Octavia Steward at the Pergamon. I'm a student at Humboldt University," Ralf said.

Nash raised an eyebrow. "What did you do for her?"

"I was her assistant curator at the Pergamon Museum," he said hesitantly.

Calla pressed him further. "Do you know what happened to her?" she asked, her tone accusatory.

Ralf shifted uncomfortably. "She was acting strange, always bringing up this ancient book about a secret city in the East. The Atlantis of the Sands, or something like that. And then, one day, she disappeared. I reported it to the police, but they said they couldn't do anything." He looked at Calla, feeling exposed under her gaze. "That was about a week ago."

Jack and Calla shared a look. There was definitely something more to this story.

"Did you know anything about her personal life?" Jack asked.

"We were work friends," Ralf replied.

"Work friends?" Calla repeated, raising an eyebrow.

Ralf nodded. "She's an archaeologist and my boss, so we didn't hang out much outside of work. But she's…distant."

"Distant? In what way?" Calla probed.

Ralf hesitated. "I don't know…she just seemed to care very little about people. But I guess that's why she's so good at her job."

Jack leaned in. "Do you know anything about the book she was obsessed with?"

Ralf shook his head. "All I know is that it was really important to her. She talked about it all the time."

"What's so special about it?" Jack asked, blocking Ralf's exit.

Ralf turned back to the group. "I don't know," he said. "But the book has been in the hands of every major government in the world for the past hundred years."

Nash raised a brow. "Why?"

Ralf hesitated, his dark eyes darting back and forth between Calla and Nash. He ran a hand through his disheveled hair, carefully weighing his words. "I don't know that either," he finally said.

Silence hung between them as Ralf looked up again, his face a mask of confusion and apprehension. "But I don't think you'd believe me even if I told you."

Calla and Nash exchanged questioning glances until Calla broke the silence. "Why wouldn't we?" she asked.

Ralf sighed again, gathering his thoughts into a coherent explanation.

"The truth is I don't know the truth—I'm just guessing," he said quietly. "But I'll bet that book is really valuable—and dangerous—to too many people. Octavia talked about a city where the impossible could happen, the Earth's resources would never run out, and there would be an energy source that whoever gets their hands on it could control the world. History calls it a sort of Garden of Eden, but real historians know more than that. They say it holds a powerful source of energy that has been flowing for centuries and is believed to come from another universe. That's what I think, anyway."

"You're kidding me?" Nash asked. "Another universe? The energy source has never run out?"

Calla pulled out the book from her bag. "This book? And every government that has studied it believes that this city has an unknown energy source and that it is an actual threat to their economic and industrial might."

Ralf's eyes widened.

The three men gawked at the frail, leathery volume tied together with a reddish yarn. Ralf remained motionless, his mouth hanging open as he stared at the leather-bound book, taking in the ancient language written on its cover for the first time.

"What's the connection between the book and the energy source?" Jack said, breaking the silence.

"That's the odd thing," Ralf said. "There are theories, but no one knows for sure. One theory is that the book has a map leading to the energy source. Whoever has the book will control it. But I think it's more complicated than that. Because if there's one thing governments have learned from the book, the city in question was part of a meteorite, perhaps from another planet that hit the Earth centuries ago."

Jack furrowed his brows. "So, does the city still exist, and does the energy source still work?"

"None of these questions have ever been answered, and all the governments that have studied the book are sure that the key to the answer lies in the seven blank pages of the book," Ralf replied.

"What did Octavia want to prove?" Nash asked.

"I don't know," Ralf said. "And you may not believe me, but I don't think it was for the reason that most people would think. She believed so much in this book that she would not use it for power or money."

"How can you be sure?" Calla asked.

"Because she told me," Ralf said. "For a long time, she trusted me more than anyone else."

Calla thought for a minute, then turned to Jack. "I want to know more about Avo Schneider. I don't think her connection to all this is just Ivan Schneider, her father."

Nash approached. "I might be able to help. Avo's NSA file suggests she's involved with a secret banking society controlled by Kronos. If I can hack into her cell phone and computer, we might find out what she's up to. Someone probably coerced Avo to work for that society; she's been with them since joining ISTF."

Nash continued. "The banking society could be using her to find the book for their own agenda."

"So she's a double spy, working for the society and ISTF," Calla said. "That's my first guess, but they're not associated with criminal activity."

"But we know they're powerful," Jack interjected.

Ralf nodded, and the three watched him amusedly.

"So what do we do now?" Jack asked.

Calla thought for a moment. "We need to learn more about the society. If they don't have Octavia, then who does?"

Nash moved to the window and stole a quick glance outside. "Multiple factions are looking for the city:

governments, the Blackhorse Group, and Kronos, who's leading the charge. We need to find out why they want the city and what they plan to do with it when they find it. Ralf, can you show us what Octavia was up to at the Pergamon?"

CHAPTER
THIRTY-THREE

Pergamon Museum, Berlin
11:03 p.m.

CALLA, Jack, Ralf, and Nash descended into the darkness. The blackness seemed to swallow them, and the air grew thick with tension as they approached the famous Pergamon archive room.

Calla's stomach churned as Nash advanced, and she followed anxiously.

As they passed display cases filled with ancient artifacts, she flinched at every strange noise or gust of wind.

Their shoes squeaked on the polished floor of the gallery as they crept down the hall.

Nash touched her shoulder to stop her and motioned toward the door with his chin.

The knob was visible in the light coming through the windows from the street.

Nash stood in front of the door, his brow furrowed in concentration and his fingers gripping the cold steel knob. He turned it clockwise, quietly clicking the lock, then pulled on the door, and it opened a sliver.

Silence.

Calla scanned the area as they entered, passing hundreds of orderly workstations until she noticed a German sign above a large door with a combination lock.

Forschung, meaning "Research," was written in bold red letters.

Nash tried to open the door, but it was locked. He muttered a curse and pulled out his lock pick set, feeling a little ridiculous as he fiddled with the lock.

After Nash wheezed and pushed open the door to the archives, Ralf led them through the stacks, searching for files referencing the city of Iram in the early centuries.

Calla turned her head, searching for the Arabian and Mesopotamian archive vault signs.

Jack pointed to a map of ancient Arabia on the wall, asking if they might be that way.

They hurried to the back and found the shelves open but empty.

Something was wrong.

Calla ran her fingers along the seams on the wall until she felt a release mechanism. Pulling on it, the panel swung open with a dull thud, revealing the ancient vault. She flicked on her flashlight and stepped inside, illuminating rows of robes, tools, jewelry, statues, and metal containers covered in thick dust and cobwebs.

As their eyes adjusted to the darkness, the intricate designs of ancient artifacts astounded them.

Secret vaults and hidden treasures gleamed in the shadows of the forgotten rooms.

They carefully made their way through the museum's long-forgotten exhibits, their eyes concentrating as they took in the immense wealth of golden jewelry and ancient weapons scattered throughout the labyrinthine pathways.

The lost city of the Atlantis of the Sands might just exist after all.

CHAPTER
THIRTY-FOUR

11:27 p.m

RALF GUIDED the group through the dusty vault, pointing out shelves filled with more ancient artifacts. They eventually arrived at a small room with a lone table in the center, on which sat a small wooden box no larger than a birthday present.

"This is all there is from Iram," Ralf said in a hushed tone. "This is everything the Kronos organization seized in 1944."

Calla's eyes widened. "What about the gala in Malta? All those priceless artifacts?"

Jack approached, examining the shelves. "I think they staged it to get money from wealthy patrons for whatever Kronos's bosses are perpetrating."

Nash paused, drumming his fingers against a shelf as he muttered to himself. "Avo runs the entire show; she may be Kronos 1."

Ralf's tone became serious. "You said you'd help get Octavia out of this mess. But you said nothing about the artifacts. I couldn't leave the Nazi loot in the museum with fake displays. Someone was bound to find and take them away, so I brought most of them here. That's what those artifacts were."

Jack pressed on. "What about the other artifacts she told you to keep in the archives?"

Ralf sighed in exasperation and shook his head. "What difference does it make? The real mystery is the book and the seven pages she couldn't translate. I think the artifact story covered what she was working on. Getting back to Atlantis of the Sands, as she called it, was what she cared about most. Most artifacts were taken by that corporation and exhibited. We still haven't received them back. I think what the authorities wanted was all of this. The real loot."

Calla retrieved the book from her bag, its symbols making her heart race. She gingerly touched the cover, feeling the smooth leather beneath her fingers. The circular runes and geometric patterns looked so strange, yet so familiar. She ran her finger over them, and an icy chill ran down her spine. "Octavia was right," she murmured. "They want the book, not the artifacts."

A sudden sound at the door startled her, causing her to stuff the book back into her bag.

She spun around, on high alert.

CALLA'S KNUCKLES turned white as she clutched her backpack.

Ralf's eyes darted between Calla and Nash as he stepped back, eventually standing shoulder-to-shoulder with Nash.

The shadows parted as Avo stepped forward, her face illuminated by pale moonlight. In her hand was a gun, which she pointed straight at Calla. "I gave you an offer," Avo said, her voice low and menacing. "You refused, and now this is out of my hands."

She advanced forward, her heavy boots echoing through the abandoned archives.

Calla narrowed her eyes and stepped back as Nash drew closer.

Jack stood rigidly between them, his eyes darting between their faces.

Avo released a deep breath, her voice tinged with desperation. "I need that book now," she said.

"It's not yours to take," Calla added sternly.

"Neither is it yours," Avo shot back. "I've been looking for it for years."

Nash stepped forward and blocked Avo from getting any closer. "You can't have it," he said in a low voice.

Avo's eyes glistened with new intensity. You don't understand," she said softly. "It's not just a book. It's the key to history—the key to everything." She licked her lips and shifted her gaze toward Calla. "Calla Cress," she continued, her voice resolute. "May I remind you I'm not letting you take anything from Berlin? I know you've been sent here to confiscate artifacts."

Avo planted her boots on the floor and squared her shoulders.

Calla glared at the woman. "Step away now, Avo."

"I can't allow you to take these artifacts or that book. Please hand it to me."

"No," Calla snapped.

"This is not up for discussion," Avo replied. "You will leave the artifacts, give me the book, and then you will leave."

"I'm sorry, Avo, but I can't do that," Calla said. "These artifacts are too important. They need to be studied and have possibly been hidden here, away from the world, for over eighty years."

"And what makes you think you're the one who's going to study them?" Avo asked. "We have people too, or is this something only ISTF's top Decrypter can do yet again?"

Avo inched closer. "Cress, maybe it's time you leave this to those who want it. Octavia Steward meddled with things she shouldn't have and people she shouldn't have. Now hand over the book," she said, pointing the gun at Calla.

The men looked on, ready to defend her.

Nash quickly stepped in front of Calla.

Avo fired a shot.

Nash spun his shoulder out of the way, and the bullet pierced the wall behind him.

Smoke drifted upwards, only to be carried away by the ventilation fans. He reached for his gun and then took a step toward Avo. "You're ISTF Germany. This isn't how we do things," he said.

"Then I'll have to shoot you, too," she said.

"Stop," Calla called out.

Nash turned. "She's not taking the book."

Calla stood between them. "I don't want anyone to get hurt over this."

"Neither do I," Avo said. "But if you don't hand over the book, I'll have to shoot everyone, starting with you."

With a roar of fury, Avo fired another warning shot.

Calla and the men dove for cover, scrambling to protect themselves from the onslaught of bullets.

Avo raised the gun once again and aimed it at Calla's head. "I warned you," she said coldly. "And now I have to do what I must."

Nash quickly stepped in front of Calla, shielding her with his body. "No, you don't," he said.

And then, before anyone could react, Nash seized Avo's pistol in his hand. With a quick twist, he wrenched the weapon from her grasp and threw it across the room.

Avo's face contorted into a mask of rage, and she charged at Nash.

He moved swiftly, using his body to pin her against the wall. His grip was relentless, and his voice was low. "You will hurt no one."

With Avo still fighting to break free, Nash put his arm around Calla's shoulder, helping her stand up.

Just as Avo made a move toward them, Calla grabbed her by the shoulder and brought her down with a swift blow.

"Are you all right?" Nash asked.

Calla nodded. "Yes, I think so." She paused for a moment,

looking at Jack and Ralf. "Let's go before we piss off anyone else."

"This way," Ralf said. "There's an escape shaft via the roof. I usually take an unauthorized smoke break there."

CHAPTER
THIRTY-SIX

THE LIMESTONE WALLS of the Pergamon's outside facade were slick with moss, and the mortar had long worn away as the group hurried through the open space at the roof's summit.

The stone blocks were rough and uneven, making a perfect ladder for the gunmen behind them.

Calla saw bullets striking holes in the ground as they hurried. Her rucksack with the book felt heavy, but she kept running, keeping up with the men.

As they reached the flat part of the roof, which seemed endless, they searched for the ledge they needed for the jump.

Dozens of gunmen were right on the wall behind them.

Calla glanced ahead at the Spree River, their only hope of escape, which wasn't far away.

She kept her head down and flew forward, dodging bullets that whizzed past her and ripped into the ground like miniature bombs.

Concrete spewed up like fireworks as the shots missed their targets.

The book bag strained to pull her back as she clambered up makeshift stairs to a higher part of the roof.

They finally reached the Pergamon's flat roof, an expanse of concrete stretching out before them.

Snipers were right on the wall behind them, their bulky silhouettes outlined against the moonlight.

Calla could hear their labored breaths.

Avo had dozens of armed men at her disposal, and the four runners didn't know where to jump to reach the river below.

Calla looked ahead at the Spree River. It was terrifyingly close, but still so far away.

They stopped running and turned to face their enemies.

Calla peered up and saw a man with tight, shiny scar tissue on his skin. His arm was a prosthetic, composed of armor plates that flexed with power and tension like an exoskeleton. The prosthetic arm was quiet when it moved, effortlessly and with precision.

Her throat constricted as the man advanced toward her.

"You're not going anywhere," he said.

"Get the book, Rion!" Avo roared.

Calla and Jack were trapped between the man, and three other assailants clustered behind him. The giant signaled to the other agents, and they closed in, surrounding Calla and Jack.

"Give me the book," the prosthetic-handed man said, who she assumed was Rion.

Calla clutched her bag close to her chest.

"Give it to me," Rion said.

"No," Calla said, glancing at Jack and Nash, who stood stiffly at her side. "The book's too dangerous to be in anyone's hands but ours."

"Give it to me, or you'll all die," the giant insisted. "If you don't give it to me, I'll kill your friends here." He shot Jack and Nash.

"No," Calla said, determination in her gut. "It's too powerful for any of us to own."

"It's just a book!" he roared. "It doesn't have any power and can't hurt anyone."

"You're wrong," Calla said.

With a roar of fury, Calla charged at the giant and struck his arm. Though the pain stung, she could overpower its mechanics.

She threw her whole body at him, but he didn't budge.

His arm moved faster than she could see, blocking every attack with the metallic beast of a bicep.

Nash raised his gun and fired at the man's arm.

Rion twisted away and then collapsed to the ground. Undeterred, he stumbled to his feet and stood still, holding up a hand to stop his men from advancing.

Rion then took a running leap at Calla and swiped the bag with the book out of her hands, sending it careening across the rooftop.

Calla grabbed a loose brick from the ground and catapulted it at him.

He dropped to one knee and dove to avoid it, but it caught him in the temple, and he tumbled back to the ground.

Calla clambered to her feet and snatched her bag back from its resting place. "Go!" she yelled to Jack and Nash as she threw them the bag. "Hurry!"

"I'm not leaving you, Cal," Nash said.

"I'll be right behind you."

"Two minutes tops, Cal," Nash said. "Then I'm back if you're not there with me."

Calla hesitated for a moment. "Go find a way out of here. I won't be a minute," she said.

She lunged at Rion, swinging her fists and kicking with all her strength.

He gasped and grunted with each hit.

She knocked him off the roof and into a pile of crates below with one final punch.

She staggered to the roof's edge, wincing in pain from the bruises she'd earned in the fight.

Peering down, she saw agents advancing toward her, weapons drawn.

She had to find the men, and quickly.

Without a second thought, she leaped from the edge of the building and plummeted into the river below.

Icy cold water numbed her skin as she arrowed through. Panic coursed through her veins as she reached for the shoreline, searching for something to grab hold of.

As her arms tired, a pair of firm hands closed around her and dragged her from the river's depths.

"Gotcha," Jack said.

CHAPTER
THIRTY-SEVEN

Berlin, Banks of the Spree River
11:56 p.m.

NASH WAS DRENCHED, and bullets rained behind him.

He stumbled toward the riverbank and, through a misty veil of rain, and saw six men spread out over a small patch of the pier. Another man, who he thought was Ralf, hid behind a torn-out tree trunk about twenty feet away, his spine pressed against the wood as though he would disappear into it.

The six men behind him were slow, but if he and Ralf didn't move quickly, it wouldn't matter.

Nash grabbed Ralf's arm and pulled him along, running up the shoreline toward a dilapidated building.

He waited for the others and saw Calla's head appear above the water, followed by Jack's.

They hastened toward them.

Once he caught up with Calla and Jack, Nash searched for a way to get up the building before they were in the line of their pursuers' fire.

The only way was on the other side, where there was a

small parking lot and a street at the end of which sat a second building with bright windows.

Nash led the group forward and scanned each side alley, but nothing stirred.

His gaze fell on the German word for 'Deliveries' painted on a door to his left, and he tried the handle.

It gave way with a click, and they rushed through.

The hallway seemed to stretch forever, lined with doors that gaped open to secrets unknown. At its end was an elevator, and Jack jabbed at the buttons on its panel wildly with his finger.

With an electronic hum, the doors opened, and they quickly climbed inside.

Nash looked up at the illuminated numbers above their heads as the elevator ascended.

The doors opened again, revealing a lobby that looked like it belonged in a grand hotel.

Two concierges were visible behind a desk, whose startled glances held still.

Nash hurried to the desk, and a concierge looked up from his computer and gave them a polite smile. "Hello, sir. How may I help?" he said, smirking at their wet state.

Nash gave him a smirk. "What's the fastest way out?"

With a knowing smirk, the concierge took a quick look behind them. "If you'd like to go out through that door and exit through the kitchen, you'll be able to walk out directly," he said.

"Thank you, sir," Nash said, nodding to Calla, Ralf, and Jack and headed to the kitchen.

Nash and his companions slowly edged the door open, and the smell of onions and garlic hung in the air.

A cacophony of voices and clanking metal filled the kitchen.

Waiters rushed around carrying trays of food, and cooks

shouted orders to each other as they flipped pans and stirred pots. The tile floor was slick with spilled liquids, and their footsteps slid a little as they stepped inside.

Realizing they had been spotted, they spun around and sprinted down a long hallway leading to a different entrance.

Doors led to other rooms. They passed some but didn't stop to look.

After reaching it, Jack opened a door at the end of the hallway.

Seconds later, they were outside and momentarily caught their breath.

"Octavia is all part of the smokescreen," Nash said as if to himself. "She's in on it."

"Really? What are you talking about?" Calla asked.

Nash looked around as if worried someone might be listening. "The Lost City of Iram. It's real, at least on satellites," Nash said. "I got intel last night from the NSA. I've also seen a meteorite stone. Calla, your father had it. It's the only thing the expedition brought back. NASA has been searching for Iram for years. They think it's in the southern deserts of the Arabian Peninsula, in Rub'al Khali. They've sent expeditions to search. But it's all top-secret. No one knows about it. It's called Ubar by some. I don't suppose you remember how you got there, Calla."

She shook her head. "We flew to Muscat, I believe, and took a very long desert ride. That's all I remember. I don't remember how we got back. I wasn't conscious after the events at the dig."

He nodded and scrutinized both sides of the street. He continued when he was sure they had blended into the evening hour. "It was a civilization that vanished over ten thousand years ago. It was said to have been destroyed by a natural disaster or as a punishment by God. The notes say it was a city of incredible wealth and splendor, a lost civilization that left behind incredible technology."

"What kind of technology?" Ralf asked, with a puzzled look.

"I don't know," Nash said. "But whatever it is, governments want it, ours included. They've been looking for centuries. Plus, they claim a signal is coming from the city, a high-tech radar signal. Octavia is in more grave danger than we thought. Governments and societies will pay for what she knows."

"But why would Octavia be involved in a conspiracy?" she asked.

Nash shook his head and clenched his jaw. "I don't know what to think, but if you're right, Octavia is in serious danger, and we have to get to her."

They ran past cars.

Horns blared, and people scrambled to get out of the way as Nash, Jack, Ralf, and Calla blended into the crowd.

Finally, they reached the safety of the train station and hopped on an S-Bahn train just arriving at the platform. Nash took a deep breath; he didn't want Calla to face any more danger, but they were dealing with a formidable enemy.

Nash had seen that giant before. From the NSA files he had read at the embassy, he was almost certain the guy was a former SAS and connected to Octavia somehow. Were they just acquaintances, or former lovers? He wasn't sure. With Stan gone and the ancient book in Calla's bag, Nash felt a heaviness of responsibility. Nothing was as it seemed, and with the Blackhorse Group's involvement, he sensed their chances of solving the puzzle were bleak. And just where had Stan gone?

They took seats in an empty car. "Calla, your father and Octavia have been abducted. Each of them knew something. I don't think the Blackhorse Group is who we're after. We need to find whoever is working and funding Avo. Those agents were no ordinary agents. They were armed with full firepower. She knew ISTF would go after her, so Avo created an army that could match them. We have to be careful."

Calla's emerald eyes bore into Nash, conveying worry. They had both agreed that until the turmoil surrounding the operatives' first arrival was resolved, she wouldn't lead the ISTF. While Nash would go to any lengths to protect her, he felt responsible and had to handle the situation. He had to keep Calla safe, yet he was conflicted as he tried to balance his past with his future.

Nash was torn between wanting to safeguard Calla and uncovering the truth. Although she had no recollection of the events in Cambridge and the desert, he feared that her return might put her in danger.

Nash wanted to keep her safe, but he also had a sense of obligation to find out what happened to his wife there. He suspected Ivan had been involved and knew Avo had got to Calla at Cambridge.

He wanted justice for his wife's suffering but seemed to face a difficult choice, to protect Calla or seek revenge.

Calla scrutinized Nash for a moment, then brushed a strand of dark hair from her face. "Alright, Marine, what's the plan?"

Nash exhaled sharply, his gaze intense"Let's get to a hotel for the night. We'll need a distraction and a car. I'll figure it out, but I think it's time we call in a favor from Raimund Eichel."

CHAPTER
THIRTY-EIGHT

Day 7
Headquarters of the Federal Intelligence Service
Chauseesatrsse, Berlin
9:55 a.m.

NASH PARKED their car and approached the towering Federal Intelligence Service headquarters, a sleek, modern building of curved aluminum and glass. In the morning sunlight, its dark green copper roof gleamed faintly.

As they entered the building after checking in with the receptionist, they made their way to Raimund Eichel's office.

Calla liked and trusted Eichel. He had risen through the ranks of the German intelligence community, and Calla remembered him well from her time in Berlin. When they arrived at his open door, a low voice invited them inside.

Eichel sat at his desk, gazing out the window at the cloudy, rolling sky. The trio sat close together at a long wooden table, waiting for Eichel to share what he knew about Avo Schneider, whose files lay open on his desk.

"Good to see you again, Calla," Eichel said as he scanned through the contents of the folder.

"We need to know more about Avo Schneider," Calla said. "Why she joined ISTF. Why her father teamed up with the University of Cambridge to search for the Lost City of Sands."

"I'm sorry, I can't help you," Eichel replied, his face unreadable.

"The archives at the university have been confiscated," Calla said. "We've come to you because you're the closest we can get to the facts."

"I don't have the authority to share any information with you," Eichel repeated.

Nash persisted. "You must have some idea why Avo Schneider joined ISTF. What's her angle? Come on, we've worked together a long time."

Eichel remained steadfast. "There's nothing I can tell you about Frau Schneider."

Jack chimed in. They weren't going to give in. "MI6 files say her father worked at the University of Cambridge without proper qualifications. And why did they let him go on the Arabian expedition anyway? What was in it for them?"

Eichel frowned. "You need to ask the university that. I'm not sure that you're going to get any answers here."

"So you *do* know something," Nash said.

Eichel was silent.

"What do you know?" Calla asked.

"I can only tell you that certain people at the University of Cambridge have a special interest in the Rub'al Khali expeditions that go back through Germany's history, one as recently as the Second World War," Eichel said.

"How can we talk to these certain people?" Calla asked. "Who are they?"

Eichel folded his arms. "I'm sorry, I can't help you."

Frustration boiled inside Calla. "You must've some idea who they are."

"I'm sorry, I can't help you, even if I wanted to," Eichel said. "So you say the university archives have been confiscated?"

"Yes," Nash said. "Who confiscated them?"

"The university administration, when the Pergamon Museum requested it," Eichel replied, surrendering. "After Ivan Schneider failed to return, the British and German governments conducted a thorough investigation. They were looking for anything suggesting he was working with an enemy."

"But they found nothing, did they?" Calla said.

"No," Eichel said. "And there were no grounds for dismissal or suspension. They were also looking for evidence of how the expedition to Arabia was funded. Contrary to what the files say, it wasn't just a simple expedition about a lost city. The German government believed there was more, but we're not sure what. Something is out there in that Arabian desert. Ivan Schneider, though an assassin by training, also had interests in artifacts that go back in his family. All the way back to the war. He intended to write a detailed report on ancient technologies and methods of Iram, and he used university funds for the expedition."

"What did he say about the funding?" Calla asked, dreading the answer.

"That they received a grant from a private donor," Eichel said.

"Do you know who that was?" Calla asked though she feared the worst.

"No, I don't," Eichel answered. "But perhaps if we could look at Ivan Schneider's report, it will shed more light on the matter."

"Where is it?" Calla asked.

"We don't know," Eichel added. "It was never found."

"What do you mean, it was never found?" Nash said. "How could something like that just disappear from the intelligence archives?"

Eichel shrugged. "I'm sorry, but I know nothing about it. The university administration just told me it was missing."

"I think I know where it is," Jack said. "ISTF. And if I'm not mistaken, Rowe Norkus, now the new Red Fox, must know. He hasn't been fully transparent. He must know the whereabouts of the report and, by logical deduction, the whereabouts of the Lost City of Sands."

Calla eyed Jack.

"He knows something, or he wouldn't have gone to the lengths of stealing the report from the university and hiding that knowledge from GCHQ. I spied through Rowe's records, and he's definitely not telling us everything. If I'm correct, the report doesn't exist anymore," Jack said.

Calla bit her lip. "Why would Rowe do that?"

Nash was the first to reply. "Because Rowe has always had eyes on two things: power in government and getting to anything that is connected to you, Calla. We can't trust him."

THIRTY-NINE

Northern Germany
3:01 p.m.

OCTAVIA REGULATED her breathing and locked her gaze onto Rion's.

He had returned to interrogate her, and her delay had only angered him.

His face was twisted in a grimace, and his hands trembled with rage.

The frigid touch of his gun pressed against her forehead, and he snarled, "You know, Octavia, we don't need you alive."

She clamped her lips together to stifle her screams.

She had loved this man once, but now she found herself in a room with a stranger who threatened her life. The ominous presence of a hidden enemy had forced him upon her, and she had to be careful not to misstep. If Rion received a signal, they were both doomed.

The waiting was unbearable.

"So, what's it going to be?" he growled. "Do you want to live or die?"

"Rion, how can you talk to me like that? We used to be…"

"Lovers? Friends? We wouldn't be in this situation if it weren't for you."

"Rion, I…"

"Shut up."

"No. Let me…"

"I said shut up!" he roared, slamming the gun barrel into her temple, causing her to flinch. "You have a chance to redeem yourself and live, but if you don't take it, you might as well give me the go-ahead."

Octavia refused to accept that Rion had turned on her. "Why?" she asked.

"You left me for dead in the desert. It was because of that girl, Cress. Everyone seems to be obsessed with her. The only reason you're still alive is you know the way back down there, and I'm only here to make sure that those who pay me get what they need from you. Look what you did to me," he snarled, hurling out his prosthetic arm in disgust.

"If it wasn't for you, I would've gotten out of there. I would have been fine if it weren't for Cress. If it weren't for you, I wouldn't have been in the fire, and I wouldn't have this." He waved his prosthetic hand at her again.

Octavia stared at the arm. She had to find the strength to keep going, but did she have the courage to do what was required? Giving up the information they were after would mean saving her own life, but it would also mean the end of the City of Sands. The source of power and knowledge would be lost forever.

She was conflicted, torn.

Octavia took a deep breath and steadied herself for what she was about to do. "I'll tell you everything," she said. "But you have to promise me one thing first."

Rion watched her curiously. "What?"

"No one gets hurt. You need me."

Rion nodded and signaled for his men to lower their weapons as well.

Octavia gathered strength. "The City of Sands is hidden in the desert, protected by something sacred. Only those who know the way can find it."

She could see the disbelief in their eyes, but she continued. "Inside the city, there is a garden. It's called the Garden of Energy, and it's said to contain a great treasure."

Rion was listening intently now, his eyes wide with greed. Octavia knew she had them hooked. "If anyone can find the city of Iram, enter the garden, and find the treasure, they'll become a great and powerful group. They will be unstoppable."

Rion nodded. "Very good," he said, "but I don't see the connection between your book and this so-called Garden of Energy."

"The secret is written in it," replied Octavia. "But I lost the book."

"How?" Rion asked.

Octavia paused for a second. "The government," she said.

Eyeshadow descended on Rion's face. He dismissed the men until the two of them were alone in the room.

Octavia observed Rion. He was tall and fierce-looking, but she had once seen him as gentle. Octavia tried to get a sense of him. He was a big, muscular man, and as she watched him now, she was aware of how much danger she was in. His strength could easily overpower her petite form. Even so, there was something familiar about him, and that strange feeling made her even more scared.

She smelled his cologne, the same scent he had worn on their first date, and tears streamed down her face. The man she had once loved was handsome. His once-white shirt was stained with sweat, and a scowl pulled at his mouth.

His gun shook slightly in his hand as Rion paced across the room, his electronic prosthetic hand twitching.

He noticed Octavia looking at him. "What? Am I not good enough for you? You had to go to the Blackhorse Group and look for their money. It's because of them and Stan Cress that I lost this arm. I used to work for them until they betrayed me. Their mission got too dangerous, and sometimes they didn't look back to see who they left in their trail of destruction."

Octavia couldn't bring Stan into this. Because of his intervention, she and Calla were alive. She didn't know what he was talking about, and a man like him would probably kill her in the morning, so if he was about to kill her, it was better to play along.

Octavia piped up, "Well, at least give me a chance to plead my case."

"Enough!"

"Did you love me?" Octavia asked as she awaited Rion's response.

Rion paused, his eyes locking onto hers for a moment before he replied. "Yes, I did. I was hurt when you betrayed me, but I understand why. I've done the same thing to my rivals several times, and now look at me." He gestured toward his cybernetic prosthetic hand.

Octavia remained silent, unsure of Rion's motives.

"Why did you give the book to the government?" Rion's voice was heavy with emotion as he asked the question.

Octavia didn't know what to say. She had betrayed Rion, and now he was questioning her motives.

Torn between what to do, Octavia thought before deciding that the truth was the best option. "My reasons had nothing to do with the government. They had to do with another group, the one you were after. The Blackhorse Group."

CHAPTER
FORTY

Kienberger Allee
Berlin Kronos Group Headquarters
4:23 p.m.

AVO HURRIED.

Her team had assembled the equipment, including lightweight tripods and a high-tech transmitter.

The laptop was running a sophisticated software program to record the results of the gas pipe experiments. The equipment cost thousands of dollars, but Avo didn't question the extravagance. The investment was sure to pay off.

Vaughn looked at her and nodded. "This will give us the stats we need. I'll record the results," he added. "It should work smoothly."

It was their first time using a software program to record the results. If the rules of quantum mechanics could predict the answers, the bankers wouldn't have needed to ask so many questions.

The group had promised a way to read the code, but Avo needed the book for that.

Rion had to have it by now. "That woman Steward better be ready to march back into the desert. Alright," Avo relented. "I'm going to take a nap. Set up a conference call for the morning with the twelve."

That night, Avo dreamed of her father, looking young and handsome with a full head of dark hair and a strong jawline.

He was laughing, and his eyes were crinkled in happiness.

Then Calla Cress appeared, and her father's smile vanished.

Avo was certain Calla had a hand in her father's death.

Calla stood over Ivan's body, and her cold, hard eyes met Avo's.

There was no remorse in Calla's expression, only satisfaction.

Avo woke up with a jolt, feeling something off.

Overwhelming rage and sorrow consumed her, along with a desire to make Calla Cress suffer for her part in her father's downfall. She wanted nothing more than to make Calla pay for losing her child, but she feared the potential consequences of her actions.

Her heart pounded, and she couldn't shake the feeling of sickness and the sourness that coated the back of her tongue.

Were her emotions guiding her decision?

She struggled to reconcile her desire for revenge with the potential cost.

It was her duty to avenge her father's death, but could she actually follow through with it?

Would it bring him back?

No matter what she decided, she could never get that time with him again.

There was no easy road forward, and no right answer, just one that would ultimately go against her conscience.

Avo's fury threatened to consume her. She wanted to lash out and make Calla pay for what she had done, but she couldn't be sure if Calla had anything to do with her father's death. Despite the injustice of what Calla had done to her, Avo questioned whether destroying another woman's life was the answer. The rage inside her blinded her to any logic or reason, yet a part of her knew it was wrong.

FORTY-ONE

Hotel Adlon Kempinski, Berlin
11:37 p.m.

NASH PUSHED OPEN the heavy wooden door to the luxurious suite at the Adlon, a five-star hotel in the heart of Berlin. He carried a tray of delicate pastries and fruit and paused in the doorway, admiring the glossy marble surfaces, leather couches, and Prussian-style architectural details.

He placed the tray atop an ornately engraved armoire and inhaled deeply, relieved that the shuttered windows provided privacy from the outside world. Lush velvet drapes hung from floor to ceiling, blocking out the city lights and creating a cocoon of seclusion. An array of shimmering chandeliers hung from the ceiling, reflecting off the gold-framed paintings adorning the walls.

He moved to the bed, bent down, and lightly kissed Calla's lips, then picked up the small tray from the nightstand. On it was a small white pill, nestled beside a glass of cold water.

She took the pill, and he held the glass for her as she drank.

He set the tray on the bedside table and eased onto the bed

beside her. His hand slid over her forehead, as he looked into hers. "Are you alright after today?"

Calla felt drawn into his gaze. The kaleidoscope of emotions in his steel-gray eyes held her captive. His hair was longer than usual, and the overhead light cast a luminous halo around his face, while the other half of his face stayed in darkness.

He moved closer, his warmth radiating like a summer sun, and kissed her forehead tenderly. His scent of musk and spice filled her senses.

She nodded in agreement, her voice barely above a whisper. "Yeah, I am."

"Good."

"I almost feel guilty that I haven't asked my father more questions about his time in the Blackhorse Group."

"Let's not think about it now," Nash said. "You need to rest."

"I can't rest, Nash," Calla said, her voice rising from a whisper. She shook her head and tucked a lock of hair behind her ear. "I had a strange memory. I've known Avo Schneider since Cambridge. She was one of the few German students in our year group. I remember her now because she was always so timid and kept to herself, nothing like what we saw today." Calla paused, her lips pursed, and she shuddered. "I didn't know her well, but I remembered something that happened many years ago. It made me feel ill."

Nash leaned in, his brow furrowed in concentration. "And?" he asked softly.

Calla thought back to the time.

It was a memory flooding back to a medical center at Cambridge. Calla had woken up to the sound of someone talking. It took her a few seconds to realize where she was. She was in a medical room, strapped to a reclining bed. Machines were attached to her body. She saw Ivan, the assistant professor from her archaeology class, talking to a woman in a white coat. The woman was Avo and had a syringe in her hand.

"What are you doing?" Calla tried to sit up, but the straps held her in place. "Let me go."

Avo looked over at her, then Ivan. "She's awake."

"What is this? What are you doing?" Calla struggled, but it was no use.

Ivan approached her, a syringe in one hand, a device in the other.

"What are you doing?" She blinked at him, confused. "What are you injecting me with?"

"It will help you relax," Avo said to Calla.

Calla, confused by what she saw, asked, "What is that? What are you doing?"

"It's okay," Ivan said, placing his free hand on her shoulder. "We're just trying to help you."

"You're hurting me," Calla jerked her head away from them. "I don't know what you're doing."

"We didn't mean to scare you," Ivan said, attempting to calm her.

Calla tried to sit up, but the straps held her against the recliner. Her panic grew as she saw the device - it looked like a flashlight with a small screen at one end - and a clear, rectangular box labeled "Kronos Plasmex." "What's that?" she asked. "What is that?"

"It's okay," Avo repeated, while Ivan leaned over her.

"Help me do what?" Calla asked. "What are you doing?"

"We're trying to help," Avo said, looking on the verge of tears. "I'm so sorry."

"Why can't I move?" Calla asked, struggling against the straps.

. . .

The memory abruptly ended, and Calla found herself in Nash's arms. She was afraid of the blank spaces in her mind, the missing memories.

"Nash, I'm afraid of the missing memories," she confessed.

"Cal, I'll do all I can to help you remember and find the people who hurt you. I love you, and I'll always be here for you," Nash said.

He kissed her deeply before pulling her close.

She felt safe and let her fear subside. Heat radiating from his body warmed her cold skin, and she was surprised by the depth of her feelings for him. She moved into him and felt the firm muscles in his chest like iron under a wool shirt.

"I know," Nash said into her ear. "I know."

"Thank you. What have I done to deserve you?" she said.

"Nothing," Nash said. "The lucky one is me. I've wanted you since the moment I saw you, but I told myself to let things happen naturally, that you needed time to get to know me, and that I needed to be patient. I'm so glad I did. I don't know what I would have done if you hadn't looked at me that way."

"What way?" she said, smiling.

He pulled her closer and kissed her lips. "This way. Now, how about we forget everything that's worrying us tonight and focus on how much I love hearing you say my name?"

Calla's lips met his, and she deepened the kiss. The need and hunger for him were so intense that she flung her arms around his neck, pulling his body into hers.

CHAPTER
FORTY-TWO

Day 8
US Embassy, London
11:26 a.m.

NASH WAITED for lieutenant colonel Masher to arrive. He stood by the window, looking down below, then turned to face the room. On one wall hung a green flag with the seal of the USA, while the other was dominated by a large bookshelf. Photo frames with pictures of family and friends adorned the room.

Masher entered without his usual smile and glanced at Nash. "They've asked me to look into a case. The Embassy needs the NSA to get involved. They want to know if we can help with the NASA files of Atlantis that have been connected to the Cambridge excursion to Rub'al Khali. It was top-secret." He gestured to a chair and seated himself.

Nash took a seat, "I'm aware. The NSA doesn't get involved in local cases."

Masher sighed. "Yes, I know, but this is different. The Prime Minister's office told the embassy that the President wants this handled. There's a good chance the local police have the information, but they don't have time to transfer it to us. The PM wants us to assist but not interfere with the investigation. It's to do with the signal from the Arabian desert, an unidentified one that's been happening for a while. The British government thinks they can use the NSA's help. The case is not just local, Nash."

He looked out the window at the rain-soaked London street, then thought back to his recruitment into KJ20-Ops, the NSA's secret operation arm, now closed until further notice.

Nash took a deep breath before speaking. "Have you seen the case file, Masher? It contains top-secret information from the CIA, MI6, and GCHQ. That's why it wasn't initially submitted for the NSA to view."

"I've read the file. I've read the information the British government and the US have."

"Why do the British need us too?" Nash asked.

Masher got up, walked to the door, and stood against it. He had a smile on his face as he turned to Nash. "The British are worried. They don't want the NSA involved in their internal affairs. They think it will worsen their relationship with the communities in the desert and those governments.

"You could be right, Nash. The British government has been compromised and thinks they're being hacked. A sophisticated virus has depleted their energy sources. In fourteen days, a hack that destroys power plants and energy reserves will deplete US energy sources. They're just looking for answers like us."

"Then, we must act now," Nash said. "There's another problem. The operatives' technology is being compromised too. They believe it started with something in the Rub'al Khali desert."

Masher furrowed his eyebrows. "It's why there's an unidentified signal from the Arabian desert."

Nash's gaze was intense as he looked at Masher. "So that's why the NSA wants to get involved?"

Masher nodded. "Yes, we want to stop whatever is affecting energy supplies."

Nash gestured toward Masher. "Masher, we don't know who is causing it. At ISTF, we think it's Kronos."

Masher's expression hardened. "We need you, Nash; it's already started."

Nash shook his head, his jaw tight. "The operatives could be the source of the problem., but I'm not yet sure."

"The operatives couldn't have hacked these energy reserves," Masher replied firmly. "Someone else has done it."

He exhaled, closing his eyes as he took a moment to reflect. When he opened them again, he gave Nash a piercing gaze. "What do you need?" His voice was low and calm, but it conveyed the weight of his understanding.

Nash shifted in his seat. "I hope you'll help with this," he said, the weight of their shared history heavy on his voice. They had been through countless missions, barbeques on the beach, pool parties at Masher's mansion, and the epic Fourth of July firework shows. Masher was like a father to him and his boss at the NSA.

Nash waited for a response, but Masher remained silent. "There's one thing I want," Nash said finally. "I want the freedom to work KJ20-Ops as I see fit."

"The men will follow your orders," Masher said. "But they need to know that the man leading them is doing it for a reason."

"I hope it won't cause any problems between us. It would mean reopening the program," Nash said.

"Not at all. You're the only one I trust to do this," Masher said, staring at Nash with unblinking eyes. "You're one of the best men I've ever worked with. I need to think about it, but I trust you more than anyone else in this business."

Nash nodded. He knew the history of KJ20-Ops was a difficult one.

As he got up to leave, Nash turned to face Masher.

"I hope you know I have your back," Masher said.

Nash nodded in silence.

"Watch out for Rodney Cook. He's still sore at you for putting him in prison," Masher added.

"He deserved it."

Masher agreed. "But be careful. Cook has a lot of powerful friends, and he was involved in the NASA project in the Arabian desert."

"I know," Nash said gloomily.

"Don't be stubborn, Nash. Know what you're up against. This man is ruthless and won't hesitate to hurt you and Calla, even from inside prison."

Nash felt a deep rage unfold within him at the thought of Rodney Cook. The former Senior Director of the Psychic Spy Program at the National Security Agency had been arrested by Nash for gambling with US government technologies under the guise of national security. Nash remembered narrowly escaping death when Cook had aimed an illegally modified black handgun at Calla's heart. Masher was right. Even from jail, Rodney Cook could come for them.

As Nash walked out the door, he remembered the resources he had at his disposal. Few knew that he had gained significant wealth running an underground intelligence security company for years, with his own team of SEALS who only surfaced when needed.

Nash worked for the government not because he needed to, but because he wanted to make a difference. The KJ20 Ops had never been easy, requiring only the best of the best to work on elite missions. They had done a lot of good in their time. But with more technology than they could handle, more cash flowing in than they had ever seen, and more questions than answers, it was getting harder to keep things under control.

It was too much to work with. The old rules no longer applied. Things were changing, and something was different now.

Something was wrong.

CHAPTER
FORTY-THREE

THE RETRO COCKTAIL lounge boasted leather banquette seating, bookshelves stocked with vintage novels and magazines, and a long, polished wood bar.

Bartenders moved efficiently, chatting with guests with barely moving lips. A sign above the bar read: *"Alcohol is a crutch for the weak."*

Avo strode to the bar, quickly placed her order, and scanned the crowded room. Spotting a small table in the corner, she hurried over and sat down. Looking around, she saw no one she recognized until the door opened, and Frau Fuhrman entered.

Frau Fuhrman glanced around before her gaze landed on Avo's table.

She strode toward Avo, her stiletto heels clicking on the nearly empty floor. Dressed elegantly in a plain skirt and cashmere blouse, her hair was styled in bouncy curls held with delicate jeweled pins.

Avo pushed her jacket back to reveal the handle of a handgun tucked into her waistband as she leaned forward, sitting tall with a poise that spoke volumes.

Frau Fuhrman's eyes sparkled as Avo took a sip from her glass of bourbon before speaking.

"Fuhrman, you've been looking for me for a long time. Why? I'm sure you're wondering why I asked you to come," Avo said in a serious tone.

Frau Fuhrman, who always found her way into government business, nodded silently.

"I have a problem with Octavia Steward, and when the city of Atlantis of the Sands is found, I want the exclusive with you on record," Fuhrman said.

"Is finding a lost city all this is about?" Avo asked skeptically.

"Octavia Steward went on national TV and acknowledged a lost city in an exclusive with RTL, a treasure that could be worth millions. I think I know where she's being held and who has her," Fuhrman said, her voice betraying nervousness.

Avo stopped in her tracks as she heard this revelation. "You do," Avo said, her voice taking on a low growl.

"Yes," Frau Fuhrman said, her eyes shifting nervously. "I do. Do you think of me as a traitor?"

"No," Avo said firmly. "I think of you as a traitorous criminal. You're a journalist, so naturally, you are nosy, but that doesn't excuse your criminal behavior."

Frau Fuhrman scowled, but Avo leaned in closer, her face inches from Frau Fuhrman's. "As far as Octavia Steward is concerned, she's safe for now. But that could change if you don't answer my questions," Avo said, daring her to challenge her. "So, what did you share with Calla Cress?"

CHAPTER
FORTY-FOUR

The Mall, ISTF Offices, London
6:32 p.m.

CALLA REVVED the engine of her Maserati and headed for the ISTF building with Jack and Nash. The concrete structure on the Mall stood as a reminder of the secret organization's power and mystery.

ISTF remained an enigma, a labyrinth of espionage linked to five powerful government agencies. According to rumor, a superior group inhabited the Earth and had created unidentifiable technologies with no one's knowledge.

MI6, GCHQ, and the NSA had all teamed up to locate where the unknown tech originated from and to assess any potential threat it may pose to the world. But it was ISTF that led the pack. The organization had the resources and tools to investigate any threat, known or unknown.

Calla clicked her key remote, and the car door locks echoed in the underground parking space as she, Jack, and Nash headed for the elevator.

With a deep breath, she turned toward the nearest entrance of the building.

"Octavia was always talking about the expedition," Calla said. "How it would be the most important thing she ever did. She said it was a chance to make history," Calla said as they stepped into the hallway of level three of the building.

"What happened when you got back from Rub'al Khali?" Nash asked.

Calla shook her head. "Not much. I woke up in the hospital with Octavia in London. She was the only one who knew what had happened."

Calla's stomach dropped, as she recalled the night in the desert, kneeling beside Octavia's limp body. There was a figure in the distance, a man wearing a dark hood and visor. He was motionless, but she could feel his presence. His arm was raised as if he held a gun.

Calla shook away the vision and opened her bag, drawing out her notes. She saw scribbles from Octavia about a man in the desert with a hooded face. Was this the same man she had seen that night? The thought sent chills down her spine as she and the men settled into the boardroom. No. There was something else. Something she couldn't quite remember. Something horrible. She tried to remember what the figure had done.

The memory returned to her, and she sank into a seat next to Jack, who had his laptop open.

"When did you first realize Ivan Schneider was a threat on the trip?" Jack asked.

Calla had seen him. "He was walking toward us, holding something in his hand on the last day. Something glinted in the sunlight. It was a gun. He pointed it at us. The next thing I remember was Octavia shouting at me to run. But I couldn't move. I couldn't run or yell or do anything to save Octavia.

She wasn't with me when I turned back. I couldn't breathe. Then everything went black."

Jack placed his strong hand on Calla's shoulder, and she felt his concern radiating from him.

His voice sounded low and gruff. "What happened? What did they do to you?"

"I'm okay," she replied, her voice shaking slightly. "Just give me a second."

Calla's body dropped further into the chair, her eyes darting around the room. Her breath felt heavy as if the atmosphere itself was a physical force holding her in place. She tried to focus on the image of Ivan in the desert. His fingers curled around the gun. She was certain that was the only way to make sense of what had happened.

She closed her eyes, and a vivid image flashed before her.

Ivan wore a black hoodie and a ski mask, the outline of his face just visible. His eyes were like chips of ice, focused on her even through the material barrier. A shiver ran down her spine.

"Ivan attacked us," Calla said.

Jack leaned into Calla. "The more we know about him and his trail, the better. Let me access the ISTF databases and see if we have anything on file." He started typing away on the keys and clicked through several menus. After a few moments of silence, his face fell. "I'm sorry, Calla," he said solemnly. "The man you described is a known assassin. We have several reports of him being connected to terrorist organizations."

"Jack is right," Nash added. "The file was closed when Schneider was believed dead."

Calla sighed, disappointment eating her. "Jack, the strange thing is, I can't even find school records for our trip. I have spoken to the university, and no one seems to know what happened to them."

Jack's lips twitched into a smile. "Let me try something."

He opened a computer window and began typing in rapid fire. His fingers flew over the keyboard as he worked, occasionally pausing to make minor adjustments.

Calla leaned in closer, watching intently as Jack worked. "What are you doing?" she asked.

"I'm looking at the records of your expedition to the Rub'al Khali ten years ago," he said without looking away from the screen.

Calla's eyebrows raised in surprise. "How did you find them?"

Jack smiled again. "I have my ways. There's nothing here," he said as he looked at his computer in disappointment. He tapped a few last keys and leaned back in his chair. "All records have been erased. Purposefully it seems."

"Why destroy records on an expedition, especially one from a university?" Nash said, shaking his head.

"The university's deans are the only people with authority to access the records. And if I had to guess," Jack said, looking at them both. "My money will be on the Blackhorse Group. Your dad's name is all over this, Cal. He knew something, and now too, he's gone missing."

Calla's face paled as her mind raced through the years her father spent away from her. "It wouldn't surprise me," she said.

She thought back to all the things she had learned about her father in the past year, a man she never got to meet until only a few months ago. He had been a spy, a master of keeping secrets, including his own. But she remembered there had to be more than that—she had seen something when she had visited Rub'al Khali.

Jack seemed to have caught on to her train of thought. "Maybe the records were just moved or closed off," he offered.

"All the more reason for us to find what's really in that city," Calla said.

Jack hesitated for a moment before crossing his arms. "So you want to go back? You *know* it exists, don't you?" Calla nodded in response.

"All I can say, Jack, is that whatever exists is something the world has never seen before. Possibly doesn't need or want to see."

Nash nodded grimly, his brow knitting. "We must figure out where this energy attack is coming from, and fast. I suspect it's all linked. I just don't understand how those resources are all gone so quickly."

Jack drummed his fingers against the table and looked at his laptop screen. "It could be something they're using to siphon it off. A giant gas pipe of some sort?"

Calla's mind blazed with determination as she leaned forward. "Kronos has been around since 1907. Let's see if we can find something in their records to help us. Dig deeper, Jack."

Jack immediately resumed tapping away at his laptop.

Calla continued. "I'm sure there is some kind of powerful energy source in the city we're headed to, Octavia knows all about it. That book and those symbols are the keys to unlocking a city that was powered by some kind of powerful and unknown energy 3000 years ago."

The Mall, ISTF Headquarters, London
8:09 p.m.

LATER THAT EVENING, Jack rushed to his office, shut the door, and leaned against it. The others had left only half an hour ago.

The place was dark, but not completely; his phone glowed with the bright blue light of its screen coming from the hip pocket of his jeans.

Jack suspected that Mason Laskfell, their ex-ISTF boss, had played a role in Octavia's kidnapping and was working with Kronos.

With trembling fingers, he sent a text message to Calla and Nash: "Laskfell's involved with Atlantis. I can't ignore it anymore."

He threw himself into his chair and looked at the ceiling, his heart sinking. He remembered his installed motion sensors and quickly logged into his computer. He scanned the room before finally landing on the screen displaying, "Welcome Agent White Wolf," in bold glowing letters.

Jack accessed the archive and clicked on the agency blueprints, searching for the X he had placed next to the archives and the hidden passageways leading directly to it.

As he scanned the blueprints, he noticed subtle differences from the designs stored in the digital archives. He searched for a way to unlock the vault but couldn't find an entrance or any sign of how to activate the hidden door. Desperate, he searched the archives for any information sent to him by agency archivists that could help him find out what they had hidden there.

After coming up empty-handed, Jack noticed two files with the same name.

He opened both, finding different blueprints.

He sent pictures of each blueprint to his computer and compared them, discovering a keypad marked on the updated blueprints on the screen.

He typed in the code and a door opened in the blueprint.

The door led to a staircase that went down twenty levels. Jack saved the blueprint to his phone and headed to the basement.

As he stepped out of the elevator, the hallway was dimly lit. He followed the blueprint on his phone until he came to a door with a keypad next to it.

He tried the code, but the handle was locked.

Jack pulled out his phone and shone the light on the door. He typed in a code, but the door didn't open.

He tried another code, but it still didn't budge. Jack leaned against the door and sighed heavily. He examined the lock and saw grime and dirt beneath it.

Using a small device with an infrared sensor, he scanned the area and entered the office.

The air was thick with dust and the smell of age.

Jack scattered tiny electronic spiders across the room that led him to an old, dusty computer on a desk. He headed for it.

After typing in a few codes, the monitor buzzed to life with a pale blue glow.

His eyes widened as a prompt demanding a password appeared on the computer screen.

Jack drummed his fingers on the desk and muttered curses under his breath while waiting for the information to be accepted.

He pecked at the keypad, entering countless combinations to unlock the mysterious terminal.

With each failed attempt, he felt hope fading until he remembered the code from the blueprint.

Jack's heart leaped as he punched in the numbers and hit enter.

Suddenly, the computer hummed, and the screen lit up with a list of files.

He scrolled through them until he saw one labeled "Atlantis".

Anticipation making his hands shake, he clicked on it, and a map of ancient ruins appeared on the screen.

Jack's breath caught in his throat as he realized he might be just moments away from uncovering the mystery of the Atlantis of the Sands.

He stared at the map for a few minutes, trying to make sense of it. It looked like three main sections of the city, each with its coordinates. He zoomed in on one section and saw it was labeled; "The Lost City of Sands."

Jack's thumb hurtled across the screen as he felt the route highlighted on the map like a trail of fire.

His heart raced faster, and his breathing became shallow as a grin stretched across his face.

He grabbed the storage flash disk he had copied, shoving it deep into his coat pocket before he sprinted out of the room, slamming the door with a deafening crash.

Just as he rounded the corner, he heard an ice-cold chuckle that sent shivers down his spine.

When Jack spun around, there was the ghost from his darkest nightmares, the former head of ISTF, Mason Laskfell, standing right behind him with an all-knowing smirk playing at his lips.

CHAPTER
FORTY-SIX

South East London, Motorway
9:57 p.m.

NASH HURRIED through the dimly lit streets of southeast London in his unmarked black Jaguar, the seconds ticking by on the dashboard clock.

Anxiety coursed through his veins, causing him to push down harder on the gas pedal, making the engine growl like a beast.

He stole a glance at his phone and felt his heart skip a beat when he saw it was already 9:57 p.m.

Nash was just two minutes from the NSA's secret headquarters, with only forty minutes to crack their secure mainframe.

His foot remained heavy on the gas until he noticed the flashing blue lights of a police car behind him in his rear-view mirror.

He realized he was going twenty miles over the speed limit.

He pulled over to the side of the road and rolled down his

window, handing the cop his license and government credentials.

The officer eyed him before letting him go, but Nash had no time to waste.

He sped off, ignoring the swerving squad car behind him, and careened around the last corner before pulling into the sprawling complex just in time.

Navigating the winding corridors of the NSA building, Nash eventually reached the lab, taking a deep breath before turning to face the computer monitor. He opened the files, his eyes widening, but it was no surprise to him. Rowe Norkus had been lying to them all as he'd suspected, and the evidence was undeniable. Nash felt a mix of relief and fury as he printed out a copy and tucked it away.

Rowe knew something.

Several moments later, Nash revved his car's engine and sped toward Rowe's house, determined to confront him.

He peered through the windshield, his eyes narrowed with purpose.

Thirty minutes later, Nash arrived at the grand porch and bounded up the stairs.

The heavy door protested as he pushed it open and stepped into the lavish house.

Muted colors of the walls, sleek furniture, and wall screens flickering with information were a testament to Rowe's wealth and power, but the stillness of the place felt eerie as if time had stopped.

Nash noticed the glass-topped end table near the entrance to the kitchen, with a soft mist of condensation on its surface. He picked up the stack of papers from its center, noting that someone had been there recently.

"NASH!" Rowe's voice echoed through the room, and Nash spun around, searching for the source.

He saw a police officer pointing a gun at Rowe's head in the kitchen, the same officer who had stopped him earlier.

The cop looked up and saw Nash standing in the doorway. "What the…?"

The cop narrowed the gun at Rowe's head, his voice was cold and unforgiving.

"You were supposed to keep things simple. But your attraction to the Cress girl has gotten us into a lot of trouble, Norkus. The Book of Iram was supposed to have been destroyed ten years ago, not sent to the NSA for analysis. That was a huge mistake, Norkus!"

Rowe slammed his hand down hard on the gun hand, and a shot rang out, shattering the front window.

As the cop aimed at Nash and fired, Nash ducked behind a recliner, narrowly avoiding the bullet.

The cop fired another shot, splitting the recliner in half and piercing the floor. He cocked the gun again, but this time Nash was ready.

In one swift motion, Nash drew his weapon and fired back.

The bullet found its mark, hitting the man's gun and sending it clattering to the ground. Nash sprang forward, tackling the cop and forcing him to the ground.

He twisted the man's arms behind his back and quickly grabbed a roll of duct tape from the kitchen drawer to bind him to a nearby column.

The cop spat at him with hatred, but Nash remained unfazed. He delivered a powerful punch to the cop's jaw, watching him slump in his bindings.

Tension filled the air as Nash turned his attention to Rowe, his fists clenched and his breathing shallow. Rowe stepped back as if preparing for a fight.

"Rowe," Nash said. "What's going on here? Who is this guy? You taking over as head of ISTF after Calla was a risky move. What's your real agenda?"

Rowe eyed Nash before lunging forward.

Nash quickly sidestepped him and delivered a punch to the gut that caused Rowe to double over in pain.

Struggling to catch his breath, Rowe threatened, "You're wrong."

Nash grabbed him by the collar and pulled him close. "Tell me what you're doing, and this can be over. You've also been spying on Stan Cress from GCHQ for the last ten years. Why?"

Rowe cowered, his eyes darting around the kitchen as Nash held him in place. His entire body trembled as if every muscle was trying to back away from Nash's grasp.

Nash's gaze settled on a button on the wall near the kitchen entrance.

He watched as Rowe reached up to press it.

An ear-shattering thump echoed through the kitchen as a black helicopter descended from the sky above the house.

Nash bolted outside, the sound of the helicopter blades pounding in his ears.

The pilot leaned out of the window, his gun flashing in Nash's direction as Rowe bolted past him and jumped into the chopper.

Nash bolted for his car and sped away as bullets ricocheted off the hood. A rush of cold air surrounded him as he drove off into the night, determined to catch the black helicopter bearing the insignia of Kronos Corporation.

He pressed on the accelerator, feeling the wind against his face and hearing the loud buzz of the chopper above him. With a burning determination in his heart, he drove recklessly after the helicopter.

CHAPTER
FORTY-SEVEN

10:07 p.m

"FIND ANYTHING?" Mason's deep voice reverberated around the room as he loomed over Jack. He was an intimidating sight, tall and broad-shouldered, his face partially obscured by shadows.

Jack stumbled back at the sight of him. "What the heck are you doing here?" he demanded.

"I could ask you the same question," Mason replied. "Although I already know why you're here."

Jack lifted a brow. "And what's that?"

Mason stared at him. "You're looking for Iram. The Atlantis of the Sands."

Taken aback, Jack felt his heart race. "How do you know that? And, so what?"

"It's my job to know things, Kleve," Mason said. "And I know that you've been searching for Atlantis. But what you don't know is that it's not just a lost city. It's a city of secrets. Secrets that many people would kill to keep hidden."

Jack's fear intensified as he watched Mason. He had heard

rumors of Mason's recent escape from prison and the dangerous men that followed him. Jack remembered the few times he had encountered Mason in the past, when the man had threatened to end not just Jack's life but also Calla's and their friends' lives. But Jack refused to be intimidated anymore.

"What have you heard about the Sands of Atlantis?" Jack demanded.

Mason's eyes narrowed. "Why are you so determined to find it? Iram is a deadly container that can only be opened to unleash destruction."

Jack glared. "And who are you to decide that?"

Mason sighed, his expression solemn. "The history of Atlantis is murky. There's no one who can be trusted with the truth. You must be careful who you trust on this quest."

Jack wasn't convinced. "And that includes you."

As Mason spoke, Jack saw a shadowy figure lurking behind him. His muscles tensed, ready to fight if necessary.

"Relax, Kleve," Mason said. "My man is here to ensure we don't have any... interruptions."

Jack eyed the looming figure in the shadows.

Before he could react, the figure lunged forward.

Jack fought back with ferocity, parrying the attacker's blows and disarming him with a swift move. He knocked him out with a few well-placed blows.

Mason observed the fight with cool detachment as if he were watching a scene in a play. "Seems you're not as helpless as I thought," he said, his lips curling into a sinister smile as he pulled out a gun and aimed it at Jack.

Reacting on instinct, Jack tackled Mason to the ground just as the gun went off.

The bullet missed Jack's head by inches, burying itself into the wall with a loud thud.

They grappled for a few moments before Jack gained the

upper hand, pinning Mason to the ground and punching him in the stomach.

Jack seized the gun and threw it across the room, out of Mason's reach.

Mason gasped for air and lay still for a moment before propping himself up on one elbow. "You used to be my best security and technology adviser. It doesn't surprise me that you found this place. Welcome to the 'seventies. A place with more secrets than all agencies put together."

Jack scanned the area for something to restrain Mason, but he had already disappeared. Frustrated, Jack noticed the panel in the wall that Mason had used to escape. He cursed himself for not being more observant. Working at ISTF was like playing an endless game of cat and mouse.

Jack hesitated, weighing his options: should he pursue Mason or continue searching for clues? Time was running out.

A loud crash outside the room made him jump, and the man he had been fighting was gone.

Jack grabbed the bag he had hidden in the corner and quickly surveyed the room for anything else of value. After copying all the files onto his phone, he ran to the elevator.

The hallway echoed with panicked cries, but the security guard was nowhere in sight.

When he reached the lobby, he sprinted out of the building, furiously tapping his phone as he ran.

Jack dialed Calla's number.

No answer.

He tried calling Calla and Nash multiple times, but neither of them answered. He took off running, hoping to find them quickly.

Day 9
Cheshire, Northwich
8:00 a.m.

CALLA'S HANDS shook as she pulled her cell phone from her pocket.

She squinted to make out the unfamiliar number on the caller ID.

Voices and the hum of traffic echoed off the walls of the government facility parking lot as she brought the phone to her ear.

"Hello?"

"Ja, this is Frau Fuhrman," said a stern, smooth voice. "You know we both want the same thing. We want world order, and I want my exclusive. I have a lead for you, and in return, you will do something for me."

"I don't take bribes," Calla sputtered. "Either tell me what's happening, or I'm hanging up now."

"Miss Cress, here's an address. I suggest you check it out before it's too late."

"This better not be a false lead, Fuhrman."

Frau Fuhrman's sharp voice filled Calla's ear as she gave her the address.

When Calla hung up, she tried Jack and Nash's numbers, but all she got were their voicemails.

She grabbed her keys and slipped into her Maserati. If she pushed it, she could get there in time.

Dread and determination were a heady mix as she started the engine and gunned the engine.

An hour and a half later, Calla pulled up to the address Fuhrman had given her. It was a gas storage site composed of several buildings perched on top of a property that stretched as far as the eye could see.

She stepped out of the car and immediately noticed the smoky stench that clung to the air. Calla reached for a thin scarf from the car to cover her mouth and nose.

Inching closer to the property, Calla kept to the shadows of the leafy trees that lined the walkways and scanned her tablet for the blueprints of each building.

With her senses acutely attuned to her surroundings, she cautiously proceeded forward.

She unlocked the front door of the main building and stepped inside, her breath catching in her throat with anticipation.

Energy pipes connecting Russia, to the United Kingdom through several countries, built in the last few years, snaked through the depths of the building.

Calla descended the dank staircase, each step peeling away a layer of dust that had settled over the years.

She arrived at the bottom and surveyed her surroundings —piles of broken furniture, shredded papers, and cobwebs everywhere.

In the corner rested a large pipe, its faded paint visible against the darkness.

She tiptoed toward it, her ears straining for any sound in the eerie silence.

As Calla approached, she felt a chill go down her spine, and a sudden dread filled her chest.

Just then, a gust of wind blew through, and the roof of the building started to collapse.

Calla saw metal pipes and debris exposed as the ceiling gave way.

She pivoted around and burst through the back door.

In haste, she clambered up the stairs and kicked down the entrance to the second level.

She traversed the hallway to get to the control room door, only to find it locked.

She yanked on the door to no avail.

Her foot bounced off the door repeatedly as she tried to kick it open, but all she heard was a splintering sound from inside the frame.

What had happened here?

She peered into the keyhole of the control room door and saw nothing but emptiness hidden behind its darkness.

"Hello!" Calla yelled as fumes began to possess the hallways.

Calla strained her eyes to see through the darkness. A gas mask hung on the wall, catching Calla's attention. She grabbed the gas mask from the wall, and, gathering all her might, kicked the door in. She stepped into the room.

Two figures in heavy black coats and gas masks were huddled around a computer, their movements barely visible in the dim blue glow.

Calla wasted no time in putting on the gas mask, feeling her operative genetic energy course through her veins.

The woman's eyes were hard and pale gray behind the

mask, and for a moment, Calla could feel the coldness of her gaze. "I'm with the government," Calla said, struggling to speak under her mask. "What happened here?"

The woman hesitated before speaking. "Someone blew up the UK's energy reserves stored in Russia and the Middle East gas pipes. It took years to complete this project and countless hours of work by the best engineers in the country. And now it's all gone."

"How?" Calla asked.

"We don't know," the woman replied.

Calla walked over to the control panel and saw that someone had turned the tap off. "Where is everyone?" she asked.

"Evacuated," a man's voice said from behind. "We're trying to repair the damage and hold on to any gas we can."

The man stepped toward the control panel and examined the dials. Then he turned to Calla. "This is only the beginning."

She glared at him. "What do you mean?" Calla stood frozen in place. It felt as though someone had punched her in the stomach.

"It's going to get worse," he said.

"How did anyone get by your security protocols?"

"We don't know."

Calla gritted her teeth.

"You're working with the government, you say? We need to know what's happening," the man said. "There's a team working behind closed doors to figure it out, but our country and others are in trouble if these gas reserves keep descending as you see here," he continued, pointing at the screen.

"Show me more," Calla said.

The man and woman exchanged a glance. "Are you sure?"

"Yes."

The man led her to the back of the control room and

pushed a button. The wall slid open, and Calla saw where the gas was collected. She counted about four controls, one for each country in the United Kingdom.

The woman came up beside her. "The process is safe, of course. Gas is gathered, filtered, and then purged into a pure gas tank that each UK nation will have access to."

Calla studied them. "An entire nation's supply evaporated? Who's capable of this? What did you see?"

The woman shook her head. "It's impossible to say. A chain reaction. A hack. An explosion. It burned out as soon as it started."

"Wouldn't leave a trace," Calla said, thinking aloud.

"Not likely. For all we know, it could be a terrorist organization wanting to dominate the world economy."

Calla moved closer to the terminals and looked behind her at the remains of the control center. When the screen lit up, she saw one terminal was still on.

She paused, her heart caught in her throat.

"Can I see that document?" Calla asked.

The man nodded, and Calla studied it. The whole thing was a mystery, but she could see the code. She pressed a key, and a program opened, showing the code in full. "What is this?" she asked.

"It's a program I developed," he said. "It's scanning the document, trying to decode its meaning. Since yesterday, it has been working around the clock. We've been trying to see if we could reverse engineer it."

Calla realized what was happening. "You won't find anything on this. You can't reverse its meaning. It has to be done at the source."

"Where is that?"

"The Rub'al Khali desert."

Private Rooms, Arundel Castle, Sussex
9:01 a.m.

AVO SQUEEZED her hands into fists and cracked her knuckles. Then, she stepped inside the door and closed it behind her, leaning on it as if to keep from being pushed back out.

Twelve members were arranged around a board table, with Paxton Maddon in the middle. They watched her as she approached them. When she was close enough to touch them, a man spoke up first. "Octavia Steward hasn't talked yet," he said.

"She will," Avo said.

She kept her lips pressed together and straightened her shoulders, proud and strong. "She will talk, or I will make her talk. I'll do whatever it takes."

The twelve group members exchanged tense glances, and Paxton spoke again. "I need proof that you have her," he said.

Avo's eyes remained fixed on Paxton as she spoke. "She is somewhere safe," she said.

A scarred Russian woman stepped forward, her hand slowly moving toward her jacket pocket.

Avo's eyes widened as the woman pulled out a gun and aimed it at her heart.

The cold metal of the barrel pressed against her, and a wave of anger surged through her veins, but she refused to show any trace of fear.

With an adrenaline-fueled surge, she wrenched the gun out of the woman's hand and yanked her forward by her blouse. With a powerful heave, she threw her across the room.

The woman slammed into the wall with a thud, and the other society members leaped to their feet, going for their holsters.

Avo was faster. "I guess you've never seen operative genetic power in action," Avo said.

Paxton scrambled up from where he had been standing.

"Put down your guns!" she yelled at the members. "Put them down!"

They stared at her.

"I said, drop your guns!"

The society members still didn't move.

"Drop your guns!" Avo yelled again.

Avo could feel their fear. She could feel their anger. And she could feel something else.

Something...

With a violent tug, Avo yanked one group member toward her. Her eyes narrowed, and her jaw set firmly as she spoke to them. "Let's get one thing straight: I'm not here to beg for things. I'm here to ensure Kronos gets its fair share of the deal."

At that moment, she picked up a noise behind her.

Mason appeared through the far door. He was watching with a cool detachment in his eyes. "Avo Schneider, you have some nerve," he said before his gaze softened, and sighed.

"And not a moment too soon; I didn't train you to be a weakling that begs for things."

His voice was stern yet comforting as he continued. "That's not how we do things around here. I brought you here for a purpose, and you know it: to ensure that Kronos does what it's supposed to—a project I started twenty years ago. Neither you nor these idiots standing before me will see it fail."

The room fell silent as the Blackhorse Group members stared at Avo. They had just witnessed her show a level of strength and power only known to operatives.

Avo struggled to contain her fury, clenching her fists to repress the urge to prove her muscle. After all, she had only seen one person with abilities like hers - Calla Cress. Avo knew it would be foolish to reveal her strength to the group.

Mason broke the silence with a commanding and authoritative tone. He made eye contact with everyone in the room before speaking. "Ladies and gentlemen, it's time to open up your pocketbooks. We'll begin the bidding at two billion US dollars."

Avo took a seat at the board table with the members, her mind still reeling from the adrenaline rush of her charade.

CALLA SLAMMED her foot on the accelerator of the Maserati, ignoring red lights and treating stop signs as mere suggestions. Despite her reckless driving, it still took her three hours to reach London from Cheshire. She juggled her phone on the wheel, dialing Nash's number.

He answered the phone. "Nash. You alright?" Calla said.

"Yeah, I'm heading back to London," Nash replied.

Calla clicked the speaker button. "Nash, I've been in the car for hours. Can we meet at Allegra's villa as soon as possible? It's important."

"Sure, I should be there shortly," Nash replied.

"Let me patch Jack. He's calling in," Calla said.

She patched Jack into the call and spoke urgently. "Listen, guys. This is worse than we thought. Somehow, the City of Sands is linked to the United Kingdom's energy reserves, and I think it concerns other governments too. Somebody is playing with the nation's energy resources. I saw the same hack in Cheshire as in Crete. They were the same symbols I saw ten years ago. They're depleting the energy reserves, and it's a hack nobody can reverse. I need to find Atlantis. Again."

Nash interrupted. "Our friend Rowe is also involved. He took off in a helicopter owned by Kronos Corporation."

"That makes sense," Jack said. "I just ran into our old friend Mason Laskfell. Kronos was one of his sub-companies. It doesn't surprise me at all."

"Okay, I'll meet you all at the villa, and we need to leave as soon as possible," Calla said.

"I'll contact Sheik Salib," Nash said. "If anyone can tell us about Arabian legends and symbols, it'll be him."

Calla arrived at Allegra's villa, her arms heavy.

Taiven was waiting for her, and he took her aside. "There's something I need to show you," he said in a low, steady voice.

"What?" Calla asked, taking a sip of water from the kitchen.

Taiven glanced at Allegra before speaking. "You have an ability operative you haven't tapped into yet. You can remember memories you never had. It can help you unlock the undecipherable code and the seven blank pages of the Iram book. Your operative genes have unlocked memories that aren't yours. You can remember people's lives and sense what they felt."

Calla's eyes narrowed as she tried to make sense of his words. "So, I could feel what it was like to be a Mongolian warrior or a Viking?"

Taiven nodded. "Yes, you could. Remember, even if you don't own the memory, you can still connect to it through tangible objects. You can find Stan; he's linked to you more than you think."

Taiven handed Calla Octavia's and Stan's phones. "Where did you get Octavia's phone?" Calla asked, her voice trembling.

"Berlin," Taiven replied.

He recounted how he had followed Octavia and retrieved her phone after she was attacked.

Calla's body was enveloped in shockwaves as she touched the objects with her fingertips.

She closed her eyes and concentrated, entering a state of penetrative vision, a power made possible by a rare silicon chip implanted beneath her skin.

The chip contained carbonados, which absorbed energy and allowed her to counteract the laws of gravity, penetrating solid matter through gaze alone. But Calla wasn't sure if this newfound ability would ultimately be a blessing or a curse.

Taking Octavia's phone in her hands, she felt the cold metal that reminded her of the gun pointed at her friend.

Calla focused, trying to find a clue about Octavia's location, but she came up empty-handed.

Desperate for a breakthrough, she opened the phone and pressed the hard reset button, hoping to find something useful.

As the phone rebooted, relief washed over her. One of Octavia's icons was missing from the home screen. At least she had made some progress.

Calla's fingers trembled as she tapped the screen, revealing a list of missed calls from an unknown number. Her mind raced as she saw an invitation from her father to Octavia to explore the ancient ruins of a temple. The thought of him made her anxious.

In a hurry, Calla retrieved her bag and opened her laptop, typing the temple's address into the search bar.

A website loaded, displaying a map of a remote desert location basking in the bright sunshine and sweltering heat. Calla zoomed in, but no roads or landmarks were to be seen. If her father was there, he was completely alone.

She looked over at Taiven and whispered, "Octavia is in danger. But I can't tell if my father is safe."

Allegra offered comfort by placing her hand on Calla's shoulder. "An impending danger usually triggers your senses. That must mean that Stan is safe... for now."

But her voice carried a hint of worry that Calla couldn't ignore.

CHAPTER
FIFTY-ONE

West London, St. Giles Square
London, 12:19 p.m.

NASH AND JACK filled the doorway, Nash carrying a laptop and Jack lugging two bags.

Nash took a few more steps into the room and took a deep breath, his eyes on Calla's face.

Jack shrugged off the bags and dropped them unceremoniously onto the chair. "Did we miss much? What's been going on?"

Calla lifted her shoulders in a slight shrug before giving Nash a soft peck on his cheek.

He flashed her a tired smile when she noticed the large bruise near his temple.

He shrugged off her concerned expression and quickly explained. "Yeah, ran into Rowe and some nasty guy in a helicopter. I'll explain later," he said.

She gave a hesitant nod before turning to Taiven as if seeking confirmation of what she had just been saying. "My area at the British Museum is more Roman and Byzantine civilizations. We're going to need more around Mesopotamia for this one. I understand the operatives have documents about Mesopotamia, including King Nabonidus," Calla said.

Taiven nodded, and his brow knit in concentration. "Yes, we have a lot of documents about him. He was one of the most important kings of ancient Babylon and may have impacted Iram's growth."

Jack's eyes shifted between Taiven and Calla. His brow furrowed as he peered at them in confusion. "What's this about?"

Calla looked down at the Book of Iram clutched in her hands. It was old, bound in a worn leather cover, and its spine creaked as she opened it to a page near the center.

She glanced up at Jack before pointing to a particular sentence. "I think there's a reference here to Babylon. What I've deciphered seems to be about a secret to some lost power or energy."

Taiven rose from his seat and walked around the desk as Calla handed him the book.

He opened it slowly, turning its crisp pages until his gaze settled on a particular section. He drew in a sharp breath and stayed silent for a moment.

Calla looked up at him. "And?"

He exhaled slowly, then shrugged. "The Book of Iram contains the secret of lost power, but it's up to you to find it."

Calla stared at the book, her mind spinning with possibilities as she remembered the story of ancient King Nabonidus and his wizard searching for a mysterious power source hidden within the Atlantis of Sands.

"According to legend, the wizard had revealed a secret that would give Nabonidus control of the kingdom and its surrounding territories," she said.

Taiven interrupted her thoughts. "And you have seen the power of the Atlantis of Sands, haven't you?"

Calla paused for a moment. "Yes. We were digging in the desert at the site of a palace. It was so powerful, so overwhelming, that I could hardly move. It was as if we were walking into an immensely strong vortex. The power was almost too much to bear. I can still feel the vibration. It felt like the earth was shifting beneath my feet, like I was losing my mind. The power of the Atlantis of the Sands still blows my mind. A man was killed that day... Ivan Schneider."

"Yes, and he came to kill you, but something saved you that day. Your mind," Taiven said.

Calla breathed hard. "I have a blank in some places, but some memories are coming back."

Taiven agreed. "Your brain was wired never to forget, so I think someone on that trip knew something and did something to you, maybe before you went there. Schneider knew you could read the seven pages... and only you."

"Taiven, I remember the parts of the trip now. The purpose and more of what Octavia was doing. Hundreds of shapes and symbols were on the walls of the city gates. These were complicated motifs, more complex than the glyphs in this book —several signs completely unlike the glyphs found throughout Arabia. While residing with Bedouins, Octavia discovered that a recent brush fire had exposed hundreds of previously unknown petroglyphs carved on gigantic boulders. I believe she couldn't fund the project and got involved with the wrong people. But what's not so clear is how she connected with the Blackhorse Group and my father. They funded that trip, not the university."

Nash settled in a chair at the desk and drummed his fingers on the wooden armrest. He glanced at Calla, perched at the edge of her seat, her gaze trained on the open book in front of her.

"That's how Octavia got it approved," Nash began. "Octavia led the exhibition with two gifted people, Calla and the former head of Archaeology at the University of Cambridge. Plus, Avo's father, the assassin, came along for the ride. The question is, why?"

Jack leaned in closer, his eyes studying the page. "What's out there, Cal?"

Calla sighed and ran a hand through her hair before gesturing to one of the ancient symbols on the paper. "It's an overgrown megalithic site," she said. "Unknown even to the state's historic preservation officer of the country. Octavia was trying to compare these petroglyphs with petroglyphs and symbols from around the world, but she couldn't find answers. She noticed a talent in me and wanted me to read the signs on that door that would open Iram... but something stopped me — or protected me."

She pointed to a section at the bottom of the page. "Do you see this section? The seven missing pages. She was trying to translate them, but they are empty — how does one know what to read? That's what I must figure out," Calla replied. "Octavia wanted to prove Iram was likely an outpost of the sunken ancient civilization or a tribute by its survivors or descendants to something even more dangerous—and when a NASA sighting happened...."

"Your father must have connected it all to the operatives," Jack said, standing. "That's why he funded it... he knew it would come back to you, and he had to be in control. He was trying to protect you, Cal."

Allegra drew in a sharp breath. "But someone else on that trip had other ideas... Avo's father," she said.

Nash spoke up next. "Avo may want a lot more from you, Calla. If Ivan Schneider didn't make it out alive—

Jack added his two cents. "She may hold you responsible."

Calla stayed silent, her hands trembling slightly. In her heart, she felt something cold and heavy, like guilt. "She does. And I'm not entirely sure I disagree. I don't remember what happened out there," she finally said in a voice barely above a whisper.

Nash placed a comforting hand on Calla's shoulder. "If you can't remember, then you can't be held responsible," he said reassuringly.

Calla wasn't sure.

CHAPTER
FIFTY-TWO

Day 10
Northern Germany
11:06 a.m.

AVO WAITED over a minute until the elevator announced the third floor. The doors opened to a pale yellow hallway, and she stepped out.

A woman with kohl-outlined eyes held up a hand and led Avo into a small interrogation room, speaking rapidly in Mandarin and pointing to a chair.

Avo nodded but said nothing as the door closed behind her, locking with an electric thunk.

Octavia sat on a bolted-down chair, blood slowly drying into a dark brown clot in small spots down the middle of her face.

"Before you ask, it's all gibberish," Octavia said. "I can't read it. I see it in my dreams and write it down in my translations, but it's gibberish to me. I don't know what it means."

Avo's emotions fluctuated between despair, and rage as she

pleaded with Octavia. "I know there must be something you can tell me," she said, clenching her fists tightly. She was desperate for the truth but terrified of revealing how much pain she was in.

Octavia shifted in her seat. "I don't know," she replied slowly. "I was hoping to solve some ancient code, but when I looked at the first page of that lost book, it was like I was looking at a different world altogether."

Octavia gauged Avo's reaction, but her eyes remained trained on a copy of a page from the book in her hands.

One her father had worked on before he disappeared. "What do you mean?" Avo asked in a low voice.

"I mean that this isn't a language from this world, but from another," Octavia continued. "It's a language only your father and Calla Cress could decipher."

Avo lifted an eyebrow. "And you're completely certain you can't read it?" she asked.

Octavia nodded. "Yes, it's a code, a language of some sort."

Avo bit her lip. "That's a strange thing to say."

"It is, but it's true. I think this ties in with a meteorite that hit Earth centuries ago. Mathematics is about the material world. This isn't about the material world," Octavia added.

"Tell me about the research you worked on with my father at Cambridge. You saw him die," Avo demanded.

"I didn't, but she did. She was just a child..." Octavia trailed off.

"You mean Calla Cress," Avo prompted.

Octavia didn't respond.

Avo's veins surged as she asked in a raised voice, "You must have some idea why he was killed!"

Octavia replied coolly, "It was an accident."

Rage burned in Avo. "Liar! It's because he was getting results!"

Octavia snapped back in disbelief. "Results? I don't know what you mean."

"He was close to a breakthrough; you can bet someone wanted those results. Why did he get results when no one else could?" Avo seethed.

Octavia met Avo's glare with a challenging stare. "Because he found the right person for the job. The girl, Calla. Somehow, he valued her way more than anything else."

Saint Tropez, South of France
9:19 a.m.

CALLA, Nash, and Jack were seated at a small, round wrought-iron table, surrounded by the remains of their breakfast.

The red and white checkered tablecloth was barely visible beneath piles of used dishes. They had just finished a meal of creamy scrambled eggs, buttery croissants, and strong French-pressed coffee. The gentle orange light of dawn illuminated the cobblestone streets and pastel villas in the distance, while a few stray cats wandered about. The cool morning air rustled the leaves of the palm trees, as Jack fought back a yawn.

As Calla stirred her coffee, she felt a sense of surreal calm sitting at the table in this place.

"Sheik Salib," Nash said, his voice hollow in the stillness. "The Sheik will help us."

"I'm ready," Calla replied, finishing her coffee. "Let's go".

Nash paid the bill, and they left the restaurant. A dark Range Rover pulled up outside, and the driver, wearing a chauffeur's cap, stepped out with a thick French accent. "We'll be at the villa in about twenty minutes."

Several minutes later, the car wound through the steep cliff roads of the French Riviera, offering stunning views of terracotta-roofed cottages, turquoise oceans, and wildflowers.

When they arrived at Salib's villa, they were greeted by a butler in a white uniform.

The two-story home was a mix of old and new, with lush gardens and an infinity pool that shimmered like a diamond in the sun. High walls surrounded the villa, but the gates were open, and a servant ushered them in. They passed through an open courtyard and entered the villa's main door.

Calla followed Nash through the common corridor that separated the main house from the guest area and emerged into an outdoor seating section next to the pool.

They found Sheik Salib in a long room lined with bookshelves, sitting in an oversized chair covered with cushions.

He rose as they entered and came forward to embrace Nash. "Nash! How wonderful! Welcome! All of you," Salib said. "I'm so glad to see you again. Come, sit down. Tell me what I can help you with."

Nash waved his hand toward three soft, velvet-covered chairs and smiled.

He settled into one chair as Jack and Calla followed suit.

A few moments later, a house helper with a white starched uniform and lace cap appeared, carrying a silver tray with a delicate china tea service and a selection of Middle Eastern pastries. The sweet aroma of cinnamon and honey drifted through the room.

"We need your help with a mystery," Nash began. "We're

looking for Iram, a lost city. Some call it the Atlantis of the Sands."

"Of course you are," the Sheik said. "And you've come to the right man. Come with me and bring your refreshments."

He led them to another gigantic wall covered with a map of ancient Arabia. "Yes. There's an old legend. Some call it an Arabian Night story of a lost city called the Eight Pillars of Iram. But it was written so long ago that it is lost, and nobody knows where the story came from."

When examining a few other maps in Salib's den, Jack pointed to one. "This looks like an ancient drawing of a city."

"You're right," Salib said. "Now, if we can just figure out what these pictures are, we'll have the key to the Lost City of the Sands."

"I think I can help with that," Calla said.

Calla reached into her bag and pulled out the Book of Iram. She opened it to a page that was covered with strange symbols. "Do you recognize these?"

Salib traced the symbols on the page with a finger. "Yes, I do. They're part of the legend. But there are so many of them. The legend says that only a woman who knows all symbols can open the gate. But that woman died centuries ago. She was the last of a long, ancient line of women knowledgeable in reading ancient symbols. She opened the gateway to the Lost City of the Sands but never returned. No one has ever returned. If you unearth the symbols on the blank pages, you can open the gates and enter the city."

"Here," Jack said, pointing to another set of symbols in the book. "These are the same ones. Do you suppose the symbols on the blank pages are the same as those in the rest of the book?"

"It's possible," Salib said. "But time is running out. With each passing day, the city sinks deeper into the sand. The sands swallow it up, the city crumbles, and the walls will soon be covered forever. I fear this will be the end of an ancient legend," Salib said, shaking his head."

"We'll find the city," Nash said. "We have to. Somehow, it's responsible for the energy depletion in the UK and now the US."

"Where did you learn about the city?" Calla asked Salib.

"One of my ancestors," Salib said.

"We think we can find it," Nash said. "We have the book."

"Then you have greater knowledge than I," Salib said, his eyes flicking over the maps spread across the table and on the wall. "I've studied them for years and haven't found it."

"Then we need to go soon. Because, like you said, we're running out of time," Calla said, her voice wavering slightly.

"I can send some men with you," Salib said, standing up. "At least they will take you as far as they can. But beware of the female warriors guarding the city—they seem as invisible as the blank pages in this book. To get to Iram, you must get through them first. It's deep in the sands, and you'll need to search for it. But first, you must speak with my wife. She's related to the tribes of the desert."

Salib led them to a spacious balcony with a sweeping view of Saint Tropez.

His wife stood by the railing, her dark eyes and olive skin illuminated by the sun's light.

Jack, Calla, and Nash moved closer, ready to meet her.

She gave them a welcoming smile, scanning their faces before speaking. "Nash, it's good to see you again, along with your beautiful wife. And how can I forget the enigmatic Jack? Salib tells me you want to know about Iram. I haven't thought about Iram since I was a girl, but it's a story we know well. To enter the city, you must pass three tests," she said, producing an ancient Arab poem woven into a shawl. "This poem is the first test; it will test your heart. The second is the Sword of Ali, designed to challenge your courage and skill. The third is a statue by the river. It will push you to your limits and force you to persevere. To reach the city, you must read the statue's lips, cross it, and solve the wall's riddle at the gate."

Calla leaned in. "Where do we start?" she asked.

"Not far. The Nazis found the sword, and it's close," Salib replied.

"Where is it?" Jack asked, his voice quivering with anticipation and dread.

His face grew pale as Calla spoke. "Just a few miles from here. In the vaults of the Palace of Monaco," she said, her voice unwavering.

The room fell silent until Salib's wife spoke up. "How did you know that?" she asked.

Calla stood tall and gave a thin smile. "I'm a curator at the British Museum, which has its perks. I know the book is worthless without the sword, and each test fills part of the book's empty pages. It was something we all thought was a myth. I've seen that poem before, in the British Museum archives, and there was a reference to it in the relics of the Pergamon archives. Together, the book and sword form the words we need to open the gates in the city."

Jack shifted with a nervous grin, his eyes darting to Nash. "How do we get into the palace?" he asked, his voice strained.

Calla put one hand on Jack's shoulder and the other on Nash's, giving a reassuring squeeze. "That's where you two come in," she said. "We break in."

CHAPTER
FIFTY-FOUR

Salib's Villa Saint Tropez
South of France
9:22 p.m.

A CHILL RAN through Calla as darkness enveloped the night. The twinkling lights of Saint Tropez cast a soft glow on the coastline and illuminated the sky.

She wanted to pause and take in the beauty, but couldn't, knowing that Kronos could change the world forever. The Sword of Ali had not been seen for decades, and the government of Monaco had purchased it, secretly from an unknown buyer several decades ago.

Moonlight glinted off the Mediterranean, creating a shimmery reflection on the water's surface. Calla stared out at the dark abyss, wondering if it could sense her inner turmoil. The waves lapped gently against the rocks, soothing her senses yet escalating her anxiety. A few boats bobbed like white flowers in a vase on the water's surface.

The French town was alive with evening activity.

The goal tonight was to ambush the Royal Palace's basement and rummage through the tunnel vaults.

Nash walked into the room with an unreadable expression. "The car is ready," he said, and Calla nodded before reaching for her holster and strapping it around her hip.

"What was the interest of the Nazis in the sword?" Jack asked as he poked his head into the room.

Calla adjusted her grip on the weapon. "The sword is special. It's said to be thousands of years old, made during the time of the Persian Empire."

"Strange timing to be carrying a Persian sword around in 1942. During that time, there was a war, and France was occupied. Not exactly a place I would collect things," Jack replied.

Calla took a deep breath and clasped her hands together. She had to tell him the truth. "The Persian Empire didn't forge the sword. It was made long before the Persian Empire existed. Let me ask you this: are you familiar with Nazi research on ancient weapons?" she asked.

"A little," Jack said, suiting up. "I do read," he joked with a wink.

"The Nazis were more interested in ancient weapons than in normal weapons. They were looking for something from history, something lost," Nash said. "Something that would win them the war. The Nazis were also interested in the special abilities of the Sword of Ali, and other mysterious weapons."

"Its abilities? It was a sword. They are just used as weapons. So how does this help us find Atlantis of the Sands?" Jack added.

Calla repeated the words to herself before speaking. "I suppose the inscription on the sword has a key cipher that opens the gates at Iram," she said. "That's my guess. But we won't know until we see it."

Nash raised an eyebrow skeptically. "According to legend?"

Calla nodded. "Yes. It's an incredibly powerful weapon, with symbols that can drive men mad at the sight of it. It was used during battle as a sword to thwart enemies, but the sword-bearer also used it in religious ceremonies. The Persians believed it held the power of God. There is a scripture in the Old Testament that discusses the Persian sword. It was the sword of Gideon."

Jack tapped his gun in its holster and laughed. "This is the same sword the Nazis were after? What are the odds?"

Salib's wife stepped into the room. "Only read the symbols when you enter the city of Iram and not before," she said in a grave tone.

Nash moved closer to Calla, taking her hand in his own. "You ready?" he asked her.

She nodded, her expression firm as she met his gaze. "Yes, let's get this done."

Monte Carlo
11:56 p.m.

THE STREETS WERE DESERTED, but several restaurants remained open, and at least two dozen boats were docked in the harbor. The spires of the palace, the official residence of the Sovereign Prince of Monaco, were visible in the distance.

Despite the late hour, the city was still bustling with people laughing and chatting in cafes and bars around them.

Mumbled conversations of tourists filled the air, and the trio carefully ducked behind streetlight poles or benches to avoid being seen.

Calla, Jack, and Nash tiptoed along the cobblestone walkway, flanked on both sides by candlelit restaurants. Ahead of them, the classical spires of the Baroque palace jutted up against the night sky. They reached a cluster of trees just as a security guard began closing the gardens surrounding the court.

They activated the invisibility feature of their electronic

suits and pressed their bodies against the dark tree bark, waiting until he had gone.

A few drunken revelers stumbled by, and Nash had to push them away. Luckily, they didn't seem to notice the three agents who trudged on, their footfalls the only sound in the night air. Somewhere, a team of ISTF agents was waiting silently.

Beneath the palace walls was the secret vault containing the Sword of Ali of Agreb, and if they wanted to get it, they'd have to find a way into the tunnels below.

"Keep moving," Nash whispered.

They advanced, and Calla looked around.

"We have to get past the guards," Jack said.

"Jack, take Calla and go to the back of the palace. There's a garden there. I'll distract the guards," Nash said.

"Come on," Jack said to Calla.

A bead of sweat slide down her forehead. Her heart raced, and her breathing was labored. She looked over at Nash, who was surrounded by three ISTF agents.

A shrill sound echoed through the air as a minor alarm went off, successfully luring the guards away from the palace.

Calla locked eyes with Jack and knew they had to act fast. She grabbed his arm, and they were off, their feet pounding against dirt and grass as they flew toward the palace walls.

Unfazed by the imposing height, Calla launched herself in a leap, frantically clawing her fingers into the stone. With a grunt of effort, she pulled Jack up to join her on the other side. Their lungs heaving, they stumbled along the cobblestone path on the other side, the tall hedges growing higher as they continued.

As they stepped into the palace courtyard, Jack and Calla were dazzled by a pond filled with multi-hued goldfish, shimmering above the cobalt and teal tiled surface below.

From a central sculpture arose two intertwining golden serpents, their scales glinting in the moonlight. Foliage swooped down from ancient trees whose leaves shimmered in shades of emerald and silver.

They sprinted through the garden and careened around the intricately carved fountain, where a cherubic water spirit held an oversized shell aloft.

They raced ahead and came to a solid steel wall. He whipped out his cell phone, his fingers flying across the screen. He threw her a grin as he activated the hack, and the massive door slid open.

Jack scrambled through, but not before tipping his head toward the entrance in an invitation for her to follow.

Calla stepped into the dark abyss, and the door shut behind them.

They were inside the palace.

Using the helmet's built-in x-ray vision, they could see their surroundings, but no one else could.

They tiptoed down a hallway and went up a flight of stairs. They were in another hallway with a door at the end.

A sign in French was on the door. Calla translated it, 'Do Not Enter.'

Jack took a deep breath as he inserted a keycard into the door, his fingers trembling with anticipation. He typed in the security code, and the door clicked open with a metallic clunk.

He gestured for Calla to step inside, and she felt her chest tighten with dread.

The room was unlike anything she had ever seen before. Rich fabrics in deep, earthy hues of brown and red draped the walls, and an enormous, heavy table stretched down the center of the room.

Its top was covered with woven cloth dyed a deep shade of burgundy that reminded Calla of dried blood.

Inlaid within its marquetry was a stone sarcophagus surrounded by dazzling gems.

At the center of the table lay a pair of identical stone boxes.

One was open and contained a silvery sword marked with dark spots along the blade. The second box was closed and had a handwritten sign in front of it: The Sword of Ali of Agreb.

Calla couldn't help but feel awed by its presence. "This must be it," she said.

Jack opened the box, revealing the Sword of Ali. It was shaped like a cross with an eagle on the handle. The hilt was gold, and the blade was silver. The edge had a golden stripe running down the middle.

"Now we just have to get out of here," Calla said, placing it in its sheath.

Monte Carlo
11:51 p.m.

RION ADVANCED through the palace's corridors, carefully avoiding the guards and the harsh light of the torches.

He felt his way to the vaults, found the right key on his ring, inserted it into a keyhole, turned it three times, then listened for any sign he had been discovered.

Aside from a distant guard clearing his throat, there was no sound. With care, he opened the door and slipped inside.

Cool darkness swept over him. After a moment to let his eyes adjust, he pulled the door closed behind him.

At first, he could only see a dull glow of light at the edge of the room. He picked his way carefully along the floor toward it until he reached a small night light that cast a warm glow over a desk.

Relieved, he saw that the first room of the vault was empty, save for a few boxes and trunks.

He walked over to the desk and picked up a pencil,

propping up some papers. Rion snapped a picture of the room and the contents of the papers before slipping the pencil back into place.

He crept to the next room in the vault, pausing at the closed entrance that separated him from the most valuable jewels.

He placed his ear against it and listened intently for any sound, but all he heard was his own shallow breath.

With a trembling hand, he reached for the doorknob, the cold brass sending a shiver down his spine. He opened the door with a soft click and stepped inside, closing the door behind him with a gentle thud.

He cursed under his breath as he fumbled for the switch in the pitch-black room. When he finally found it, he clicked his flashlight on, and its beam shot through the room like a ray of hope, glaring in tiny pinpoints against the thick blackness. He moved cautiously in a slow circle, examining every square inch of the room. There was nothing but a rickety wooden table and a small object in the corner. Where was the Sword of Ali?

As he moved closer, he could make out the shape and realized with alarm that it was some kind of weapon. He stood frozen in place.

CHAPTER
FIFTY-SEVEN

CALLA AND JACK scrambled down the palace until they stopped in front of an imposing wooden door with an intricate lion's head lock.

Jack grabbed the lion's mouth and yanked it with determination, but the door remained tightly shut.

Calla backed away from the door, noticing what he was about to do with the Sword of Ali of Agreb in his hands. With a deep breath, Jack hoisted the sword above his head, and with one swoop, it split the door in two.

"Well done," Calla said admiringly.

They scurried inside and were enveloped by thick darkness.

Calla couldn't see a thing, but she could feel an ambush behind them.

"There's a light switch on the left wall," she said, knowing her voice would be the only thing that could guide them in the dark.

They hurried across the room, their footsteps slamming against the stone floor.

Suddenly, a motion sensor came on and illuminated the room.

They surveyed the shelves full of chemicals and equipment lining the walls.

Two tables sat in the middle of the room, their surfaces hosting computers, microscopes, and other scientific equipment.

"Where are we?" Jack whispered, checking the blueprints on his e-watch.

Calla knew immediately. "We're in one of the palace labs," she said. "Two guesses they've been studying the sword."

A door opened, and the muffled laughter of several voices filled the hallway outside the laboratory.

They froze in their steps, and Jack quickly motioned to stay low and duck behind the tables.

The bright lights of the lab cast long shadows across the floor, leaving little room for them to hide.

"We have to find a way out," Jack whispered as he studied his phone. "The blueprints show a trap door leading to tunnels. Let's go."

They crept along the walls, staying as still as possible and barely breathing.

Calla saw a door and tried the handle.

It opened with a small click.

She pushed it open slightly and peered outside, then quickly shut it again. "There's a courtyard with another high wall surrounding it. If we crawl through the tunnels you mentioned, we can get away with no one seeing us," she said, pointing at a nearby metal trap door.

They pulled it open with a loud creak and saw a tunnel with stone steps that led below the palace.

They advanced in the darkness as they crept into the inky depths below.

With Jack at the lead, they stumbled along the narrow

tunnel, forced to press against each other in order to pass through.

After what felt like an eternity, they found a wider tunnel and finally spread out to walk side-by-side.

The air was heavy and thick, each breath a struggle as they descended further down.

Ahead of them in the darkness, they could make out glistening concrete and murky water. Then they heard voices around the corner, and they stopped in their tracks.

Jack peered cautiously around the corner as Calla crouched behind the concrete wall.

CALLA AND JACK burst out of hiding, sprinting as fast as they could.

Calla covered her nose against the musty odor of the underground tunnels, her feet slipping on the smooth floor.

Sweat soaked through her shirt, and her lungs felt heavy, but she kept running, keeping up with Jack.

Fumbling for her gun, she clicked off the safety with her thumb.

Her footsteps skidded along the worn concrete floor, which glimmered in the light of a single bulb hanging from a stone pillar meters ahead.

They quickened their pace, their boots clicking as they moved forward.

Dark tendrils of fog glided across the floor, disappearing into unseen shafts, enveloping them in a blanket of darkness they navigated through.

For a moment, Calla struggled to keep up, trying to breathe as the fog thickened the air with moisture.

Suddenly, they were surrounded by two stern-faced guards

with swords drawn, and pistols cocked in front of another imposing wooden door with an intricate lion's head lock.

The first guard stepped closer, pressing the cold steel tip against Calla's throat. "Give it to me."

Calla shook her head and stepped protectively in front of Jack, her eyes blazing with defiance.

The man's face hardened, and he cocked the gun.

From the shadows behind the guards, Nash burst out with an animalistic determination in his steps.

He dove for the man's legs, sending him staggering. In a single swift motion, Nash tore the sword from the guard's hand and leaped back to his feet with a triumphant cry.

But then, the blow to Calla's head came swiftly, feeling like a thousand needles piercing her skin.

With her eyes stinging, Calla watched as Nash lunged at the man, taking him to the ground.

"This is your last chance," Avo roared from the opening of the tunnel with a sword in hand, possibly the one they left in the vault. "Give me the Sword of Ali, or there will be consequences."

Where has she come from?

Calla took two guesses. Avo had to have had Octavia's help. She had to be responsible for her disappearance. It all made sense. Octavia would've known about the sword— perhaps even the three tests.

Nash leaped in front of Calla, shielding her from Avo's wrath. "You need to stop coming for things that aren't yours," Calla said.

A squad of Monaco Palace guards suddenly surrounded them, leaving Calla to think fast.

She signaled to Jack to take the Sword of Ali and disappear to the meeting point using the invisible suit, then looked at Nash and gave him a knowing look. They would fight their way out.

"Fine, we will do this the hard way," Avo said.

Calla watched as Nash charged at Avo, the silhouette of their fists clashing against one another in a heated battle as the sword she held dropped to the floor.

Calla quickly disarmed one guard with a roundhouse kick and charged toward the fight.

As she reached them, she saw Nash lunge and Avo block.

Taking her chance, she delivered a swift kick to Avo's leg, followed by a sharp kick to her head.

Calla adjusted the straps of her invisibility suit tightly. She could almost hear Nash's breath behind her as they hastened toward the opening of the tunnel to the outside.

Jack and Nash had already passed through, leaving behind the deafening sound of the heavy grate clanging shut.

Calla's body lurched at the sound, every muscle tensing up as the men took on the other assailants.

She heard a noise.

The blow to Avo had not been hard enough.

She raised her gaze to find Avo sneering down at her, her sword held high and ready to strike.

With unbridled agility, Calla dropped to the ground and spun on her heels, propelling herself toward Avo's feet in a flurry of movement.

The clash of steel meeting concrete echoed through the outside walls of the palace as Calla dodged the blow and the sword made contact with the ground.

CHAPTER
FIFTY-NINE

"SO YOU THINK BEING an operative makes you special... well, guess what? You and I are not too different. We both were abandoned by parents we should have adored. Left to fend for ourselves in this world as operatives and not knowing it. The only difference between you and me is that I discovered my strengths. I've had time to practice and understand who I am. This isn't something I can say about you."

Calla could barely make out a slender ray of light above her.

Her stomach twisted into a knot.

She remembered feeling the same emptiness as a child, the feelings of loneliness and abandonment that she had never been able to shake off.

The darkness seemed to embrace her, pulling her into its depths and teasing her with memories. Her heart raced as fear crept up her chest, threatening to overwhelm her. Yet, despite the fear, something called out to her with an irresistible yet familiar pull.

She recalled the pain of being abandoned as a child and struggling to survive parentless in this cruel world.

Slowly, she gave in to the darkness around her and its power over her.

In that moment of vulnerability, she was reminded of those who had left her behind and hurt her in the past. And yet, in that dark abyss, she yearned for their forgiveness and love.

Tears streamed down Calla's face as she looked through a black cloud of despair that seemed to swallow her whole.

She felt its powerful pull, tugging at her heart and mind until it had stripped away all of her defenses, and only raw pain and anguish remained. Despite the torment it caused, there was a strange comfort in giving in to the darkness.

Avo lunged forward and delivered a thrust to Calla's stomach.

She gasped in pain as an electrifying surge raced through her veins.

In one swift motion, Avo brought forth her sword and plunged it deep into Calla's flesh.

Calla recoiled in shock and pain as a red river spilled from her side, traveling down her leg and pooling around her feet.

She screamed in agony, feeling like her life was being sucked away.

"The moment we got word you were going to have a baby, I swore to kill your child, the same way you killed mine, and now you can never have that privilege again!" Avo spat.

Calla felt confusion wash over her. When had Avo had a child? Had she been pregnant?

"When my father didn't return from Rub'al Khali, I went into shock, then I lost my child!" Avo hissed.

Calla's eyes widened as she pieced together what had been said. "You were pregnant when I went to Rub'al Khali?"

"I begged my father not to go, knowing I'd always have a difficult pregnancy. He was all I had."

Tears welled in Avo's eyes.

Calla gasped in pain as her vision blurred. Her body

convulsed against the ground. She had been stabbed, and she felt the warmth of her own blood pooling around her. With every ounce of strength, she had left, she looked at Avo and coughed out blood, "Is that why you and your father tried to kill me back at Cambridge all those years ago?"

Avo raised an eyebrow and sneered. "Is that why you did it, left him to die in the desert?"

Calla struggled to remain conscious as she felt her life slipping away. The pain was unbearable. With blood-stained lips, she shook her head defiantly. "I don't know what you're talking about."

Avo bellowed with rage and rushed forward, her fists pounding against Calla again and again.

Calla lay broken on the ground, blood trickling from her nose, but she refused to surrender. Summoning all of her strength, she struggled to push herself up, but was too weak to move. As every ounce of energy seeped away, she still clung to a faint glimmer of hope.

Then Nash's voice rang out in the darkness, drawing her out of the black abyss that had consumed her.

He was like a beacon, and she stumbled weakly into his arms.

He quickly drew his gun and placed it against Avo's temple, his voice booming with authority as he commanded Avo not to move.

Calla felt a surge of relief as Avo backed away.

Suddenly, Avo stumbled, and Nash fired a shot in the dark.

Calla heard a thump and hurried footsteps before Avo was gone, and ISTF agents flooded back into the tunnel.

"You can see in the dark, Nash, can't you? I thought only operatives could do that," Calla whispered.

"There's a lot mere agents can do," Nash said, his voice serious as he lowered the gun.

He put an arm around Calla's shoulders and gently pulled

her closer. His hand brushed against her forehead, and he gasped when he saw her blood. "Calla, you're hurt. Your temperature is spiking, and you're burning up."

Calla's voice was strained. "No," she said with certainty, her body shaking with pain.

She glanced down and saw a steady stream of crimson spreading from her arm and dripping off her fingertips.

Nash's hands moved to her side, and he gasped when he saw the wound. "Oh, God!" he said desperately. "Calla, stay with me."

Her heart beat against her ribcage as she attempted to take a step, but she was pinned in place and felt severe pain in her abdomen.

Her vision blurred, and before she could react, she lost control of her body and fell into Nash's arms.

CHAPTER
SIXTY

Day 11
Off the Coast of Monaco
Scorpion Tide Yacht
1:29 a.m.

A DARK HAZE slowly enveloped Calla, and she struggled to figure out who or where she was.

The pain in her side intensified, and she heard muffled voices echoing in the distance. She felt her body being lifted and knew vaguely that she was being carried somewhere in warm arms, but the pain in her gut was excruciating.

A team of medics anxiously waited, pacing and wringing their hands.

They quickly lifted Calla onto a stretcher and rushed her back into the treatment room of the Scorpion Tide. Calla could feel the blood flowing out of her body, soaking her clothes, pooling around her.

Struggling to open her eyes and see the people gathered around her. Their forms were blurred.

As the seconds passed, the pain in her stomach

intensified. She felt the tugging of a needle as it slid into her arm and the reassuring pressure of the IV bag flooding her body with medication. It was meant to calm her and stop the pain.

Calla felt herself floating, finding it more and more difficult to stay conscious. Her eyes felt heavy, and she had trouble keeping them open. She closed her eyes and drifted again.

Nash stalked the hallway, his broad frame heaving with labored anguish.

Jack crouched at the threshold of the treatment room, his face drained of color and etched with dread.

Both men were covered in blood, in their own prison, with strained eyes glued to the flurry of medical activity filling the room.

The medical team quickly assessed Calla's condition and began tending to her, but she remained unconscious, her features slack and unresponsive.

Despite their frantic efforts to save her, Calla was already slipping into the darkness.

As she floated in an in-between state, visions of her past, her childhood, and her relationships with the people she loved haunted her. Calla's mind was fuzzy and disoriented as she lay on the medical examination table.

She could barely open her eyes, and when she did, she could only see a bright light shining down on her.

She tried to move, but her body felt heavy and sluggish as if she were wading through molasses.

Her mind was hazy, and she couldn't quite recall what had happened.

Then, she heard a voice she recognized. Jack's.

He leaned over her, urgently imploring her to stay awake and fight.

"Don't you dare slip away from me," he said. "Stay with me, Calla."

Struggling to keep her eyes open, Calla strained to make out his face.

Nash stood off to the side, his fingers interlaced and worry lines creased across his forehead. He looked as if he were holding on to a thin shred of hope while dread threatened to overtake him.

"I'm so sorry," Calla whispered, her voice barely audible. "I tried my best. I did."

"Shhh," Jack whispered back. "It's okay. You're going to be fine."

Calla knew the truth.

She was dying, and there was nothing she could do to stop it.

The medical team worked frantically around her, but Calla could feel herself slipping in and out of consciousness.

A wave of sadness swept over her as she thought of her parents and the life she had been denied.

Then she thought of Nash and their last embrace. She had promised never to leave him, but deep down, she knew it was no use now.

Tears stung her eyes as regret consumed her.

She also thought of Jack, her best friend, who had always stood by her side, no matter what.

Both men were trying to remain strong, but Calla could sense their despair, even as she was slipping away... Somewhere.

Her vision faded to black; the end was near.

She thought of all the lives she had touched and all the people who loved her.

She wished she could have done more for them. But most of all, Calla thought of the mission and how Atlantis might have taken everything from her.

CHAPTER
SIXTY-ONE

NASH'S FISTS clenched as he watched the medical staff struggle to save Calla's life.

The scene was a blur of activity, and he felt like he was watching from outside his own body as the nurses and doctors worked to stop the bleeding and stabilize Calla's condition.

Every second felt like an hour, and he stood frozen, unable to process what was happening.

Pain racked his body as he watched the last moments of Calla's life unfold before his eyes. Paralyzed with fear as he stared at the incision in her abdomen, the blood dripping in rivulets onto the white medical bed beneath her.

Bitter tears slid down his face, but he did nothing, unable to move or think of a way to help her as she slipped away.

Finally, he forced himself to take a step forward, unable to bear the sight of Calla's suffering any longer.

With trembling hands, he reached out to take her hand, holding on to her with desperate strength as the medical staff brought in more equipment.

"Come on, you can beat this," he muttered, wiping the

tears from his face and trying to stay strong for her. "You're the strongest person I know, Calla. Don't you dare give up now."

In the back of his mind, Nash knew it was a long shot. Calla had been in a vicious fight and had sustained severe injuries, but he refused to believe that she was going to leave him, refused to let himself give up hope.

As the minutes ticked by, he gradually became more aware of the reality that Calla was battling a losing fight. She was fading fast, and her vital signs were dipping despite the medical team's efforts.

Terrified and heartbroken, Nash stood helplessly by as his wife slipped into a coma, mere inches from his fingertips.

Still, he refused to give up.

Nash refused to let go of Calla without a fight, determined to do whatever it took to keep her alive. He would make any sacrifice, even if it meant risking his own life.

Each breath she took gave him hope, and he clung to it with all his might, praying that somehow she would pull through.

Dr. Bertrand, Calla's specialist who had rushed from Paris to be at her side, solemnly placed a hand on Nash's shoulder. "I'm so sorry, Nash. She's gone. It's over. We did all we could. We can't bring her back from the coma she's in now."

Nash's chest heaved with despair as he stared at Calla's lifeless body, tears streaming down his face. Despite the finality of reality, Nash couldn't let go of his last shred of hope that Calla would survive against all odds.

As her vital signs continued to dip, even that flicker of hope faded away.

With a heavy heart, Nash turned to Dr. Bertrand and reluctantly nodded, knowing he had to make the hardest decision of his life: to let her go. He gently squeezed Calla's hand one last time before softly closing her eyes.

She was gone now, leaving a gaping hole in his soul.

"Only the machine is keeping her alive now," Bertrand said, "but not for long, just mere hours."

Nash called Taiven, hoping the operatives could help. Taiven could offer no solace. "I'm sorry, Nash, but there's nothing we can do. We're too far away, and she only has a few hours left," he said into the phone.

Nash's body quaked with agony, and grief overwhelmed him. He could hardly believe his one true love had been taken from him so suddenly and savagely. But even in his anguish, he found minor comfort in knowing she had been freed from her suffering.

"Nicole has been trying to reach you for days. She may already be on her way to you," Taiven added.

Nash disconnected the call and slumped to the ground, burying his face in his hands as he let himself grieve for the loss of his wife.

The medical staff dressed Calla's final wounds placed her on a clean bed, and wheeled her out of surgery.

Jack stumbled forward and grasped Nash's shoulder tightly. "I'm so sorry," Jack's voice trailed off, and an excruciating silence ensued.

Nash looked up, recoiling. His eyes glazed over with grief, and he clutched onto Jack's shirt, holding onto the last shreds of hope.

A palpable sadness settled between them.

CHAPTER
SIXTY-TWO

"NASH?"

He thought he had heard his name, but he wasn't sure. His body was stiff, and his mind was foggy as if he had been sleeping for an eternity. He wanted to move and answer the call, but his limbs were heavy, and his thoughts wouldn't come together.

Slowly, he raised his head.

Nash didn't know how long he had been sleeping on the cold floor.

"Nash, it's Nicole," the voice said. "Nicole Cress."

He saw Calla's mother in the doorway, her eyes brimming with tears. Before he could blink, she crossed the room and embraced him fiercely. Her lips met his forehead in a desperate kiss, a silent plea to be strong and brave.

He thought he had just experienced a hallucination. Nicole was a vision of an older version of Calla.

As Nash unsteadily withdrew, Nicole made her way to Calla's bedside.

She pressed a gentle kiss to Calla's pale cheeks, asking everyone in the room, other than Nash, to leave.

The machines hummed around her, keeping Calla alive and stable, but Nash could see it was bittersweet for Nicole.

Everyone quietly filed out of the room, leaving only her and Nash.

Nash collapsed into a chair by Calla's bedside, feeling numb. He couldn't believe Calla only had moments of life left; it didn't seem real.

Nicole sat with him in silence for a while before finally speaking up. "Nash, I'm so sorry," she breathed, her eyes shining with unshed tears.

Nash tried to process everything that had happened. It felt like a nightmare he couldn't seem to wake up from. Calla was gone in every way but a few last breaths, but he wouldn't accept it. Part of him wanted to rage at the world, to demand why this happened to them when they had finally found happiness together. He knew it wouldn't bring her back, so instead, he just sat by her silently, stroking her hair, and trying to imprint her image onto his mind so he could never forget her just as she was. He looked at the machine that kept her alive and wondered what it would be like once they turned it off.

He couldn't bring himself to accept it for a long time, but finally, he knew he had to admit that she was gone.

As a tear rolled down his cheek, he leaned down and kissed her lips. "Goodbye, beautiful," he murmured. "I love you."

"You can't say goodbye yet," Nicole said, softly.

Nash looked up at her, eyes stinging with tears.

She squeezed his hand reassuringly and gave him a sad smile. "You're the only one who can bring her back to us, Nash," she whispered. "Love is stronger than any operative science and has always been." Nicole touched his cheek, wiping away the tears that had fallen there. "Don't give up hope yet."

"What do you mean?" he said. "She only has moments to live."

Nicole held his hand tighter and leaned in. "Love is the only thing that keeps an operative alive because it's the one thing that is inherently denied them."

"Come again."

"If it weren't for Stan's love for me over the years, I'd be dead by now. What's inherent by nature in other humans is foreign to operatives. Love."

"Not sure I understand, Nicole."

"As operatives mingle with humanity, they begin to crave the one thing that keeps the human race alive and reproducing. Love. Your love for Calla is much stronger than any operative science or medical intervention. Remember that. What keeps a baby alive? Isn't it surely touch, a kiss, a cuddle, a caress, intimacy? Calla has craved that all her life, everything we denied her, and it comes from you. It's what makes her strong."

Nicole reclined in a bedside chair next to him. Then she looked straight at Nash. "Stan and I have always loved Calla from afar, and I know now it was a mistake to leave her as a baby. She needed human touch, a family connection. Mama and Papa Cress, her foster parents, gave it to her, but she needed more. When you came along, you strengthened her more than she could imagine. She is a force to be reckoned with, even more so with you by her side."

"I..."

"You need to hear this, Nash. Ten years ago, I broke into GCHQ and took the Book of Iram out of that place. I knew Calla was the only one who could read it, but she was not ready, and it would have killed her. Ivan Schneider was a second-class agent, a scoundrel with a chip on his shoulder, and he made it personal for us. Now his people have taken Octavia. Stan and I worked undercover with Octavia, but she was weak. We don't blame her at all. She is only useful to them because she is the only one who knows her way back to the City of Sands, to Rub'al Khali."

"*You* took the book?"

"Yes, and gave it to Octavia to use it to help the Blackhorse Group. It's been ten years, and we still have not found what is in that place. The book, the symbols, all the things only Calla can help with. But she was not ready. They would have found and exploited her if I hadn't taken the book from GCHQ. Ivan Schneider and his daughter Avo tried to get hold of the book for months before that trip."

The words hurt, even as he said them. "Avo did this to her."

"Avo has been after Calla for ten years now and has hidden her true identity within ISTF. Her allegiance is with Kronos, an organization born out of exploiting science, history, and heritage. When I heard Stan couldn't stop that expedition, I knew I had to interfere and get the book to Octavia so she could protect my child. If they got to the city with the book and the artifacts, it would distract them from what was really in that city. The real dangers of Iram. I knew they needed the book, but I didn't count on what darkness could do to Calla. Taiven explained that darkness took over her life when we left her as a baby, and I'll never forgive myself for that."

"What do you mean, darkness? Calla fell still in the tunnels under the palace. I think it had something to do with darkness."

Nicole took a deep breath. "Calla's operative subconscious is afraid of the dark. It's something she took from her childhood when we, her parents, abandoned her. She can learn to control it, but now she has to fight for her life first, and that starts with you."

"I… You were…"

"No," she said, her voice tight with emotion. "I wasn't with the Blackhorse Group, but Stan needed me, and I'd do anything a mother could do for her child." She looked away, her eyes filling with tears, and drew in a shuddering breath. "I didn't lose Calla then, and I won't lose her now."

Nash felt his heart catch in his chest as he watched her struggle to hold back the grief.

Nicole wasn't finished. "It's clear to all of us. You, too, didn't have the easiest of backgrounds, Nash, with parental divorce and constantly moving from one place to another. When you met Calla, both your hearts found a home. You found each other. Belonging. Two abandoned souls were now beating together in unison. You are one-half of her, so your heart needs to keep beating for her when hers can't. And the one thing you both can't live without is each other's touch; in this case, you are literally the air she needs to breathe."

Nash gulped, feeling hope returning to him as he stared at Calla's peaceful face. "I don't know how to bring her back, Nicole," he confessed, his hope fading.

Nicole smiled. "You do. I'll be back to check on you both." After giving him one last kiss on his forehead, Nicole rose and left, leaving Nash with his thoughts.

Nash was determined to bring Calla back from the edge of death.

Not knowing what to do, he removed his shoes and slowly climbed into the bed next to her unconscious body. As long as there was love between them, nothing could stop them from being together again.

He remembered the words he and Calla had always shared. As he settled next to her, he whispered them over and over again. "You and me against the world." It had been their mantra.

Gently stroking her face, Nash felt her pulse still steady, but weak.

She was so pale, her skin ashen and lifeless. Nash held her

hand to his face and gently kissed her palm. Then he laid his head on the bed by her side and held her hand in his, just as he had when they were new lovers. He took a deep breath and let it out slowly, trying to calm his racing heart and giving himself the strength to do what he had to do.

It wouldn't be easy, but he was ready to fight for her.

Nash spoke softly, "I love you. I hope I've told you that every day I've been with you, Cal. And I won't stop now. There's so much I still want to tell you, to share with you. My heart found yours when we met by the Rameses II statues in the Egyptian Room at the British Museum in London."

He held her face in his hands, his shoulders shaking with emotion.

Nash drew in a breath, his heart heavy, thinking back to their past. "Though we didn't properly meet that night, our hearts did. Three years later, when you found out you were an operative and a damn powerful one at that, one who many people wanted to hurt, I swore I would take care of you and love you even when they wanted to force us apart."

He paused.

"The day we eloped in the mountains of Colorado was the best day of my life. It's you and me, fighting against anything that comes our way. We do it for ourselves, but we also promise to leave this world better than when we entered it. I know you would punch me now if I didn't ask, but may I kiss you, Beautiful?"

His words stuck in his throat, not knowing how to continue. "Find your way back to me."

Nash watched her and thought he saw some color return to her cheek. He leaned down and brushed his lips across hers, then pulled away and held her hand to his chest, feeling her pulse fluttering against his fingers.

After lacing his fingers through hers, he pressed his lips

back to hers, then pulled back and watched her face. She was more beautiful than he'd ever known.

After a beat of silence, he gave her a gentle kiss on her fingers. "I love you, Calla. Please come back to me. Choose us. Choose life."

CHAPTER
SIXTY-THREE

7:21 a.m

"NASH?"

Nash opened his eyes at the sound of Jack's voice. He shook his head, still disoriented, and sat up slowly, feeling the pounding headache and neck pain.

Shadows in the room gradually came into focus, and he realized he had spent the entire night by Calla's side.

Jack approached him with a look of pain and understanding in his eyes, and Nash could sense the anguish in the air even before he spoke.

"How is she...?" Jack asked, his voice trailing off with the same sadness Nash felt inside.

"I don't know," Nash replied.

"She's too far gone," Jack said with a hint of exhaustion in his voice. "Her pulse is weaker, but it's holding," he added, his words carrying a sad smile.

Nash and Jack watched over Calla together as the machines kept her alive.

Taking Nash's arm, Jack suggested, "Come on, man, let's get some food in you."

Nash hesitated, but he leaned over to kiss Calla one more time before leaving the room with Jack.

They headed to the stern of the ship, where they were greeted by a staff member wearing a white uniform and cap.

He nodded and waved them over to a long table, where a tray of sausages, eggs, bacon, fruit, and freshly baked bread awaited them.

"It's tough," Jack nodded as he sat down. He ran a hand across his dreadlocks and shook his head. "But you gotta keep on trucking."

"I know," Nash said, placing his hands on the table. "I don't know what to do without her. She is my entire life."

"We're gonna fix it, Nash," Jack promised.

Nash let out a sigh. "She's not out of the woods yet."

"I know that." Jack gave him a pat on the back. "Now, come on, let's get something to eat. You need your strength."

"Thanks, Jack."

As they ate, Jack continued. "We're going to get her back. We always do. You know you have to keep yourself together. You are a strong guy, Nash. Don't forget that."

After finishing their meal, they walked to the ship's railing and looked out over the water, silently watching the sunrise.

CHAPTER
SIXTY-FOUR

8:23 a.m

SHE GASPED for breath as if she had been holding it in forever.

Calla opened her eyes, blinking against the sudden brightness. Her head throbbed, and a wave of nausea washed over her, making her body sway unsteadily.

She lay on a simple cot, her body covered by only a thin sheet.

The room was dark, except for the soft glow of recessed lighting from the ceiling.

Gradually, she noticed other details. The room was empty and quiet, with no one else present. A machine next to her bed beeped, the sound sharp and insistent in her ears.

She forced herself to sit upright.

Her head still spun, and a tightness in her chest as if something were constricting her breathing.

A rush of images and sounds flooded her mind as she struggled to remember where she was.

She moved her hand to the side of her abdomen and felt

around, sure she had sustained something powerful. She couldn't explain it, but her body felt stronger.

Calla looked around the room, and then she remembered his voice in her ear, keeping her strong throughout the night. She had felt his touch and known his love, and at that moment, she had found the strength to keep fighting.

The words echoed in her mind, and she whispered them, *"You and me against the world."*

CHAPTER
SIXTY-FIVE

8:45 a.m

NASH STEPPED AWAY from the breakfast table.

He hesitated, looking back at the breakfast buffet, seeking reassurance that the world wouldn't fall apart if he left. "I'm gonna go check on her," he said, moving toward the yacht's interior.

"Check on who?"

Calla's voice came from behind them, rocking him to the core.

He whipped around and saw her standing in the gangway. The arc of her smile radiated.

His jaw dropped. "Cal?"

"Haven't I told you two never to have breakfast without me?" she said with a small smile that relieved them both.

Calla slowly approached them, her tears turning into sobs that racked her body.

Nash ran toward her.

Without a word, she threw herself into his arms.

It felt too good to be real; a reunion that was both unexpected and miraculous.

Calla laughed and cried burying her head in Nash's chest.

He lifted her chin and examined her face.

Her eyes were swollen with crying, and her skin was flushed.

He cupped her face in his hands, blinking as if he couldn't believe his eyes. "Calla," Nash said, his arms wrapping around her. He held her close and buried his face in her hair. "I thought I lost you. I thought you were gone," he whispered into her hair.

She smiled weakly. "I'm here now."

"We thought we'd lost you," Jack said, his voice rough with emotion. "We were so worried."

"I'm sorry to have worried you," she breathed. "I think I'm fine now."

Nash held her close, letting out a sigh of relief. "Thank God you're okay."

"I love you," she said, trying to draw a full breath as she met his eyes again. "I love you so much. You saved my life. You didn't give up on me."

"I'm here, Calla," he replied, taking her hand in his and kissing it. "I'm right here."

Nash stood and pulled her into his arms again as she fought to keep her eyes open.

She was exhausted, so he pulled the blanket she had dragged out of bed around her and held her close. "I feel so weak," she admitted, her head resting against his chest. "I'm starving," she said suddenly, pulling away from him. "Is there anything to eat? Nash?" she called weakly.

"Rest, Calla," he said. "It's okay. I'm not going anywhere."

She gave him the faintest smile and closed her eyes. "I knew you wouldn't," she said.

He didn't know how long he held her, but he wouldn't leave her side until she was strong enough to walk on her own again.

Jack laughed and came over to hug her. "Welcome back, kiddo. You had us all pretty worried there for a while. Let's get you fed."

"Yeah, well, I guess I needed the rest," she said with a shrug. "What's been going on?"

Nash's eyes were fixed on her, ensuring every inch of her was okay. "You still in pain?"

"No, none. My head feels a little fuzzy, but I'm fine otherwise." Her words were spoken softly.

"You wanna go back to bed?" Nash asked, exhausted and relieved.

"No," she breathed, then smiled weakly at him. "I think I'd rather have some food."

"Yeah. Food." Nash smiled back and went to get her something, returning with some fruit and seating her down on the deck.

"Thanks, Nash."

Jack turned his eyes away from her to give them a moment of privacy, but he listened intently.

"Last night," she began, still trembling slightly as if she were still terrified. "Did you... kill her?"

"No, I'm not that kind of assassin," Nash replied with a quick shake of his head.

Calla reached her arms around him, clinging to him.

Nash backed away slightly and gazed into her eyes. "You're my soul."

Jack watched quietly, listening and smiling.

"Nash?" Calla said.

"Yeah?"

"My mother..."

"Is someone you should thank," Nash finished her sentence. "She may not have always been there for you in person, but she has always been there protecting you from the moment she conceived you. She's on the yacht, and I'm sure she would love to see you."

CHAPTER
SIXTY-SIX

Kronos Corporation, Berlin
3:26 p.m.

"ATLANTIS of the Sands is so important to you because it means control over the world's energy resources," Rowe said.

Avo nodded. "We need alternative energy sources, and Atlantis of the Sands is the key. If we find and control the city, we control the world's energy."

Rowe leaned back in his chair, considering her words. "You're willing to let humanity destroy itself to hold energy sources over its head. Is that it?"

Avo glanced at him, then looked away. "Humanity will destroy itself anyway. Greed will do that. Kronos is speeding up the process by using sources few know about. And that gas pipe you authorized at GCHQ was the key. That was when I knew we could pull this off. Can't you see? Your time at GCHQ under Compton proved convenient for this minor operation. Atlantis of the Sands solves an unsolvable problem."

"You're talking about genocide, using energy," Rowe said.

Avo turned toward him. "What?"

"Genocide," Rowe said again, his voice level. "You're talking about killing almost every human on the planet, starving them of energy."

Avo stared at him for a long moment, then slowly shook her head. "No, I'm not, Rowe. That's not true at all."

"I don't believe you," Rowe said.

Avo shrugged. "That's up to you, Rowe." She looked away. "I'm sorry if my plans disappoint you."

"It doesn't disappoint me," Rowe said. "It scares me."

"You're the next generation," Avo said. "You're the next industrialist to take over the world. You're part of the mess we're talking about. The part that will destroy the world if things keep going as they are. You knew what you were getting into."

"So you're saying you could stop this from happening if you wanted?" Rowe asked.

Avo nodded, betraying a hint of pleasure.

Her eyes darted away from his. "It holds the potential to control the world's energy supply, yes."

Rowe's face hardened, skepticism written all over it as he crossed his arms tightly. "And you'll use Atlantis to get people to follow the plan?"

Avo shook her head and swallowed hard, her jaw set in determination. "No, I won't have to," she said firmly. "I don't need to convince people to follow the plan at all."

The surprise in Rowe's eyes was quickly replaced by a look of shock, his jaw dropping. "You don't?"

"No," Avo said, shaking her head. "I'm not the one who's going to lead this expedition. With the former Red Fox, I believe you call her the Decrypter out of the way, Octavia Steward can lead this expedition, whether or not she knows it."

**A Week Later
Scorpion Tide
1:27. p.m.**

CALLA LOOKED up as a distinguished silver-haired man with dark skin, clad in a tailored blue suit, strode onto the balcony of her master bedroom. His pale eyes, identical to his suit, took in the Monaco coastline from the balustrade with serene self-assurance. His voice, a familiar and comforting sound, rang out.

"Dr. Bertrand? You're here?"

"Yes, Nash asked me to come. Luckily, I was in Paris and came as quickly as possible," he replied with a warm smile. "Calla, I'm here to tell you something about yourself."

Calla studied the doctor, wondering what information he had come to give her. "What is it?"

"This is the second time someone has tried to stop you from having a child. I want you to be careful. But the good news is that you're exceptional. Your genes are scientifically intriguing."

Calla pursed her lips, admiring Dr. Bertrand's expertise. A distinguished professor in psychiatry, neurosciences, and psychology, he was also a Medical Institute investigator on many scientific committees, including the Committee for the Scientific Investigation of Claims of Unexplainable Science and the affiliated Commission for Scientific Medicine and Mental Health.

Dr. Bertrand opened his briefcase and withdrew a folder. "Within you, you have a gene. A unique and exceptional gene that empowers you to heal yourself, so to speak."

Calla felt her heart skip a beat, and her stomach churned. She had been stabbed in the stomach just a week before, and the wound still ached slightly, but Bertrand was correct. It had healed quicker than anybody had expected. Could this gene be responsible? Could it be the reason a child she could have would be so threatening to some people?

"What do you mean by 'heal'?" she asked.

Dr. Bertrand adjusted his reading glasses. "This gene has a self-healing mechanism. When you undergo any physical trauma, your body can repair itself and regenerate tissue. It has the ability not to age, and you can fight off any disease."

Calla gaped at the doctor. This was impossible. How could she possess such a gene?

Dr. Bertrand nodded. "It is quite rare, and we think you are the first of your kind to have this gene."

"You mean no other operative has had it?"

He shook his head. "Not according to my work with some of their scientists."

Calla felt a wave of emotion as she realized what this could mean for her. She had gone through so much; now, she could protect herself with this gene. She could defend herself against any foe, any illness, and any pain. What did it imply? Would she never be hurt again?

Calla felt an intense sense of gratitude toward Dr. Bertrand. "Thank you," she whispered.

Dr. Bertrand smiled. "You're most welcome, my dear."

He closed his briefcase and stood up. "Now, I think it's time for you to rest. You've been through a lot and need to recover."

Calla nodded and escorted him to the main deck area. "Thank you again," she said as he disembarked from the yacht.

Dr. Bertrand nodded in response and turned to leave.

Calla watched as he walked away, feeling a warmth in her heart that she hadn't experienced in a long time.

She had been on the brink of despair, and now she had a way to protect herself.

As if on cue, the sun emerged from behind the clouds, casting its rays upon the waters of the Mediterranean.

Calla watched as the waves glistened in the sunlight and felt a sense of peace wash over her. She had been through so much, but she was not defeated. She had overcome her fears and was ready for whatever life threw her way. No matter what happened, she knew she would be okay. She was strong; she was brave, and she had to become mentally invincible.

One Week Later
Scorpion Tide Yacht
6:22 a.m.

NASH UNLOCKED the yacht's gym door, flicked on the lights, and hung his keys on a hook.

The punching bag had been hanging for months, and the leather was worn and thin, glinting in the sunlight that shone through the metal rings at the end of the bungee cord that held it.

Kicking off his shoes and pulling his shirt over his head, Nash headed straight for the punching bag. He needed to think.

Half an hour later, Nash was drenched in sweat, with thick beads clinging to his body and dripping onto the tattered canvas mat beneath his feet. He wrapped a hand around one cord on the bag and pulled it until it snapped taut with a pop. Then he drew back his arms, bringing his fists down hard on the punching bag.

The air was heavy with perspiration and the smell of leather and steel.

Nash leaned against the side counter, resting his head in his hands and catching his breath.

As Calla entered the room, Nash could see her face blushing, and she bit her lower lip. She was wearing a workout bikini and had a towel wrapped around her midsection.

Nash tossed her a smile, and although she seemed unsure how to approach him, she felt the need to.

She reached up to wipe the sweat from his face, and he felt a quick flutter in his chest as he leaned down to kiss her.

Calla was his wife and had seen him this way many times, but she had that glint in her eyes.

She turned and looked at the two samurai swords hanging on the wall across the gym. The blades were positioned vertically, facing at an angle like the tips of fangs.

Nash watched her stare. His sword handles were made of dark wood, and their handles were wrapped in leather.

She admired the clarity of each katana as if they had been polished with a fine cloth.

Calla dropped her things on a nearby chair and rubbed the towel over Nash's shoulders and back, slowly, in circles.

Nash stared at Calla, the light streaking across her body, outlining her toned curves, smooth skin, and bright eyes.

The wound on Calla's tummy had healed nicely in the past week, and Nash breathed a sigh of relief.

He looked down at her and saw the tenderness in his eyes reflected in hers. It had been a brutal week. The wound had been cruel, malicious. Had he known, he would have finished Avo right then for doing that to Calla. What kind of woman takes that away from another woman? He still didn't know if it had ruined any chance of Calla ever conceiving again.

Calla drew near, put her hands on his chest, and looked up into his eyes as if she had read his thoughts.

Nash kissed her forehead, and as she drew him close, no words were spoken. He held her in his familiar warm embrace for several long minutes until she broke away.

"I spoke to Dr. Bertrand again yesterday," Calla said.

Nash listened carefully.

She looked up into his eyes. "He and a couple of medical operatives checked my vitals. Nash, I can have children." Her eyes were glistening. "We can still..."

Nash breathed a massive sigh of relief, held her close, and felt her tense up. He pulled back. "Am I hurting you?"

She shook her head. "No."

"What's wrong?" he asked.

"I don't know how to explain it. I need skill and strength to defeat an opponent stronger or more skilled than me."

Nash nodded, understanding. "Sounds like a fight."

"Okay," Nash said, nodding again as he tried hard not to admire her physique. Calla always did that to him. "You're in great shape, Cal."

"Am I?" Calla said. "I need to get better with my hands. I need to win fights with my hands alone. Strength and skill are required for that."

Calla looked at him, biting her lip. A moment passed between them.

Calla looked down and then up at him. She stood close to him and reached out. then slid her hand down his chest and abs.

Nash looked at Calla, his heart beating faster. He could see the curves of her body through the thin material of her bikini, the muscles moving as she backed away from him.

He felt a stirring, trying to look away.

Calla sighed, and he held her gaze as she came closer, leaned in, and massaged his neck. "I don't know if I can do this," she mumbled, her eyes shining with intensity. "I'm not strong enough. I don't feel fast enough."

Nash shook his head. "You're stronger than you think you are, Calla. Believe that you can do this."

She paused, searching his eyes. Then she nodded.

He leaned closer, pulling her scent deep into his nose. Then he held her hand, tracing her lips. "Okay," he said, his eyes lingering on the swell of her hip. "Then I know just what to do."

The thought of her body made him pull back again. He felt himself getting distracted and then moved away from her toward a cabinet on the far wall.

Grinning, he opened the cupboard and pulled out a strip of black cloth as soft as feathers.

He came back toward her and turned her face away from him, out toward the large windows of the gym. "I'm going to cover your eyes with this blindfold and teach you how the samurai pick up their enemies' weaknesses. No one is stronger than you physically. The only reason you freeze when it's dark is that you hand over control. I need to teach you how to take away your sight and depend on your other senses. I once told you that you have the same supersonic speed as any other operative, and it kicks in when you sense danger. Use that inherent adrenaline to fuel your other senses. Don't depend on sight. It's not the best judge of your opponent."

Nash turned Calla away from him and bound the cloth around her eyes.

"Okay?" she said.

"The blindfold focuses your mind. To stop you from thinking of anything else and to make you feel me and be one with me."

Calla was quiet.

He pressed his body against hers as his fingers moved around, binding the blindfold around her head.

CHAPTER
SIXTY-NINE

CALLA TOOK a deep breath and traced the outline of Nash's shoulders and chest through his t-shirt, hearing the sudden change in his breathing.

"Do you trust me?" he asked.

"I trust you," Calla replied.

Nash picked up a wooden sword with a leather grip and a leather sheath from the far end of the room and stood behind her, placing the sword in her hand.

"I'm going to teach you how to sense your opponent," he said. "To predict their moves and actions. Most of all, to have the physical and mental strength to defeat them."

Nash placed her left hand on his shoulder and her right hand on his back.

She was scared, but she trusted him.

He squeezed her hands lightly and stepped to the side, explaining what he wanted her to do as she stepped with him.

Encouraging her gently, Nash turned to show her, placing his hands on her hips and guiding her. "Pivot off my body," he whispered, his breath in her ear.

"I can't see anything," Calla said, sounding like a child.

"There's no judgment here," Nash replied.

She stumbled forward, feeling her arm brush against his chest and tracing his muscles.

Feeling his hand holding her arm, she asked, "What happened?"

Nash smiled. "I told you to trust me."

"This is a lot of trust," she said, still sitting on the floor.

"I know," Nash said. "But it will help you."

She rose, the blindfold still covering her eyes.

"Pivot off my body," Nash said.

"Okay," she said.

"Be quick and accurate, and use your senses to find the weakness."

"I don't have any eyes," Calla joked.

"Well, use your ears then," Nash said.

She could hear his heavy, rhythmic breathing and smell his woody scent. His strong hands grabbed her shoulders, and he spun her around. Taking in the rhythm of his heart beating, Nash's voice was soft and low in her ear.

"And you're getting better," he said. "There's a secret to defeating an opponent stronger than you. It's all in your mind. When you face them, don't think about how strong they are or how many there are. Just focus on your strength and what you're capable of. The enemy will doubt themselves and their abilities when they see that you're not afraid of them. And that's when you'll have the advantage."

There was a thrill in her body. She wanted to turn around but didn't want to break the spell and tried to stay in this moment.

"Is that what you did in the military?" she asked.

"It's one thing I did," Nash said. "But it's not just physical strength that you need. It's also mental strength to control your fear and use it to your advantage."

"How do you do that?" she said.

"Understand your fear," Nash said. "And then you have to use it."

Calla gripped the wooden sword with white-knuckled hands, feeling the humid heat of his body just inches away and the steady rhythm of his breath.

"Focus, Calla," he said, his smooth voice calm and soothing. "Set your mind completely on the task at hand. Learn to use your other senses if you want to be good."

Calla nodded, trying to steady her nerves. She had been looking forward to this moment since Nash had first told her about the deadly art of the samurai sword, determined to master it and prove she was strong enough to face any challenge, no matter how difficult or impossible.

He took hold of her forearm and positioned it in front of her with three fingers beneath the other hand.

She flinched, but he soothed her with a murmured, "Relax." Then, he instructed her to use her mind to access her peripheral vision to follow the circle he traced in the air.

He explained the basic movements of martial arts, including footwork, stances, and strikes, and guided her through them. As he demonstrated how to deliver a strike, he placed his palm softly against the back of her hand, pushing down to show her how to leverage all the power in her arm and shoulder against his abdomen.

A unique combination of fear and strength swelled within her.

Nash held her hand and flexed it to show the correct stance. He showed her how to grip the sword, then walked her through the moves again and again.

Unable to see, he gently corrected her when she stumbled in her movements until she moved with the training sword as if it were an extension of herself.

As she became more aware of her other senses, she

naturally moved from side to side, creating a figure-eight pattern, and she startled herself with how well it worked.

"It's all about control," Nash said. "If you can control your fear, then you can control your opponent."

"It's the same thing in a sword fight," he continued. "Focus on your opponent, not on your fear. If you can do that, you'll be able to defeat them."

"Okay," she said, nodding.

She didn't need to ask him because she trusted him. He would always be there for her, no matter what happened. She knew she could defeat anyone, no matter how strong they were, as long as she had Nash by her side. Everything was going to be okay.

Nash's words echoed in Calla's mind as she pictured her opponent and could see the fear in their eyes. She knew they were trying to control their fear, just as she was, but she was not afraid.

Focused, she wouldn't let her fear to control her. Instead, she would use it to her advantage.

With her sword raised, she charged forward, soon dancing in the dark with Nash and drawing on her inner strength.

She focused her mind and could make out faint shapes in the darkness.

She could hear Nash's footsteps, but couldn't tell where they were coming from.

She sensed the air around her and could alter her movements accordingly.

Nash showed her how to use her other senses to guide and navigate her movements. He instructed her to listen to the sound of her opponent's footsteps and use it to anticipate their next move. He told her to feel within herself for the confidence she knew she had, despite the blindfold that prevented her from knowing where Nash stood.

"That's good," he said. "I can feel your confidence growing."

Soon, Calla was fighting with two swords, moving through the darkness with her eyes closed.

She pumped her arms and legs, feeling the strength of her muscles and the adrenaline in her body. Power surged through her mind, and strength entered her body.

Nash breathed behind her. He was there, in the darkness, with her, and they were one. Calla was now in control of her fear and would not let it control her or ruin the moment.

"You're doing well," Nash said.

"Let's finish this," she said.

Nash set his hands on her shoulder, and the energy in his body moved to hers. His confidence transferred to her, making her feel powerful and focused. Together, they could do anything.

"You ready for the final cut?" he asked, his voice low.

"Ready," she replied.

He slowly stepped forward, demonstrating the movement and angle of the last cut.

His hand moved gracefully as he guided her sword, teaching her how to move away from his reach and use the momentum of the swing to gain an advantage.

The intensity of their fight had made the air between them crackle with energy. She could feel the heat radiating off of him, and for a moment, she forgot why they were there.

Calla wanted to stay in this moment forever with him - learning and exploring.

He took a step back and removed her blindfold, revealing the strength etched in his body with every movement.

Calla felt the power emanating from him; she knew this was where she belonged.

Her hand moved up to his, their fingers entwined as she looked into his eyes.

The desire between them was palpable as they stood face-to-face, only inches apart.

She closed her eyes and moved closer to him.

He shivered from her closeness and anticipation as he placed his hands on her hips.

She tilted her head and pressed her lips against his, and he responded with fervor.

Her fingertips delicately traced his body, taking in the feel of his firm abdominal muscles, the softness of his shirtless body, and the warmth of his kiss. Her heartbeat quickened as he kissed him. She kissed her harder.

She slid her hand up to his chest and felt the heat growing between them, and she knew he felt it, too.

He broke away from her and kissed her neck; this was one training he'd never done.

She was training him, training his senses to something deep between them.

Monte Carlo
7:27 a.m.

SET LIKE A STUNNING PORTRAIT, the magnificent Hôtel de Paris Monte Carlo stood tall on the Casino Square, commanding attention. The ravishing building anchored in the Mediterranean with the Prince's Palace and sapphire blue sea as a backdrop to the breathtaking scenery.

Avo took in the beauty from the balcony of her room, then spun around and backed into the room, pulling out an aluminum suitcase that Rion had delivered that morning.

The musty smell of old paper filled her senses as she stepped closer to the writing desk, studying the familiar handwriting on the yellowed pages. The careful script that filled the cramped margins of countless books throughout her childhood was the same one on the diary pages, and she felt a chill run down her spine as she realized whose signature was at the bottom of each page.

Her father had always been a distant man who showed

little emotion and devoted himself fully to his work and, to this, his grandfather's diary.

Despite his devotion, her father had never given her any reason to think he was anything other than a brilliant German scholar like his grandfather before him.

Had he been hiding something?

There, laid out before her, was proof that her father had faked his death.

The paper with the expensive silk-screened Kronos logo lay on the table next to a picture of her and him sitting on the deck of their old house.

She stared at the papers in her hands, trying to make sense of them.

Avo blinked hard, feeling her knees buckle, but she stayed upright, glued to the spot. The papers blurred, and her head felt light, so she sat on the arm of the chair and breathed deeply.

He had lied to her, her mother, and everyone. The documents lay before her, a swirling sea of information, and she knew she needed to read more.

Avo rested her fists on the desk. Her eyes raced across the lines of text of her father's research as her mind spun with possibility. The more she read, the more her plan solidified, and she knew she had to keep going.

She lifted the documents off the desk, placed them back in the suitcase, and opened the top drawer, removing the folder from it. Then she returned the suitcase to its place in the closet and sat back down at the desk, opening another file.

The folder contained copies of more documents, each with a date and a place, and a schedule of where he had been in all the years since his research began stared back at her.

Avo flipped through the pages.

She searched for any sign of where he might be if he were

still alive. She put her head in her hands and forced herself to breathe deeply. As she scanned through the remaining pages of the file, she saw that there were no other entries and hadn't been in over ten years.

CHAPTER
SEVENTY-ONE

Day 19
Salahah, Sultanate of Oman
6:17 a.m.

RIDING in the back of the jeep, the warm desert air blew through Calla's hair. She tried to concentrate on the book she was reading, but the dry dust of the road made it hard to focus.

The jeep crunched over the soft sand of Oman's Rub'al Khali Desert. Calla, Jack, and Nash saw nothing but a vast expanse of orange and bronze for hours until they approached the place believed to hold ruins of ancient Iram.

In the distance, she saw an enormous sandstone peak looming on the horizon. As they got closer, she made out a ruined city with broken pillars and walls that the desert sands had long since reclaimed.

Calla remembered snippets of a lecture from her days at Cambridge. Claudius Ptolemy was one of the first to mention Atlantis of the Sands, a city known as the City of Pillars. It was an important trading outpost for merchants and travelers, providing supplies and shelter. Islamic poetry described its beauty and its eventual decline and fall. Today, it remained a mysterious reminder of its past glory.

Calla sat in the jeep, hypnotized by the vastness of the ruins. She asked the driver to halt, and they drove no further.

The ISTF jeeps stopped at the edge of a city where the river met buildings slowly being consumed by foliage.

Jack, Calla, and Nash climbed a steep path, weaving their way around crumbling walls and tumbled rocks.

In the distance, they saw a solitary statue standing atop a tall hill, its details lost in time. They could feel the warmth of the sun on their faces and hear the steady trickle of the ancient river running through abandoned streets.

They kept walking alongside it, never taking their eyes off the lone statue that stood overlooking the river's length.

Calla edged closer to the aged figure and realized it was a sculpture of a man with three lions' heads perched atop his shoulders. After hundreds of years, the elements had taken their toll on the colossal stone—patches of lichen clung to the crumbling walls while cascading stone sheets littered the ground.

The statue watched over its domain from high atop a jagged slab of rock, three fierce lions' heads surveying the scene beneath them from centuries past.

Calla recalled something. "The blank pages are connected to the poem that Salib's wife told us about. I knew I had heard the poem before," she said.

She bent down and squinted, tracing her finger along the symbols etched into the weathered stone. The faintest whisper of a breeze danced around her as she read the forgotten words aloud. She felt a chill run through her body, and the syllables hung in the air of the ancient poem. The statue was telling her something.

She had to read its lips. How?

Calla spun around to face the group. She noticed Jack had a magnifying glass on his compass, and she took it from him, positioning it over the statue's lips. On them, etched in minuscule symbols, was ancient Arabic.

She glanced at Nash. "Nash, you speak Arabic. How is your ancient Arabic?" Nash shrugged but approached.

Calla peered through the magnifying glass and read out each symbol one by one as Nash translated.

His voice was steady and sure as he deciphered each one. "No one can enter the city without the Sword of Ali. The Sword of Ali is the protector of the city. The sword gives courage, and it gives protection."

Jack hurried back to the car and fetched the Sword of Ali from the jeep, bringing it to Calla.

She stared at it for a few moments, trying to figure out what to do next. Then, she faced the statue and noticed it had all its components except for a weapon.

She carefully removed the sword from its sheath and placed it in the statue's grasp.

As the statue shifted on its base, a low rumble shook the air, and a path opened up behind it.

Calla locked eyes with the men, and they took the hidden path through the ruins of the ancient city, dodging scattered bits of rubble as they ran.

White stone walls crumbled, and broken arches spanned over the pathways. Gigantic towers, once used to defend the city, were now buried by sand cascading off their peaks like a waterfall.

The wind whistled through cracks in the walls, creating a melody that was almost like a chorus of ghosts singing a soft song. With every step closer to a lonely tower, Calla felt a sense of familiarity in her chest.

She had been here before.

The thought of whatever unwelcome fate awaited them in this long-forgotten ruin made her heart sink, and her gut told her that no good would come of it.

"What was that?" Jack said.

CHAPTER
SEVENTY-TWO

Rub'al Khali Desert

AVO'S TEAM buzzed with soft murmurs at their camp as the temperature dropped. She'd spent the trip from Monaco poring over her father's secrets.

Hackers, archaeologists, and workers were assembled and prepared to venture into Iram, the lost city.

Avo surveyed her team and wondered if this was how her father felt when he arrived. She was determined despite the relentless heat and urged her team forward.

Rion confirmed his earlier findings to Avo, stepping up to her. "We've pinpointed their location near the statue in Iram. She's still alive. Not sure how she survived after your last encounter with her."

Octavia approached Avo with a face full of dread. "We must not go in there. The city is filled with a mysterious and dangerous force. No one has ever returned alive after venturing in."

Avo pushed Octavia aside. "We're leaving now, and this one's leading the way," she said, pointing to Octavia.

. . .

Twenty-five minutes later, they reached the statue. Avo observed the Sword of Ali already in its grip. "Move!" she ordered, with her gun trained on Octavia.

Pushing through the ruins of the ancient city behind Octavia, Avo felt the pressure of leading the inexperienced team.

She weaved between sharp edges that jutted out from the ravaged landscape, with the desert reclaiming parts of the once-mighty metropolis.

Avo led the way with agility and poise, seemingly oblivious to the treacherous footing.

Her agents struggled to keep up as she forged a relentless path forward.

Avo's footfalls sank into the powdery earth, and the deep grooves between the stones seemed to whisper warnings with every step.

Her team kept their eyes on her in the unfamiliar place.

They ventured deeper into Iram's core, feeling their way through hidden crevices and barely visible pathways. The dread in the air thickened, and Avo felt her team's anxiety rising.

A sharp noise pierced the silence, jolting Avo to a stop.

She raised her hand, signaling for everyone to be still and silent while they searched for the noise's source.

"Get a load of this," Avo said as she and the team slowly cleared a large chamber covered in a thick layer of dust and debris.

Before them, a wall painting appeared. It was a vibrant red-orange that had faded over time, but the image was still clear.

The painting depicted four people sitting on a stone bench. One person was clearly a king, wearing a crown and holding a scepter. He sat at the back of the bench, flanked by four other people.

"It's a family portrait," Avo marveled. "Look at how regal the king looks."

The person on the left was a woman wearing a beautiful purple robe embroidered with silver patterns. She held a small box made of gold in her hand, but it was hard to see what was inside. The person on the right was a man dressed in sandals and a simple white robe. His right wrist was wrapped in a cloth bandage, hiding a tattoo. His sad expression made it almost painful to look at him.

Avo couldn't take her eyes off the painting, which was so lifelike that she felt she could step right into it and join the family.

"Hey," Avo said. "Who are these people?"

Standing nearby, Octavia pointed to the man on the right. "That's Mai, and the woman on the left is Fez. They were the first king and queen of El-Kara."

"Did they have any children?" Avo asked.

Octavia nodded. "Yes, three. A girl named Sailah was the oldest, followed by another girl named Odiya, and a boy named Masam, who was the youngest."

Avo continued to stare at the painting, feeling like she was looking at an old photo of long-lost relatives. "If that is here, then there is more treasure in this city. Keep moving."

CHAPTER
SEVENTY-THREE

CALLA, Jack, and Nash crouched low behind a jagged rock formation, their eyes keenly focused. All three held their collective breath as they prepared themselves.

With a sudden nod from Jack, Calla, and Nash sprang to their feet and scuttled across the dry ground. Ducking behind a tall stone pillar, they listened for any telltale signs of detection.

After a few moments of silence, Nash peered around the corner and motioned for them to proceed.

Walking as fast as they could, they made it to the side of the temple with a crack running through it and hid in the shadows to catch their breath.

Their footsteps echoed off the walls, and they noticed two figures emerging from the shadows, brandishing weapons.

Octavia turned to run, but Avo tackled her to the ground.

Desperate to escape, Octavia wriggled free and delivered a sharp elbow to Avo's jaw, sending her tumbling over a nearby rock.

Avo was knocked unconscious by the impact.

Calla, Jack, and Nash rushed over to help Octavia.

Without hesitation, Nash delivered a powerful kick to an assailant making a run for Octavia.

Octavia quickly got up and brushed the dirt from her clothes. "Thank you," she said, her voice trembling.

Calla held her breath as Octavia's eyes burned with unanswered questions.

Octavia studied Calla's face, searching for remnants of their past friendship. It had been a decade since their last encounter, but the familiar feeling of their bond was still there.

"Are you alright?" asked Calla softly.

Octavia nodded, unable to find the words to express what she was feeling. "So you found Iram?"

"We were lucky," Calla said, not wanting to reveal the details of the map, the book, and the sword.

"You're good at what you do," Octavia said.

Octavia shook her head and studied Calla. "You're lucky to have friends like this."

Calla smiled.

"You can't celebrate yet," Octavia said. "We have to stop Avo from getting to the walled gate. If she reads the inscription on the wall, the secrets of the Lost City of the Sands of Arabia will be hers."

"We need to move! Avo won't stay down for long. And I can hear the team moving," Nash urged.

"She'll never make it through the gate," Calla said as they ran deeper into the ruins.

"It's impossible," Octavia said, panting.

Jack kept up his pace next to Calla's. "Really?"

"Calla has to open the gate. Only she can read the puzzle written just for her," Octavia explained.

They stopped running when they reached an embankment.

The embankment was a looming gray expanse, towering high and encircled by seven towering gateways.

Calla approached the walls, her feet dragging through the shifting sands. She ran her hands over the inscriptions carved along its surface, heavy with dread at the thought of what had happened the last time she had done this. Just as she was about to decipher the symbols, a desperate scream pierced the air.

She spun around to see Jack and Nash being swallowed by a swirling pit of sinking sand.

Octavia stood stunned, her body shaking as she watched the men being dragged into the blackness.

"Hang on!" Calla shouted, flinging herself onto the ground to help the sinking men.

Octavia, who had been standing back, moved forward and yanked Calla's arm back.

Without another thought, Calla removed her shirt and threw one end toward the men in a last-ditch effort to reach them. She held tight. Nash grabbed for it but couldn't reach it.

Just as she had resigned herself to failure, she saw Jack moving in the sand, struggling to keep his head above the surface.

Calla stretched out her arm as far as she could, but she knew in her heart that there wasn't enough time for her to make it across before both men would be gone forever.

With a deep breath and a silent prayer, she watched as Nash reached for her shirt one last time... but missed it by mere inches.

Jack had disappeared beneath the sand.

Calla remained outstretched on the edge of the sand pool, her heart thumping in her chest, eyes wide as she watched Nash's head slowly get sucked under.

Calla gasped in horror as Jack, and Nash disappeared into the depths of the sand.

She stood paralyzed, not knowing what to do as a million thoughts raced through her mind.

Tears ran down her face, a mixture of sorrow, guilt, and confusion.

Octavia's face was ghostly pale, and her eyes were glazed with tears. She let out a loud, shuddering breath before saying, "I'm sorry, Calla. It's all my fault. This wouldn't have happened if I hadn't convinced you to come here all those years ago."

Calla felt like the air had been knocked out of her lungs, and she couldn't stop the tears that came flooding out.

The sound of buzzing drones startled Calla, and she turned around to find herself surrounded by Avo's men, who had caught up.

Ten of them stood with assault rifles pointed at her, and one of them lunged toward her and threw her to the ground near a beam of light emanating from a hovering drone.

The blow to her head sent a flurry of stars across Calla's vision, but it paled compared to the desperate anger and shock burning inside her.

Soon after, everything went black.

CHAPTER
SEVENTY-FOUR

CALLA OPENED HER EYES, and darkness seemed to press down on her.

She tugged at the rope that bound her to a chair, and her heart sank to her stomach as she realized what had happened.

Calla strained her eyes and made out the shadowy shapes of pipes and valves that lined the walls, illuminated by a faint sliver of light seeping in through a high window.

The room was filled with the smell of engine oil.

This had to be the engine room for Kronos's gas collection project in the desert.

As she regained consciousness, Calla focused on the clanking of metal pipes, a rhythmic staccato that echoed in the dark expanse.

Realizing Avo's plan, Calla noticed a faded blueprint on the wall, showing something that looked like Nazi architecture.

She felt a sudden rush of air and heard a sharp whistle as multiple assailants headed toward her.

Her wrists were roughly untied, and she received a powerful boot to her stomach, sending the chair and her to the ground.

Two sets of hands lifted Calla from the chair and shoved her into a long metallic tube with sharp edges.

She was now in Avo's hands.

The engine roared, and sparks of electricity shot through the tube.

Calla had no time to think or react as the whirring of the machine grew louder and louder.

The electrical surge trapped her in the metallic tube. It was a gas pipe, a giant one, and they were going to dispose of her in the desert.

They were going to take advantage of the power of electricity and the tube's strength to shoot Calla out into the desert. If she survived, she would never find her way back.

Suddenly, she found herself in an expansive space, blinking away the darkness with hurting eyes. The tube's walls were constricting, and the vibrating walls muffled her screams. The electrical surge grew even stronger, and she felt herself lift off the ground and charge forward at lightning speed.

As she spun around and around, she could feel the electricity pulsing through her veins.

The spinning stopped. With a jolt, she felt herself launched out of the tube and onto the sand.

She was in the middle of the desert, far away from the gas collecting center. Where exactly? She didn't know.

Desert heat surrounded her, and she fought the urge to collapse from exhaustion as sweat trickled down her face.

Heat scalded her skin, and her mouth was so dry she could hardly swallow.

She turned to look at the end of the tube that had spat her out. The engine's roar was still there, but a rolling sandstorm that tinted the sky a deep orange muffled it.

Grains of sand clung to her skin as she squinted. Without

warning, the tube shot back, creating a vibration that threw Calla to the ground before it disappeared underground completely.

The engine's thunder faded until all that was left was the buzz of cicadas.

Her knees buckled, and she collapsed onto the sand, too tired to find the strength to stand.

The heat from the pipe had baked her clothes to her skin, and salt from her tears dried on her cheeks as she lay there, wondering if Jack and Nash had survived the quicksand that had swallowed them alive.

A blanket of darkness from the sandstorm had descended, making it nearly impossible to see beyond a few feet in either direction. She could only make out swirling sand dunes stretching endlessly.

CHAPTER
SEVENTY-FIVE

Kronos Gas Facility
Rub'al Khali Desert

A FAINT RUSTLING noise brought Calla out of her stupor.

She surveyed her surroundings, the vast Rub'al Khali desert, where the sun had already set, and the sky was turning a darker shade of red by the minute.

The desert ground beneath her feet was rough, made of sharp stones and dust, and she stumbled as she scrambled up the sloping dunes.

A chill wind blew around her, sending grains of sand flying in all directions.

She hugged herself tightly and continued, straining to hear the sounds of life.

Calla sat, her eyes focused on nothingness. She had to do something.

As she hugged her knees, a glimmer of hope came over her; she caught sight of a birthmark on her ankle, resembling an intricate tattoo that seemed almost as cryptic as the inscription she had tried to read in the lost city.

She realized the wall of Iram was written for her to read. Her birthmark had something to do with it. The key to overcoming Avo and saving her friends was not in the legendary Sword of Ali or other riddles, but in the birthmark tattoo on her ankle.

The endless expanse of dunes seemed to go on forever. She had been walking for hours, and her throat was painfully dry. Her heart leaped when she finally spotted a figure riding a tall horse in the distance.

He was still far off but heading in her direction.

Calla waved toward the approaching horseman, and he responded with a raised hand. As he slowed his horse, she realized the group following him comprised six Bedouin women dressed in traditional clothes and faces decorated with intricate patterns of kohl.

A helicopter descended from the sky as if following, sending a flurry of dust. When the chopper landed, Calla concentrated.

Calla knew that face and covered the dust from her eyes as she squinted to get a better glimpse.

The door opened.

She knew the man who stood before her.

He approached her as he spoke, "I have been reading the history of the Arabian desert and how it endured wars and several excavations, including one conducted by the Nazis. They kept good files, and thanks to them and this tribe, I found you, Calla," the man shouted above the roaring blades.

Raimund Eichel rubbed dust from his face as he finally reached her.

CHAPTER
SEVENTY-SIX

EICHEL DISEMBARKED FROM THE HELICOPTER, followed by several agents, and then Calla saw her father, Stan, jump off the chopper. Her eyes were still burning from the sand, and a female warrior, Bedouin, handed her a water bag to wash her face.

"Father? Where? How? We thought someone had…"

"No. I staged it. To disappear, so I could go within Kronos's organization, posing as a banker. Once a spy, always a spy. During the war, MI6 had many moles surveying German transmissions, and Raimund's intelligence offices had even more to tell us. When I realized what Avo was up to, very similar to what her father Ivan had been up to, I knew I had to go to the source without telling you. To keep you safe. The source lies in the inception of the Kronos organization, Project Mercury. Are you hurt?" Stan asked, taking in Calla's disheveled appearance.

Her face was pale and sweaty, and her clothes were torn and stained. "No, I'm fine," she whispered, her voice trembling. "I lost Jack and Nash at the ancient city gates.

Father, it was horrible. It happened again. I should never have brought them here."

Eichel moved into view and took her arm, his gaze shifting nervously. "Calla, we must get out of here. There's a storm coming. One of the energy pipes ruptured—Kronos has several pipes under this desert, just waiting for you to discover the source of the unknown energy's origin. They were trying to kill you with it." He looked up at the sky and then back at her. "Can you walk?"

She remained expressionless, her eyes wide and unblinking.

Stan filled his lungs with a deep breath. "Let's get some more water and help for her," he motioned to two ISTF aides off the chopper.

The agents approached and wrapped her tight in a blanket. They carefully led her toward the awaiting helicopter, her plaited dark hair spilling down her back like a curtain of ebony.

Eichel glanced at Calla as Stan held her close as Stan locked eyes with her. His expression was solemn. "Calla, the missing files from Cambridge University. I think I know what happened. Kronos needed them, stole them, and used Jack's research to build the energy pipelines to power the desert's energy. They plan to drain all the energy from the lost city and cut off the world's supply."

"I know," Calla said. "I've seen the UK's reserves. They are depleting fast."

Stan stared at the files on his phone for a long time. Finally, he reached for her hand. "I'm sorry about Jack and Nash. They are like sons to me."

Calla held back a lump. "I saw them go under the sand, just like Ivan did all those years ago when I was at Cambridge. And he hasn't been seen since. It's been ten years."

Stan took her hand, reassuring himself she was alive.

"They used Jack's research to build the energy pipes for the desert. That's how I could find you, Calla. We connected to the systems of the energy pipe. When we found it, your phone was still on you."

"Any connection to Jack or Nash?" Calla asked.

"None," Eichel replied as they headed to the chopper.

**ISTF Desert Camp Base
An Hour Later**

EICHEL HELPED Calla to a tent at an ISTF base camp in the desert and urged her to rest. As they waited for reinforcements and other agents to arrive, Eichel went outside to fill a bottle from a makeshift well. He returned to find Calla looking at a laptop.

"What is it, Calla?" he asked.

"I don't know," she said, touching the screen gently. "I've seen nothing like it before."

"Can I see?" he said.

She handed the laptop to him.

Eichel studied the files on the screen carefully.

"This is the Lost City of Atlantis of the Sands, an ancient metropolis rumored to have been destroyed by a catastrophic meteor strike thousands of years ago," she said.

"The Nazis were after it too. They believed that harnessing its power would give them an enormous advantage in the war," Eichel said. "There's a mystery about its origins. It was a futuristic place made entirely of slate and sand. That file you're looking at is the only surviving file in the German archives about the city."

"My connections in German Intelligence and other classified files," Eichel replied when Calla asked how he got the file. "Most of the Nazis who went in search of Atlantis of the Sands never returned. Strange, powerful forces guarded it that no one could seem to penetrate. But one man made it back. That man was Dietrich Kronos, an engineer and inventor who later founded the German technology group Kronos GmbH. He was the brains behind the Nazi expedition in 1942, and spent years trying to unlock the secrets of this ancient city."

As Eichel spoke, Calla's fascination grew. "If anyone had the skills and knowledge needed to crack open the mysteries of Atlantis of the Sands, it would be him. His grandfather had been part of a mysterious group, the Blackhorse Group. Do you know them?"

Calla nodded, looking at Stan. "They were formed in 1903 after its members discovered the secrets of the operatives and allied with them to protect the operatives' secrets. This group comprises historians and explorers, setting up expeditions to retrieve historical artifacts and exploration from history around the world. The group is also super-secret and heavily funded by its members with their own personal interests. But along the way, Dietrich broke from the group and the mandate. He had his own plans."

Eichel took a seat "I didn't know."

"My great-grandfather told me stories about the Blackhorse Group discoveries," Stan said. "He was convinced that the answer to finding Atlantis of the Sands lay within the hieroglyphics that covered the city walls. According to legend, only one person, a special operative, could read them."

Eichel stared at Calla for a moment, realization dawning on

his face. "That's why they took you as part of the Cambridge expedition," he said softly. "They must have known about your connection to the Blackhorse Group."

"I'm not sure," Calla said. "Nash told me I had to find the answers for myself. And now I think he was right. I want to find them in whatever way I can."

Eichel's jaw tightened, his eyes shining with determination. "Then we will find them together," he said firmly. "The power of this city could change everything. We must protect it, no matter the cost."

Eichel's eyes were focused on the laptop screen, and his fingers raced across the keys, searching for clues.

Calla leaned closer, as they sifted through the information.

Eichel suddenly looked up. "Calla, do you have a tattoo of a key on her ankle?"

Calla's stomach churned at the thought of revealing her secret. She had a birthmark that resembled a small key at the base of her ankle and had kept it hidden from most people since childhood. Rumors had circulated that she was strange because of it, but she never understood why.

"Calla?" Eichel called out.

She looked down at her ankle, where the birthmark was, and sighed. "Yes, I have the birthmark. It's not a tattoo."

"The Nazi files also state that Kronos barely escaped with his life. When Dietrich returned, he was a changed man. He would not speak of what happened and refused to reveal the location of the city. The only thing he would say was that it was guarded by strange, powerful forces that no one could seem to penetrate."

Eichel's brow furrowed in thought. "Do you think your grandfather's group knew about these 'strange, powerful forces'?"

"I'm not sure," Stan replied. "But I think they might have had some idea. After all, they could keep the secrets."

Eichel processed the information, and his voice trembled with excitement as he spoke. "We must take extreme caution. If Kronos told the truth, we might face something far more insidious than we initially thought."

Stan confirmed, "It's true. Calla, the Bedouin warriors here, are a group of powerful female guardians who have sworn to protect the secrets of Atlantis of the Sands at any cost. They know every corner of the ancient city and could help us navigate through it in moments."

Eichel pointed to the laptop screen, and Calla leaned in closer, her eyes scanning the blueprint spread across the screen.

It was a map of the desert, and more than that, it was the blueprint for an energy pipe, a relic of Nazi Germany's past attempt at tapping into the desert's energy supply.

Calla felt a thrill of success, followed by a wave of fear. What if the Nazis had succeeded in their mission? What would it mean for humanity? She shook the thought away and focused on the task at hand.

Eichel pointed to a small box on the blueprint, and Calla squinted to read the text that was too small for her to see from across the table.

"What is it?" she asked.

"It says here that they found the energy in the desert," Eichel replied.

"So they could extract it?" Calla asked, her voice rising with excitement.

Eichel shook his head. "No, they found a spillage," he said, pointing to another box on the blueprint. "It says here in German that they could test the gas and oil, but its source was never located. They could never get it to work."

"So what happened?" Calla asked, her stomach tightening with dread.

"The Nazis had scientists working on it," Eichel said, "but they stopped."

"Why?" Calla asked.

"It doesn't say," Eichel replied, scanning the document. "I don't know why they stopped, but judging from the rest of these documents, they were trying to harness the energy for themselves. This blueprint is dated October 1944. There are tons of documents from the war in the intelligence archives in Berlin, but none of them mention the desert's energy."

"So the Nazis were trying to harvest the energy?" Calla asked.

"Yes," Stan interjected. "They were trying to harness the energy *and* hold the world hostage."

"Harness it for what?" Calla asked.

"I don't know," Stan said, shaking his head. "But this is it. This is what we've been looking for."

Calla's breath caught in her throat. "Now the energy depletion in the UK and the US energy reserves makes sense. What if Kronos thought they could drain the Earth's resources and become the only energy supplier for the world? That was one way to ensure their survival and a monopoly on global energy resources," Calla said, her mind racing.

As Calla stood in front of the computer, the head of the satellite department at ISTF entered the tent. "What do you need exactly?" he asked.

"I need to know if there's any underground activity in southern Arabia," Calla replied. "Can you see anything more on your satellites than what NASA shared some twenty years ago?"

The man looked perplexed. "Underground activity?" he asked, raising his eyebrows.

Stan intervened. "Yes. We need satellite imagery."

The man sighed and leaned forward. "We don't have satellite images of southern Arabia," he said. "ISTF has contracts with news agencies in the area and other officials who have satellites. Someone must have something. If not, we need to patch into NASA."

Calla squinted at the man. "We all have these satellites, and we don't have a single one monitoring the southern tip of Arabia?"

He shook his head. "We do," he said. "We just don't have a satellite close enough to get good images of it. And even if we did, the frequencies for the radar would interfere with the other satellites we have. With so many satellites orbiting the Earth and their frequencies overlapping, it's difficult for us to get good images."

"But a desert town would radiate different frequencies, wouldn't it?" Calla said. "Radar frequencies that wouldn't interfere with the other satellites."

The man nodded. "I'm sure you're right," he said.

He sighed and turned away from her. "I'll get the images you need from ISTF," he said. "They'll take care of getting them into your system."

Calla nodded but didn't have time to think about it any further.

Eichel rose and moved to where Calla was. "Everyone is ready. We have our men, and more ISTF are about an hour away."

"Thanks," Calla said.

"I have Allegra on a secure line. She asked if she could speak to you," Eichel said as he handed the phone to Calla.

Calla's voice was hushed, almost a whisper, as she settled herself in a secluded corner of the room. She held the phone close to her ear, and Allegra explained. "It was fourteen days after you returned from the university trip. That's when Taiven and I flew to the newly discovered city of Iram. We had been tipped off by the satellite feed NASA had picked up. We had to move quickly; we were the only ones who could do it,"

Allegra said urgently. "Several operatives helped us, but we knew it was dangerous. We didn't know what to expect."

Calla's shock turned to disbelief as she realized Allegra had known about her before they had officially met. "You knew me before we met in London?" she asked.

"Yes, Calla," Allegra replied. She paused, and her voice grew serious. "It was our duty to do this."

Calla's curiosity was stirred. "You're saying that you two went back to the ancient city?"

"Yes," Allegra said solemnly. "We had to. We couldn't trust anyone else with this. We didn't know what we would find, but at least it was a chance to find out what happened to Ivan." She swallowed hard before continuing. "So, we crossed the barren desert and walked past the broken fragments of houses and crumbled buildings until we reached the ancient city destroyed years ago by a meteorite impact. We searched every crevice, but all we found were broken pieces of rock from the meteorite and empty streets with no signs of life. Our only theory was that Ivan was caught between worlds, stuck somewhere in limbo because of the meteorite. Energy attempting to replicate something using its energy. Perhaps making a copy of the place of the universe, it came from. We studied the rock, which is not found on Earth."

Calla listened. She didn't know what to believe anymore. "You saw nothing?" she asked, holding her breath.

"No, we didn't. Perhaps the energy was just too much for him." Allegra replied, breathing deeply. "Calla, we won't know for sure until we go back. What we need are more answers."

"That's why you've been trying to get back there," Calla said. "How are we supposed to return to a place that doesn't exist in our world?"

"I don't know. But I know we have to try," Allegra said, her voice tight with worry. "We must send a team of scientists to help you open the gates of Iram. And if they can't do it, physical force may be necessary."

Her words sent a chill down Calla's spine. She knew she was asking for a lot, but Calla had to do it – for Jack and Nash.

Calla leaned forward, her voice heavy with fear. "If I open the gate, I'll be opening the floodgates of the source… straight into Kronos' energy pipes."

"I know, and we need you to close the gate before Kronos gets close. Avo's agents are in place waiting for those gates to open, and they have an army behind them." She paused, waiting for Calla to answer her next question. "Are you ready to try?"

At that moment, the tent flap lifted, and a woman with shining bronze armor entered. Her face was shrouded, and her voice was low and urgent. "We must go now," she said, her gaze flickering between them. "My sisters and I are on the move, and we must get you out of here before they find us."

Calla's attention lingered on the intricate henna tattoos that ran in an endless pattern down the warrior's arm. Clouds, birds, and vines intermingled with crescent moons and the unmistakable symbol of Calla's own birthmark. She realized with a start that the symbols were written in the same ancient language that had been used in the peculiar book found in the archives of GCHQ, the book with seven blank pages.

A thrill of discovery rose within her as she remembered the symbols and understood their meaning. This hidden tribe of seven female warriors had to be connected to the mysterious forces guarding the Atlantis of the Sands.

"We have to go now," the warrior said again, breaking Calla out of her reverie.

Calla nodded firmly, and everyone followed the warrior out. Calla trailed behind the measured strides of the six women as they walked in single file through the cool night.

The moonlight bathed the desert in a soft silver glow, and Calla knew that time was not on their side.

The Bedouin warriors all wore masks, but Calla could feel their determination and was one of them.

Each of the women had been selected for a special purpose, and Calla was eager to do her part.

She had to reach the heart of the hidden city before it was too late.

Calla acknowledged what she had suspected. She was one of the warriors.

Each of the book's seven blank pages was connected to one of the six female warriors.

Calla was the seventh.

CHAPTER
SEVENTY-EIGHT

Iram
Edge Site of he Ancient City
5:01 a.m.

A GENTLE WIND swept across the desert, brushing against the agents' faces as they moved rapidly through the sand toward the outpost.

Calla led the way, her heels sinking into the shifting dunes, her finger hovering over the trigger of her weapon as she scanned the horizon.

The team emerged into the bright sun, outfitted in their state-of-the-art uniforms. The lightweight fabric was designed to keep them cool and comfortable, and each agent had shoes with extra cushioning and air-sole technology to minimize shock while running.

Helmets with air vents to regulate body temperature fit snugly on their heads, and cushioned pads provided extra protection. Prepared for combat, the team marched forward.

Calla looked over her shoulder, straining to see the agents' faces against the backdrop, memorizing their positions before focusing on the magnificent structure in the distance.

Squinting, Calla could make out a faint outline of a tall wall surrounding the energy facility structure, with guard posts and armed soldiers stationed at the entrances.

The ISTF team had arrived in the ancient city of Iram and was met by several other undercover agents who blended into the crowds of local diggers and tents surrounding the area. All of them were dressed in traditional garb but were armed with handguns concealed beneath their clothing, ready to use at a moment's notice.

Using satellite technology and ancient maps as a guide, Calla was confident they had finally found Iram's gates.

Calla motioned for her team to move forward with an upraised palm and curled fingers, and they spread out around the ruins and approached the outpost.

As they drew nearer, Calla saw three large tents in the center of a bustling camp, with armed guards in uniform patrolling the perimeter, guns slung across their shoulders.

A convoy of vehicles approached from the opposite direction and came to a halt, with more people disembarking.

Calla recognized the Kronos emblem on their uniforms. All of them wore dark glasses and camel-coloured suits and hats.

They were Avo's agents.

"Looks like they're getting ready to start the dig," Stan said. "Calla, look around and check if you see anything out of the ordinary."

"Okay." Calla moved away from them, blending in with the commotion of the dig site.

She wore her keffiyeh and hid her face behind a scarf, but still had a sharp eye for detail.

She saw guards walking around the site's perimeter, surveying the equipment. Calla then noticed a group of workers gathered around an area secured with thick yellow ropes.

She crouched down, peered through the ropes, and saw heavy pipes with gas lines running through them. The pipes seemed to be cut or tampered with at regular intervals, and Calla sensed that something was off.

She felt a chill run through her as the crunch of boots on gravel grew closer.

Peeking out from her hiding place behind the rocks, she saw the Kronos agent's prosthetic arm glinting in the rising sun. He stood there with a gun in his other hand.

She drew her gun. She leaped from behind the rocks in one swift move, tackling him to the ground.

She pummeled his back with every ounce of strength she had, sending them both tumbling to the ground.

His curses filled the air as they rolled together in a tangle of limbs and dirt.

She scrambled on top of him, grappling with him to control his gun.

Their bodies burned in the hot sunlight, and sand stuck to their sweaty skin.

Suddenly, Calla felt a chill run down her spine as he reached into his jacket. He drew a small gas canister, and Calla instinctively held her breath. She lunged forward, gripping him by the throat until he went unconscious and dropped the canister.

She knocked it away from them, her heart pounding.

Calla took advantage of the opportunity and bolted at full speed down the rocky path toward the ancient ruins. She got close enough to make out the peculiar sight of the group of Bedouin women with sharp, modern-looking weapons standing guard at the ruins' entrance.

They were clearly a highly skilled and deadly force and had agreed to meet here.

Calla felt her breath catch as their intense gazes turned toward her. Yet they didn't move to stop her as she passed them by, stepped over the threshold, and entered the heart of the ruins.

Iram's resting place seemed darker and more decrepit than she remembered from her last visit.

Calla felt an uneasy sense of foreboding as she walked deeper into the heart of Iram behind the women, following the winding paths through jagged stone arches and crumbling statues that loomed over her like silent guardians of the past.

Finally, she came to a narrow tunnel that led underground. She descended into the dark tunnel and felt a rush of adrenaline coursing through her veins.

Determined to find anything, even Jack and Nash, dead or alive, nothing would stand in her way.

As she approached the heart of Iram, Calla heard the hum of high-tech machinery coming from deep within the ruins.

Kronos agents streamed into the area, their faces illuminated by the harsh glare of flashlights. The air was heavy with sweat and anticipation as they surveyed and mapped the ancient site.

She whirled around in shock to see the prosthetic man standing behind her, his weapon raised and pointed directly at her head.

He glared down at her with icy contempt. "You're not going anywhere, Calla Cress," he said sternly, trying to push her backward.

A deafening explosion echoed deep in the tunnels, shaking the site violently as bright flames erupted from an opening nearby, engulfing everything in their path.

Panic-stricken workers scrambled for safety as smoke filled the surrounding air.

Calla seized the opportunity and decided to run.

"Over here!" a female voice shouted from ahead.

CHAPTER
SEVENTY-NINE

CALLA FOLLOWED the voice of the Bedouin woman through the tunnel. The tunnel ended, and she blinked, taking a moment to adjust to the sudden brightness.

In front of her was a gate covered in ancient writing, and the air had a musty smell like a tomb that hadn't been sealed properly.

The scent didn't bother her, but she was too focused on her task to pay much attention.

The gate was made of black metal with jagged, serrated edges that glinted in any available light. Its surface appeared to shift like a shadow underwater.

Calla stood before the ancient wall in awe of how much time had worn down its surface.

Symbols of unknown origin and meaning were carved into the weathered stone. She couldn't decipher the language, which was not English, Arabic, or any other modern language she knew. It was a code, a set of ancient rules that seemed to stretch beyond the heavens and her sight.

She wanted to unlock the mysteries of the code, but fear prevented her from exploring further.

Calla needed to open a gateway on the wall using letters and symbols she had seen before but never understood. The wall was too high to read, but she started identifying a few individual characters.

Some symbols looked like scratches from a sharp metal tip. Others were as tall as a man, and Calla's heart raced when she finally recognized one of them as an 'L'.

She stood, the memories of the events that had taken place there a decade earlier still fresh in her mind.

Calla approached the ancient wall made from large slabs of slate decorated with symbols, stretching across time and space.

A chill ran down her spine as she felt the immense power radiating from this place. What mysteries lay beyond the wall.

Calla looked at the women, her heart pounding.

They had bright olive skin and midnight hair, and each had a tattoo of a symbol on their arm. She raised her pant leg to reveal an identical birthmark on her ankle, the same intricate pattern of seven circles she had seen in the Book of Iram.

The women nodded in recognition, and one of them spoke. "You have a unique power within you that has been passed down through the ages. When you first arrived ten years ago, you called us and are now here again. You're the only one who can access the wall's mysteries."

In the center of the circle, with the six women, Calla raised her hand. "What if I open it and can't come back?"

The woman who had spoken before looked at her. "You have to try. Your friends could still have a chance."

One woman turned her arm over and let it rest on her forearm. "You can only open it with this," she said, pointing to the symbol design on her wrist that wrapped around her entire arm. "See the birthmark on your ankle? All of us have a mark like that, and they match the pattern of those Iram pages we kept from becoming lost. These symbols belong to no culture, no one dynasty, but that of mankind and what lies ahead."

She moved closer to Calla and put a comforting hand on her shoulder. "You're here because it is time to return to Iram in order to restore it to its rightful place in the world."

Calla blinked, and a wave of recognition swept over her. "You're the one who saved me ten years ago," she exclaimed.

The woman pointed to the wall of symbols, her fingers shaking with urgency. "Hurry, it will only be open for fifteen minutes. If your friends are in there, you must bring them out, or they won't be able to return since this place only appears when the rock activity reacts with the sand every ten years."

Calla nodded and stepped closer to the wall, inspecting the mysterious symbols. She compared the familiar pattern etched into her ankle tattoo to the shape of the plaster on the wall's edge. Her mind quickly realized what she had to do.

At the sound of a distant explosion, Calla spun around and saw Avo emerge from the end of the tunnel, gun drawn and eyes narrowed. Avo was now only a few steps away, and Calla could see the determination that contorted her features.

The women had been there moments before, yet there was no trace of them now.

The air felt thick with anticipation, yet the area was completely silent. Not even a faint rustling of fabric or a whisper of conversation remained.

Avo glared at her. "Once you lead the way and open Iram, we switch on the pipes. We need only open the wells now, and then Project Mercury will be activated. We will be the world's only energy supplier. You'll open it now. You will read the code," Avo spat.

Calla didn't move but stood in front of the tall, slate wall, eyes narrowed in concentration.

The man with the prosthetic arm hovered close to her.

The wall seemed to hum with energy, a blend of what appeared to be ancient and futuristic technology.

Calla took a deep breath. She had to do this for Nash and Jack, not because a gun was in her back. She placed her palm on the wall and pushed, feeling its surface warm from the electricity coursing through it.

A symbol appeared in the corner of the wall, followed by others. An invisible hand seemed to write them as they flowed on the surface.

Calla traced her fingers on the rock, searching for patterns similar to her tattoo. When she spotted one, she pressed her fingers into it, then drew a symbol on the corresponding place on her wrist as close as she could to the original.

Calla's head was spinning as she stared at the code on her tattoo.

She knew her ancestors had been here before, but the operatives had tried to keep them away and had hidden the secrets of Iram. Yet here she was, holding a code that could unlock something centuries old.

She wasn't sure if it would work, and if it did, it would trigger a reaction that could create an entirely alternative energy source. It seemed almost too good to be true, and Calla wasn't sure if she could trust the science of her ancestors or even herself.

If it failed, the world would remain in darkness. She had to take the risk.

Calla stepped back, her mouth agape at the sheer size of the gray stone wall. It practically vibrated with electricity, and something stirred within her as she felt an ancient knowledge, long forgotten, bubble to the surface of her mind.

Taking a deep breath, she reached out and placed her palm on the wall, letting the ancient symbols carved into the stone seep into her consciousness.

She could feel the memories of this place, of the ancient

scientists who had opened and sealed it centuries before. She remembered the code written on the women's tattoos and instinctively ran her finger from symbol to symbol, pressing as she went.

As she did, the wall shimmered and shifted inwards, creating a small opening.

She remembered more of the women's words and followed their instructions, running her finger from symbol to symbol and pressing as she went, imitating the movements and thoughts of a long-gone culture. As soon as she finished with the last symbol, the wall shifted inward.

Avo deepened the gun into Calla's back, and she turned around to face her and the man with the prosthetic arm.

Calla thought back to the woman's sword that had nearly killed her.

With a determined look, Calla met their gazes.

Avo's eyes flashed with amazement, while the man seemed disbelieving, realizing that Calla intended to face whatever lay ahead alone.

The low hum of energy intensified within the ancient wall, causing it to shimmer and shoot dust upward. Avo stumbled back with a gasp, and Calla's eyes remained fixed on them.

The air crackled with heat, and her mind quieted as her feet moved without her will.

She felt a force pull her forward as if gravity had reversed, and she was being pulled into the unknown depths of space beyond the wall.

In the next moment, she disappeared within the wall, and darkness consumed her.

CHAPTER
EIGHTY

CALLA LANDED hard on her back.

She found herself in a vacuum, surrounded by pitch-black silence. Whatever had brought her there weighed down on her, and she couldn't move.

She took shallow breaths, her heart pounding in her chest as she felt a wave of claustrophobia wash over her.

A faint light pierced through the darkness, and Calla scrambled to her feet.

She crept forward carefully, each step echoing through winding passages that seemed to stretch on forever.

The air grew chilled.

The walls around her were made of tall slate-gray stones, their edges strangely smooth as if burnished by an unseen force. They seemed to blend with the floor, creating an infinite void. As she looked around, she had the disorienting sensation that time and space were merging and swirling into a bottomless abyss, an endless maze where time and space seemed to merge in a swirling black hole of nothingness.

Finally, as she emerged into a vast gray maze of twisting passageways and endless hallways, she realized this was no ordinary place built by man. This was something far more mysterious and wondrous than anything she had ever imagined.

Utterly alone, Calla shot through the narrow pathways of the maze, her feet pounding against the cold slate floor as her lungs heaved in a desperate panic.

Everywhere she looked, there were a million identical walls that shifted and transformed, kaleidoscopic reflections of her wide-eyed face looking back at her in horror.

No matter how hard she tried or which way she turned, she couldn't find a way out.

Calla zigzagged through the shadowy labyrinth, navigating its twists and turns with surprising agility.

The further she went, the more the air seemed to choke her with its suffocating darkness.

Ahead of her, she could hear something, like someone moving. She halted at the sight of a lump lying limp on the ground.

Her legs felt like lead as Calla ran toward it, every step amplifying the thunderous beating of her heart.

Nash!

She knelt beside him and brushed her fingers against his shoulder. "Nash?" she whispered.

His eyes fluttered open hesitantly, and his brow creased with confusion.

He groaned and winced as he sat up, carefully feeling the bump that had formed on his head. "Cal? What happened?" Nash asked, covered in sand dust and glancing around the unfamiliar setting.

The walls of the maze-like chamber seemed to close in around them. "You were here one minute, and then I woke up in this strange place," he added.

Nash looked around at the strange maze. "Where are we? What is this place?" he said, pushing himself up.

"I'm not sure," she said with grim tone. "But, I'm so glad to see you," she said, clinging to him. "We must see if we can find Jack and get out of here."

Calla turned and looked back the way she'd come.

The hallway ended in a featureless slate-gray stone with a single, solid-looking entryway.

When she tried to retrace her steps with Nash, however, the floor gave a strange, electric buzz, and she was suddenly at the far end of a long, vaulted corner.

With a sense of dread, this place reminded her of a dark place in her past.

The air smelled vaguely acrid and burned.

Calla looked at the endless passageways stretching out all around them. She didn't know where they were going but knew she would never leave this place without Nash.

After what felt like an eternity of racing through the maze, Calla and Nash emerged into a large circular room with a massive metal door set into the wall.

As they approached the door, a loud rumbling sound came from behind them.

Calla turned to look over her shoulder and saw that the maze walls were closing in on them. If they didn't get through the opening soon, they would be trapped forever.

Calla heaved the heavy stone doorway open with every ounce of her remaining strength, and they stumbled into a new space.

The landscape stretched out before her as far as the eye could see, illuminated by an eerie silvery moonlight that seemed to come from all sides.

Then it hit her. this wasn't natural light but a glow emanating from a large metal globe in the middle of the wasteland.

This was no ordinary place. The meteorite that had hit Iram and embedded its DNA deep beneath the sand had created it.

The ground seemed to move as if the meteorite was reproducing itself, creating air pockets beneath its surface.

"That's what caused the quicksand," she said.

Nash raised an eyebrow. "Come again?"

"That's not a desert," she said. "I know what's happening."

He looked around, curious. "The meteorite did this."

"Yes. The meteorite has some kind of energy that created this place underneath the desert. It doesn't seem real that we are underground in a maze created by a primitive machine-learning entity from the meteorite's energy. The meteorite learned to replicate itself and created this source of energy, but we only have a few minutes to get out," she said, turning to Nash. "Nash, we're caught somewhere between reality and not. We have to stay focused and find Jack." She looked at her watch. "We only have a few minutes."

The maze walls seemed to shift and slink closer, giving her no room to escape.

The faint silhouette of a figure emerged on the horizon, and with each step it took, the figure grew ever closer. Its looming shadow cast a long stretch of darkness on the wall as more than one person's heavy, thudding footsteps drew nearer. Anticipation rippled through the air as their presence grew.

Calla felt a surge of hope that it might be Jack, that he had somehow made his way out. But as she got closer, her hope crumbled into despair.

It wasn't Jack. Avo had followed her. The woman who had lured them into this wretched place, stood with a grin as she watched Calla.

Avo let out a sharp yell, its shrillness echoing off the walls. The man beside her had his prosthetic arm raised, a pistol pointed shakily at Calla and Nash.

Calla's eyes widened, her heart beating wildly in her chest as she registered the danger.

Nash lunged forward, his muscles clenching as he moved with a speed that defied logic.

The man reeled backward, his prosthetic arm up in defense. But it was too late. Nash had his fingers clamped around the gun, and he yanked it from Rion's grip.

With a flick of his wrist, Nash spun the weapon around and pointed it at Avo, his finger twitching on the trigger.

Jack materialized from the shadows, a firearm in his hands that he brought straight down on Avo's head with a resounding crack. She dropped unconscious.

Nash leaped forward and kicked the man in the gut as Rion's body slumped to the ground, limp and motionless, next to Avo's.

Jack turned to Nash and Calla with a smirk. "It's about time you two showed up," he said. "I've been wandering around this place for hours now. What kind of place is this?"

Calla grabbed his arm, conveying the urgency of the situation. "Jack, I'm relieved you're okay. We're inside a giant meteorite rock that has been replicating itself for centuries beneath the desert using an unknown form of science. It's creating a planet within Earth, and it will consume the entire planet in a few more centuries. The side effect is it's releasing a certain type of energy, and Kronos plans to hold the world hostage with it."

Jack's gaze was intense as he looked at her. "Where did it come from?"

Calla spoke quietly. "Outer space. It could even be like carbonado diamonds from an alternate existence. Remember the meteor shower that created the Divide? They must be related."

Jack stared at them both as realization dawned on him. "So, a meteor hit the Earth, sank under Ubar, and started replicating and growing… and the energy here is what it uses to build this maze?"

Calla smiled, relieved to see both men alive. "Yup, I knew you'd get it. This is a whole new geology lesson. Jack, Kronos used your technology too. They stole it."

"I suspected as much," he hissed.

Nash dusted off his combat pants. "So the Nazis were exploiting this place."

Calla nodded. "Right, but while the energy is enough for our worldwide supplies and resources, it's also simultaneously destroying the planet. Jack, you know this better than anyone. The composition of this meteorite, though charged with natural gas and energy, may be good for energy depletion now, but in significant quantities, it also has a dangerous composition for Earth's ozone layer. This is Kronos's plan: to be the ultimate supplier of gas. Think of the meteorite as a parasite embedded in the Earth, and at any point, it could grow so large that we won't be able to contain it."

Jack took a deep breath and slowly exhaled. He looked at Calla with newfound respect. "That's how you got in here. Cal, you amaze me."

Calla nodded slightly and tucked a strand of hair behind her ear. "I had help. I'll tell you all about that later, but yes, the symbols are embedded in the fabric of the operatives' world and my birthmark. But the energy this place is giving off is worrisome. There have been no signs of life here. It's as if this is where the Divide happened."

Jack rubbed his chin contemplatively. "The Divide explains a lot of the operatives' science, but with the energy depletion and the planet nearing... who knows what, it's dire out there."

Nash crossed his arms and raised an eyebrow. "We can't let that happen."

Calla looked up at him, her face serious with determination. "If we close the Divide, the meteorite will be destroyed, and Earth will have a chance to be saved from its destruction."

Jack shifted and looked from one person to the other as he posed his ultimate question. "How do we do that?"

Calla frowned and paced across the ground, her hands tucked inside her pockets.

Jack then projected a display on the dark slate in front of them. It displayed blueprints of Project Mercury and satellite images. "If we create an opening, energy will travel through, and the Divide will close,"

"I'm working on it," Calla said, still pacing. "The opening to Earth's surface is sealed, but we need a door for the energy to travel through. That's what the Nazis were working on. The pipes are in place. I know this because Avo's people put me in one. If we allow the energy to travel through, the meteorite will keep growing under the Earth."

Jack scratched his head. "So we need to slow the energy down?"

Calla shook her head. "No, we have to shut the whole thing down and destroy the meteorite activity in the sand."

Nash took in a sharp breath. "We better get started. If NASA's sightings are accurate and your calculations are correct, we need to shut it down at the source. I can't believe Kronos used your blueprints for this."

Jack's face lined with worry. "I didn't know they were so advanced. My findings at the ISTF labs explain a lot. This energy extraction plan has been in the works for years. I found the plans in the archives just before I ran into Laskfell."

"So, what's the first step?" Nash asked, looking between Jack and Calla.

Jack took a deep breath. "We need a massive influx of power to shut this place down."

Calla nodded. "The same kind of power that created the walled city in the first place. That means finding the original meteorite rock, removing it from this place, and destroying it.

If we do that, it'll stop expanding, and nobody can exploit its energy again."

Nash nodded solemnly, his face grim as he considered what needed to be done. "Yes, we have to put a stop to this now."

CHAPTER
EIGHTY-ONE

JACK GAZED AT CALLA, his eyes wide with anticipation. "How do we find the original meteorite?"

Calla looked off into the distance, her brow furrowed in thought. After a few moments, she gave a decisive nod. "If the meteorite expanded from a single rock, that rock must be in the city's center," she said. "Based on NASA sightings, the center is located at 21 degrees north longitude and 48 degrees latitude. Do you have your compass with you, Jack?"

Jack reached into his backpack and sighed in relief when he felt the compass. He smiled up at Calla as he withdrew it.

"Take us to that spot, please," she said. "That's where the original rock is. Like a cell of an organism. This place first divided from one cell and is still intact somewhere; otherwise, the meteorite rock would not be growing."

Jack adjusted the settings on his compass until he got a reading and a direction. He struggled to his feet, pointing ahead of him. "This way," he said as he began walking.

Calla and Nash followed close behind.

They navigated through the strange, convoluted landscape of slate and rock until they finally arrived at a spot.

"This must be it," Jack said, gazing out.

The ground ahead of them was flat and even. Soft dirt and dust were packed so tightly that it was like walking on a black-and-white linoleum floor.

The city around them had been built entirely of white stone that glowed in the sunlight. Carvings were still visible on crumbling walls. Some buildings towered over them, but the ceilings were open and high above the ground. There was nothing but an empty landscape surrounded by a sunken Arabian ancient ruin of a once prosperous city.

A flat, level area lay before the group. It was vastly different from the rest of the strange, distorted landscape. The city walls were made of shiny blue tiles that glimmered in the light from their flashlights.

Stones were broken and weathered, and ornaments were torn down and vandalized as if they were idols that had been permitted to stand for too long.

The front gate had been taken down during a war with nature centuries ago, and the only movement came from the still air that carried the fragrance of history.

The place appeared to be breathing while it slept, hiding its treasures in the shadows, but there was still no sign of the rock.

Calla walked up to the edge where the slate rocks ended, and nothingness began.

She stepped onto the stretch of empty ground and held out her hands. "Can you feel it?" she asked Jack.

Jack shook his head.

"Try," Calla urged.

Jack approached the edge and placed his hand on the ground. He looked back at Calla and shrugged, then took a few more steps forward and stood right up to the edge. "What's that?" he asked, pointing into the space.

"I see it," Nash said.

"I see it, too," Calla said.

"Step back," Jack said, then bent down, squinting hard.

Calla and Nash stepped back a few paces, but they strained their eyes to see what Jack was looking at.

"The energy source is here," Calla said, her voice revealing her anxiety. She gestured to the shimmering air around them, showing the space that was almost a reflection of the space they had left behind. "This is what the operatives' energy can do. Kronos needed the energy to control everything, including dark matter."

Jack continued where Calla had left off. "This was Kronos's vision. When resources became scarce during the war, German engineers started exploring alternative sources for exploitation. We're surrounded by natural gas production, but it could mean a new world order, with Kronos having the upper hand with natural gas supply."

Calla shook her head. "A world with an energy shortage."

Nash narrowed his eyes and pointed to a spot in the distance. "There it is--"

"You're right," Jack said. "According to my compass, the original meteorite is about twenty meters from here. That's where the strongest signal is. How do we get to it? I'm not sure I trust that ground over there."

Before anyone else could respond, Avo called from above. She had caught up, dripping with venom. "Don't touch that!"

CHAPTER
EIGHTY-TWO

AVO FIRED.

Calla dodged the bullet. She had to get to the rock.

Her shoes pounded against the hard ground as she raced. She felt the energy of the crater pulsing through the slate tablets beneath her feet, as if the lifeblood of the crater, gave it strength and vitality.

Avo fired again.

This time, the bullet zipped by her shoulder.

She could feel an invisible force rising in the air, pressing against her skin like a physical presence.

It was her job to close the meteorite source, but it wasn't like the other places she had been. This was different somehow.

What the meteorite had created was like a spider web, a trap, a snare. It drew energy from the Earth's veins and arteries as if it was feeding it to another world. It was a drain, a leech. Sucking life from this world, the meteorite had to be stopped.

The only way to stop it would be to close off its source.

Calla's breath came in ragged gasps. Her lungs felt like they were on fire, and her legs gave out from under her. She closed her eyes and tried to focus on nothing but her breathing and the sensation of air flowing in and out of her lungs as she jogged.

Calla sprinted to the heart of the crater, where the meteorite glimmered in the center of the space. With trembling fingers, she reached out to pick it up, her hand closing around the cold, smooth surface.

But then, a firm grip clamped down on hers.

She froze, her heart pounding in her chest as she stared into the deadly eyes of Ivan Schneider, the assassin who was sent to kill her ten years ago.

He was the man from her nightmares, standing right before her.

The tension in the air was palpable as they both prepared for a life-or-death confrontation.

He had been waiting for her to come and take the rock. He was very much alive. How?

"You think food is the only sustenance? This place has something no one can explain, and not just energy!" he spat as if reading her mind. "You should've stayed away," Ivan said, his voice like ice. "This isn't your business."

"It's my mission," Calla responded, still clinging to the rock. She could feel its power coursing through her veins, giving her strength even in this moment of danger. "I'm here to close the crater and restore order."

Ivan laughed bitterly. "Order? That's impossible." He sneered at her. "The meteorite has already changed things in ways no one can control or predict. It's too late for you to do anything now."

Still gripping Calla's hand tightly, he leaned closer to her face, his voice low, and set his hand on the rock. "But I'll let you live if you promise me something: Don't interfere with what is happening here again."

Calla felt a chill run down her spine as Ivan released his

grasp on the rock and stepped back. She clutched it against her chest tightly, feeling its energy pulse through every cell of her body.

Ivan snatched it from her grip.

She had just made an involuntary deal with a dangerous man, and this was only the beginning of a much bigger battle ahead of her, one that would test all of her skills and courage if she wanted to restore nature's balance and order in the world by destroying the crater's power.

Ivan still wore the jacket Calla had seen on him ten years ago. How could she forget the smell of that leather as he held a hand to her neck? Now she remembered. He had tried to kill her. She recognized the hoodie and the red mesh shirt. His hair was still buzzed short. His face, however, was older, with lines that sagged at the edges of his lips and eyes. He seemed to think he had only been there for a few minutes but had been there for ten years.

Time slipped away, and each day felt like months. Each minute felt like a week.

Calla dove forward, snatching the meteorite from Ivan's grip. Before he could react, she slammed into him with a feral growl, sending them both sprawling to the ground.

Ivan was strong, but Calla was faster.

With an expert twist of her body, she got on top and pinned his arms to the ground.

Time seemed to slow as they struggled, the air crackling with tension. He fought to break free, but Calla held firm.

A gunshot echoed through the maze, and a bullet landed by her boot.

Ivan sprinted off, leaving behind the rumble of collapsing rubble from the cave's ceiling.

Calla was frozen in place, her gaze locked on the man with the prosthetic arm until he fully emerged from the rubble. His expression was stony and unreadable. Despite that, Calla could see his pain.

"You're Rion," she whispered. "Now I remember... You and Octavia..."

Her voice trailed off as her legs buckled beneath her when she turned and saw Avo behind Rion.

Avo's hand thrust a grenade of vengeance that sent them all flying. The force of the blast sent them all tumbling backward.

Calla landed hard on the ground.

Splinters of slate and fragments of exploded stone flew in all directions.

In an instant, the place had filled with dust and rubble. The entire place shook with the explosion's power, sending a plume of dust and debris into the atmosphere.

All Calla could feel was darkness and dust in her mouth. When the dust cleared, and the roaring of the explosion faded away, the place had been mangled, and the floor was now unstable.

Calla staggered to her feet and surveyed the damage. The place had been transformed from a dimly lit den of secrets into an open, broken shell.

She felt the impact of the blast throughout her entire body, and in a blink of an eye, she was engulfed in more darkness.

CHAPTER
EIGHTY-THREE

NASH TURNED SLOWLY, taking in the destroyed remains of the cave. Debris filled the air, muffling sound and blocking his vision. "Where's Calla?" he shouted over the ringing in his ears.

Jack coughed and spat as he wrestled with a device in his hands. "I can't see or hear anyone."

Nash retrieved his gun from his combat pants holster. "We have to find her."

But before they could move, Avo coughed through the dust and rubble, a new explosive clutched in one hand.

Nash spoke in a low voice. "The blast has sealed off the passage between Calla and us."

They watched as Avo and her men moved through the debris, their weapons held tightly.

The smell of smoke lingered in the air, and Rion wasn't with them.

Avo ran to Ivan when she saw him. "I knew you'd come back!"

He held her tightly for several moments. "I always believed in you. Now let's finish this."

"That should have taken care of her," Avo muttered, referring to Calla. "Let's go back and work on the energy before this place is obliterated."

Jack looked at Nash with a determined expression. "Let's follow them. It's the only way we can help Calla. The Nazis built shafts down into Rub'al Khali. I saw it in my research and maps I found in ISTF archives. I never knew what they were for, but I guess now I do. That must be how they got down here. Those shafts go down hundreds of feet, but these debris slates are high, and we need something to drill through."

Avo and her team staggered through the mess, Jack and Nash close behind.

After what seemed like an eternity, they stopped as a few more agents joined them.

Avo turned to a man named Vaughn, who had made his way from the surface to meet them.

"See?" Jack whispered from their hiding spot. "He must have come down in one of those shafts. If we can get to the end of the shaft, they might have something we can use to help Calla."

"The gas pipes should be ready," Vaughn said.

"Blow up this place and the shafts once we are back at the energy center. I don't want anyone to reach her," Avo replied.

Vaughn gasped. "Listen, the engines are running, but we can't destroy this place," he pleaded, desperation lacing his words. "You've made this personal. This was about the energy, not Cress, not you."

Vaughn watched as Avo raised a handgun to his head.

Nash paid attention to the number of explosives on one of the agent's belts. "He's seriously going to do it," he muttered.

Before he could act, Avo flung one of the bombs into the tunnel where Nash and Jack were standing.

In a split second, Nash pushed Jack out of the way, and

they threw themselves out of the tunnel, seconds before it exploded.

Sparks flew and flashed as the explosive charges detonated, sending shockwaves rippling through the underground maze.

Nash and Jack were thrown out of the tunnel as debris rained down on them, and smoke filled the air.

The two men coughed and groaned as they clambered to their feet, Nash shouting, "We have to go back for Calla before it's too late!"

They scrambled outward and raced to the shafts after Avo and her team.

But they both knew it was a futile effort. Another blast shook the tunnels, sending them hurtling still higher as they threw themselves into the elevator shaft.

Nash eyed the two elevator cars in the shaft, each one large enough to carry five people.

He waited until the debris settled and then reached for the elevator button. He pounded his fist against it several times, the dull thuds reverberating up and down the shaft.

However, despite his efforts, the doors still wouldn't move. He slammed it again, and miraculously it opened.

"Stay here," he commanded. "I'll try to find Calla. If I'm not back in two minutes, go!"

An explosion from an undetonated explosive device interrupted his sentence, throwing him back into Jack. The doors slammed shut, and the elevator shot upward.

It raced past ancient corners of the city and clanged to a sudden stop, flinging open its doors and expelling them out with a crash. They landed on concrete.

Jack and Nash surveyed their surroundings as a thick cloud of dust and smoke cleared.

The two men were in a wide cavern filled with tables, chairs, and a massive screen.

"Where are we?" Nash asked.

Jack looked up at a screen. "You think this is Kronos?"

"It must be."

Jack and Nash looked around. What seemed like the crater's center was destroyed, and walls smashed in. This was the control panel room of Kronos' archaeological dig and control room.

Smoke and dust filled the air, and the smell of burning metal was heavy in the back of their throats.

A radiant energy surrounded them, pushing them further above ground and into the room.

Still, inside the rock maze, Calla was far away from Nash and Jack and out of reach.

Nash turned to Jack. "We have to go back and get Calla."

Jack hesitated, scrutinizing the control panels with a critical eye. "We can do it, but there's no way we're doing it alone." His eyes lingered on the monitors. "Calla is the only one who knows how to control the energy inside that place."

Nash furrowed his brow, his jaw tight. "We have to open it, Jack. We have to get Calla back."

Before Jack could respond, there was a flicker of movement in the room's corner.

Nash and Jack froze, their eyes widening as they watched.

Avo and Ivan emerged from the shadows, making their way toward the energy center's control panels.

Jack cursed, and he and Nash took cover, with Nash holding his breath, realizing that if they were caught, they wouldn't be able to rescue Calla.

Nash leaned forward and whispered, "We have to stop them. I can activate the control panels, but you'll need to provide me with cover."

Jack nodded and grabbed a long metal bar from the ground, positioning himself in front of Nash and raising the bar in defense.

Avo and Ivan discharged their weapons, spitting fire, and causing the ground to shake with a thunderous roar.

Jack and Nash leaped for cover as bullet holes peppered opposite walls.

"We need to get to the control panels! We have to stabilize the energy center!" Ivan shouted, whipping his head toward Avo, and they took off to an adjacent room, arguing.

Nash glanced from his hiding spot and saw Jack taking cover beneath a counter.

Avo and Ivan spoke rapidly in German, their voices laced with urgency as they discussed how to get the energy running in the conduits as soon as possible.

A gunshot from one of the team echoed through the room, causing Nash to whip around.

Avo and Ivan spun and headed directly for him, with their weapons raised and ready to fire.

"*Vater*, I'll take this one!" Avo shouted, kicking Jack's body. Ivan ran over to Nash and raised his gun.

"Get up!" Ivan shouted.

Nash stood up, and Ivan advanced. "Now, no one goes anywhere. The energy has started moving. The machine is working. I knew we would get Kronos's project running."

Avo and her team closed in on Jack and Nash, their guns trained on them with unwavering focus.

Nash stared at the control panel, already formulating a plan.

The humming and whirring of Kronos's machines were almost deafening, and the floor vibrated from their power.

Avo's team took up positions around the high-tech control panel, the world's only future global energy supply if it was activated.

"Ivan said, moving as he spoke. "The system is ready." Avo gave a decisive nod. "Activate it now."

Nash glanced at the control panel and quickly sidled up to

Jack. Once the machine was online, getting to Calla would be difficult unless he could come up with something quick.

He took a deep breath and whispered, "Jack, I have a plan."

Jack gave a curt nod. "I'm listening."

The control panel of the Kronos machine glowed blue in the center of the room. Nash pointed at it, gesturing for Jack to make a move.

The surrounding machines churned and hissed like an oncoming train.

Nash lunged forward and grabbed one guard by the shoulders, wrenching him to the ground.

Jack used his shoulder to tackle the other guard, sending him sprawling. Nash sprang toward the second guard and thrust him into the wall.

The man reached for a weapon that was not there as he slumped against the wall in defeat, and Nash secured the guard's discarded firearm.

Jack put his hand on the control panel, steadying himself for the job ahead. "Okay, we can do this. Just follow my lead," he said.

"Okay," Nash said, his voice strained with urgency.

Jack closed his eyes and clenched his fists tightly as he leaned forward and put his hands on the control panel.

The lights on the panel flickered and sparked, and the machine whirred as it drew energy from the ground.

"It's working, Nash. I can feel it," Jack said. "We need to get to the other side and find Calla."

"Let's go," Nash said. But then he realized something was wrong.

"Nash, the machine took more energy from the wells than expected. The energy is being diverted to the crater. We have to go! It's going to explode!"

Nash seized Jack's arm and flew toward the door, but Jack halted. "We can't leave yet! We need to have all the energy on this side!" he shouted.

EIGHTY-FOUR

CALLA FELT A HAND NUDGE HER.

Rion stepped close, and she flinched away.

Her arm was bleeding, and he reached for her, but she held out one hand as if to fend him off.

With his good hand, he took a step toward her, and she leaped back, slamming into the slate so hard that the soft flesh of her backside hit with an audible smack.

He stopped, furrowing his brow.

She stepped back again.

"It's all right," he said. "I won't hurt you."

"You tried to kill me a minute ago," she said.

"I know," he said. "First, let me help you with your arm."

He reached for her arm and applied pressure with his fingers until the wound stopped bleeding. "It's only a flesh wound. It should be better in a second."

"How did you end up with people like Avo and Ivan? You didn't start out this way."

"It's a long story, one to do with Octavia."

She looked around through steam, smoke, and darkness. "Now what?"

Her arm throbbed with pain.

"Calla," he said. His voice was firm but kind. "We're beneath the desert, several thousand meters deep, but the slate slabs are rising through to the Earth's surface. In a few centuries, this desert will be gone if we don't do something now, and if we extract energy from the meteorite center as Kronos hopes, it will slowly kill the Earth."

"The only way out is with this," she said, pulling the meteorite rock out of her pocket. "This rock started everything and hit Earth with force," she said, staring at Rion. "I know how it works. I can destroy it the same way it created itself."

Rion stared at her. He looked at the space looming over them, pulsing with energy and power.

"It's our only chance," Calla said. "We must shut down its energy and find a way out of this place."

Together, they cautiously approached the glowing crater. Its ethereal light mesmerized them, and Calla could feel its energetic force emanating deeply.

"What now?" Rion asked, his voice quivering slightly.

Calla thought hard and focused her energy on the rock she was holding. "Well, if the power with which it hit came from impact, then impact is what we need."

Rion opened his mouth to speak, but before he could, Calla gathered all her strength and hurled the rock with all her might into the center of the glowing crater.

A deafening roar shook the ground, and a blast of searing heat swept outward from the crater, creating a shockwave of pure energy that ripped through everything in its path.

The force of the blast sent an unstoppable wave of power toward them.

Calla grabbed onto Rion as they tumbled into the center of the space and felt an immense force pushing against the walls of their surroundings.

Electricity sent their muscles into spasms. They levitated an inch above the sand and then slammed back down. Back and forth they went, thrusting upwards through the sand.

The force of the collision was like an explosion, a cacophony of chemicals that sent them careening through the air and sand.

Calla felt her chest constrict with each breath she managed, a smothering fear of the unknown propelling them further upwards until they breathed fresh air again.

"WHAT THE HECK WAS THAT?" Nash shouted over the thunderous hum that seemed to grow more and more powerful.

The ground pulsed with electricity, funneling unknown energy from the lost crater in the desert to the Western World.

"This way," Nash shouted as he leaped to his feet.

An earsplitting explosion shook the control room, shattering fluorescent bulbs and spewing sparks.

The air filled with the smell of burning plastic as the room descended into darkness.

Nash had seconds to recuperate and take stock of the situation. He sprinted to the control panel and saw something on the screen—the blueprints of the energy center—a deep tunnel with shafts.

Jack joined him to look at what he was staring at. "I was right," Jack said. "Kronos has been using the shafts the Nazis built to access the energy source, but they couldn't get past the walls to get the energy."

"I guess that's where Calla came in," Nash replied. "I'm going back."

Before they could react, they heard a noise behind them.

Calla stepped out of the shadows, her face set in determination.

It was Nash who spoke first. "Cal?"

"Hey," she whispered.

They met each other's gaze and were silent for a long moment.

Despite all his training, Nash felt overwhelmed. He stared at her in stunned silence, his eyes focused yet distracted as if he were looking at something he couldn't understand. His heart seemed to swell to where he thought it would burst.

Calla's arms around him filled him with relief, and he sighed deeply, feeling the tension drain from his body. It was as if nothing could ever destroy them.

As he returned her embrace, he unconsciously sensed movement in the corner of his eye.

Desert sunlight broke through the now-blasted control room and angled into the space. The brilliant light assaulted their eyes, and they squeezed them shut, trying to block out the pain.

Avo had returned to the room and rose from her corner amidst the destruction. "I'll be back," Calla hissed as Nash tried to speak.

Rion emerged beside Avo and reached out for her throat.

"No!" Calla shouted, her voice echoing through the destruction. "Avo started something long ago in a lab in Cambridge that I need to talk to her about."

The men stepped back as Calla gently released Nash and took a deep breath.

She had to focus completely, pushing away all the clutter of the last several days from her mind. She focussed her energy with a burst of strength, ready for this moment.

Avo's fists slowly unclenched as well, and they stood facing each other in silence, the hot air heavy and oppressive in the space.

CHAPTER
EIGHTY-SIX

CALLA FELT THE TENSION, anticipation, and hostility radiating from Avo, but she tried to ignore it.

Instead, she focused on her breathing, surroundings, and how her muscles felt with each movement.

She felt a shift, a surge of adrenaline coursing through her body. Calla charged forward and attacked without hesitation, landing a flurry of punches and kicks.

She sensed Avo's movements before they happened, using her opponent's labored breathing and sweat as cues.

Avo went down with a sickening crunch, and the sound of bone against metal filled the room.

Avo was not done. She got back up, blood trickling from her nose, and charged forward.

As they exchanged blows, the control room erupted in flames, and the sound of crackling wires filled the air.

Avo staggered back, blood dripping from her bruised eye, and advanced on Calla.

Calla was ready, and with a powerful punch, she sent Avo crashing to the ground once again.

Blood dripped from Avo's bruised eye as she advanced toward Calla once more, who stood in the center of the room.

Avo's eyes widened in pain as Calla's fist sent her to the ground.

The sound of crackling and snapping filled the air, and the fire quickly spread across the control panels, filling the room with the acrid smoke of burning wires.

Although it seemed the fight was over, Avo rose with a savage growl, her muscles tensing as she charged toward Calla.

Calla dodged Avo's blows, and the fight filed out into the desert sands, but the bright sunlight made it difficult to focus on the attack. She couldn't dodge fast enough, and Avo's fist connected with her shoulder, causing her to stumble.

Calla scrambled away, but Avo's rage gave her the speed and power to pursue her relentlessly.

Eventually, Calla was cornered by an ancient wall, unable to escape the onslaught.

As Avo lunged for the kill.

Calla reached blindly for something that would give her an advantage.

The two highly trained operatives tore at each other.

Calla's hand shot across the ground and closed around a small, jagged rock. With a single, swift motion, she pulled back and flung it as hard as she could.

It connected with Avo's shoulder, barely slowing her momentum, but it was enough.

At that same moment, Calla darted back into the darkened recesses of a room in the abandoned, taking a moment to catch her breath and regroup. Nash and Jack watched close by from the outside, ready to intervene when needed.

The two women grappled fiercely in the darkness of the control room, their bodies intertwined and their breaths mingling.

Calla could feel sweat dripping from her face and the chill of the surrounding shadows.

Both women were cut and bleeding, neither willing to give in. She tried to locate Avo in the darkness, hoping to gain an advantage with her little knowledge of the space, but Avo seemed to be just as lost in the darkness as she was.

Neither spoke, each waiting for the other to make the first move.

Calla steadied her breath and tilted her head up. Nash's instructions were a whisper in the back of her mind. "Don't use your eyes in the darkness. Listen to your surroundings. Your other senses will be sharpened in the dark."

Calla swung her fists, connecting with Avo's body with each blow.

It was working.

Her hands struck their targets again and again, and the other woman suddenly pivoted behind her.

Calla stepped back as she let go of all her senses except for touch and sound. She spun around to meet Avo's counterattack, and the two women crashed into one another.

Although little more than a silhouette, Calla could sense the other woman's movements weakening, and a wave of relief washed over her.

Every second counted.

Avo struck Calla's chest with a sickening thud, stealing the wind from her lungs as she stumbled back.

All she could make out in the darkness were a few jagged rocks scattered across the floor. She reached out and grabbed one, holding it like a talisman as Avo advanced upon her.

Calla felt the other woman's energy like a wave ahead of her and heard the heavy breathing coming closer and closer.

Avo lunged, and Calla evaded each strike with amazing speed and grace. Then, pushing her advantage, Calla unleashed a flurry of fists, raining blows of hurt, pain, and wounds down on Avo until she collapsed to the ground.

With a reverberating crash that echoed through the space, Calla stood over Avo.

This had to stop.

The only way was to keep Avo from causing further harm.

Calla lowered the rock slowly and held a hand to help her adversary up off the ground.

Avo rose to her feet, her chest heaving with exertion. She snarled.

Calla reached for the woman and dragged her out into the sunlight. It was then that Calla opened her eyes.

Avo heaved and struggled under Calla's strong grip.

"You came for me to take away the greatest gift that could be given to me. I will not do the same," Calla said. "We've both suffered enough."

In a flash, she saw danger.

Ivan had drawn a knife and was advancing on Calla, but she stood her ground.

Before she could escape harm's way, she watched Nash appear out of thin air, charged toward Ivan, and slammed a fist into the man's gut.

Ivan fell backward into the sand.

Calla turned to Avo. "I know it's hard not to have a father in your life, but that doesn't mean you have to do this. I, too, grew up without a father, but I won't let it turn me into a monster, and neither should you."

ISTF forces filled the space, their guns aimed at the three figures in front of them, Avo, Ivan, and Rion, and their teams.

Calla stepped forward. "Wait! Rion is with us. He helped me get out alive."

The agents' fingers remained firm on their triggers but eventually relaxed and allowed Rion to step away.

Ivan defiantly raised his head and whispered to Calla as he was being dragged away. "You can't stop what's coming."

"Neither can you," she said, "This whole thing began with a rock. This is what I saw in the crater. It's what I saw at the Cambridge dig. It was code and just physics. You set those bombs in Greece, at Knossos Palace, didn't you? To test me. To see if I could decipher them to bring me back here. You faked your death to lure me."

Ivan was barely conscious, but he nodded. "So? Did you? decipher it?"

"I guess you'll never know."

She turned when Eichel and Stan approached with the ISTF team. "We need to reverse this. If we cross-pollinate the energy through the Kronos network, we can replenish the energy in the reserves around the world. They won't even know anything happened," calla said. " It will take days, but we need to start."

Stan's eyes twinkled as he scanned Calla's face. "Calla, look at you," he breathed, shaking his head in awe. "You're the best thing I have ever done, and I wish I could have seen you grow up."

Calla leaned into her father's embrace and took a moment before she whispered. "Can we start again? And no more secrets, Dad. That must be hard as a spy," she mumbled. "You get to see me live the rest of my life."

Stan pulled Calla into a hug as he nodded.

Jack cleared his throat and stepped forward, breaking their embrace. "Kronos was crazy to think they could take all of Earth's energy without consequences," he declared, gesturing at the destruction around them. "But we can use the same network to restore what has been taken. I will use the plan I had originally intended before Kronos turned it into a weapon. Let's reverse Project Mercury."

"And then we shut this thing off permanently," Calla said,

turning to the destroyed facility. "The meteorite has stopped using Earth's soil beneath the Arabian sands to grow, but we can't take that chance again." She slowly pulled away from her father and gazed out at the archaeological dig that had been consumed by the meteorite several centuries ago. A ruined city burned in the sand intertwined with meteorite activity.

A determined look appeared in Nash's eyes. "Okay, let's get to work."

Iram Ruins
One Hour Later

CALLA STUMBLED THROUGH THE RUINS, her footfalls echoing off the broken walls, the crumbling foundations, and the scattered stones that littered the ground like ashes.

The signs of once-vibrant life had been reduced to dust and debris everywhere.

Calla felt the weight of grief and guilt in the air like a heavy fog suffocating her.

As she picked her way carefully through the ruins, her eyes took in the broken remains of what had been. Through the haze of grief, she noticed a small detail: the bright yellow petals of a flower still blooming despite the destruction.

It was a reminder that amidst the ashes, life still existed, a faint glimmer of hope in an otherwise desolate landscape.

She relived the time she had visited, believing she could save Avo's father from certain death if only she could decipher an ancient code, but now realized the code had been a part of her all along. The realization shook her to her core, and her footsteps kept leading her through the ruins, almost of their own volition.

A flurry around the camp was in full swing as ISTF arranged for the dig to be shut down.

Nash and Calla watched as the operatives worked tirelessly, stringing up a web of wires to form an invisible field around the crater, ensuring its secrets would stay beneath the surface.

Nash's footsteps crunched in the sand behind her, and they surveyed the activity. She slowly turned and saw him silhouetted against the sun, his hair whipped by the warm wind.

She took a deep breath. Calla finally understood that her guilt had been unfounded and recounted what Mason Laskfell had done months ago. "Laskfell hypnotized me several years ago, and then his work was carried on by Ivan Schneider, and I believe he made me believe everything about what happened ten years ago."

Jack joined them. "Yeah, I ran into Laskfell. I still don't understand how we can't find him and who is helping him."

"All these years, I had been living with the guilt of being unable to save Avo's father," Calla said.

Nash held her hand. "But you never actually did anything wrong. It was all Mason's doing. He drugged you and Avo, and her father brainwashed her into thinking you were responsible, but you have always been strong and stood up to them, even unconsciously. Your brain and mind are incredible. I hope Avo knows the truth, lets go of the past, and moves on with her life."

Realization hit Calla like a ton of bricks as she drew in a

breath. "I was never supposed to save Avo's father; it was all just a lie that was fed to me."

The guilt and shame she'd been carrying around all these years evaporated, and she felt lighter than she had in ages. Nash's touch brought hope to her heart. "Avo's father wanted to stay in the lost city because of his greed and recklessness—not because of anything you had or had not done."

Calla exhaled deeply, feeling the weight of worry dissipate in the warm air.

Nash stepped closer and looked out at the desert scape before them. "We will fly out to Berlin tomorrow," he said. "Lots we need to deal with there."

As nightfall arrived, they sat around the campfire in the desert. Calla watched Octavia as she took a seat next to the fire.

Octavia leaned slowly into Calla. "I'm sorry, Calla."

"Don't be. If you hadn't insisted on returning to Iram, to this place, we would have a planet growing inside our Earth like a parasite."

Octavia nodded slowly. "They wanted to make you feel you were responsible. The guilt would make you want to help. They experimented on you when they realized they couldn't break through to you all those years ago."

Calla took a deep breath, her heart heavy, knowing that Mason Laskfell had poisoned Avo's mind against her. But why bring her on such a perilous journey if the code had been a red herring? Could it have been to uncover her true potential as an operative? She remembered how Ivan had acted so oddly during their expedition, obsessing over the code, not even paying attention to the lost city itself.

Octavia's voice broke through her thoughts like a light piercing through a storm cloud. "When Ivan didn't find the city, he was enraged. He manipulated Avo's mind to make her believe you were behind her father's death, turning her into a dangerous woman on a revenge mission."

Calla leaned into Nash, her eyes still on Octavia. "Yet, I can understand what it's like to lose a baby you never had."

"Where did you get the Book of Iram, Octavia?" Calla asked.

Octavia smiled wryly. "A Bedouin who asked to meet in Muscat, claiming that he had found it in the ruins of the lost city. He said he would only give it to me if I came alone. I made a mistake, and I came with Rion."

Calla listened to Octavia's story. As she looked into Octavia's eyes, she knew without a doubt that it was all true. She knew what love could do. Maybe Octavia and Rion could start again. That was something for them to work out, perhaps regain what they had lost in the madness of Atlantis and its power.

No one should ever have that much power.

She knew that now.

Stan sank down into a seat next to her and held Calla tightly. She could feel him tremble as he held her close. His nose brushed against her forehead and settled in her hair, breathing in its scent as he pulled away. "I'm so sorry, Calla, for the Blackhorse Group. I should have done more. But I couldn't risk putting you in danger."

Calla looked up at him, searching his eyes for an answer, but all she saw was a deep sadness. Her hand moved to his arm, giving it a gentle squeeze.

Octavia leaned forward and placed a reassuring hand on Stan's shoulder. "It doesn't matter now. We can't change what happened in the past."

"I understand now, Dad. I don't think you should stop." She winked at him. "The Blackhorse Group has done me more good than harm."

Calla searched Nash and Jack's faces. "Did you know? About the Blackhorse Group?"

Nash shook his head, his eyes fixated on Stan's exhausted face. "No."

Calla's brow furrowed. "Dad, why send me to Iram if you knew I would be in danger?"

"It doesn't matter now. We can't change what happened in the past," Octavia said.

Nash intervened. "Because he loves you and knew you were the best person for the job. Look what you did here. Only you could have figured it out."

Eichel settled on the ground beside the fire, holding a mug of warm cider.

"Yes, I think the Blackhorse Knights can be trusted with our secrets," Calla said, and then her stomach knotted. "Dad, did my mother really steal the book out of GCHQ?"

He released a heavy sigh and rubbed his jaw, seemingly resigned to answer her question. "Yes, she did, but you didn't hear it from me."

Calla, Jack, and Nash chuckled until their stomachs ached and tears formed in their eyes.

"Well, I suppose we know what to do with Rowe now," Calla said.

"No," Nash replied. "Let him be. From now on, he will be more useful to us than he realizes. He doesn't know we're onto him. Let's keep it that way."

Pergamon Museum, Berlin
Two Days Later

THE COLD AIR bit at their skin, and Nash held Calla close to him, offering her silent comfort. Despite the weight of their actions, they knew they had done the right thing and that kept them moving forward.

Somewhere in the darkness, Mason Laskfell watched their every move. They knew he was still out there, but perhaps that was for the best. They needed to track down the full extent of his operation, and keeping him on the loose was the only way to catch him.

Frau Fuhrman marched up to them, her face gaunt and her long coat draped over her figure. "So, I guess you found Octavia, but not the lost city?" she said slowly, her gaze shifting to Calla. "I never heard from Avo Schneider."

"That was your contact?" Calla raised an eyebrow.

Nash stepped forward. "Frau Fuhrman, I suggest you stick to journalism and leave government business to us."

"Not on your life," she said with a smirk. "The public has a right to know what ISTF is up to."

Calla's lips curved into a hopeful smile. "How about you cover the story of the recovery of dangerous criminal Ivan Schneider and his daughter Avo Schneider, who were involved in money laundering with bankers using manufactured stories around ancient artifacts and cities?"

Nash nodded in agreement. "Ivan was a wanted assassin."

Frau Fuhrman's eyes widened with interest. She stared at the three of them one by one.

"We can grant you an exclusive interview with special agent Raimund Eichel," Jack added with a smirk.

"German Intelligence? That's a big exclusive," she said, smiling. "Thank you," she added and bowed slightly.

"You're welcome," Calla said.

Jack cleared his throat. "I'll arrange your meeting."

"No need," Frau Fuhrman said, turning on her heels and making her way back across the museum galleries with large strides.

The three watched with amusement as she disappeared around a corner.

Jack, Ralf, Nash, Calla, and Octavia descended into the musty, narrow museum vault filled with old scrolls and maps.

Calla's finger glided over the faded paper of an ancient Nazi map as Nash and Jack leaned in to inspect the markings. The thin red thread they were searching for snaked around the edges of a circular crater around Oman.

Nash held each map and scroll before carefully rolling it up, adding it to the ever-growing pile on the long table.

They continued their work even as their eyes grew heavy. By evening, they had collected all the maps and scrolls related to Iram. With precision, they took apart each one beneath a lone lamp, carefully removing any signs that could lead them to the City of Sands with no trace left behind.

Locals referred to it as the "Dark Zone," warning of treacherous sandstorms and shifting quicksand that made navigation nearly impossible.

The Ubar desert crater had become notorious among a select few journalists as the hidden source of a global energy crisis. Not anymore.

No one wanted Rowe to know the truth of what had happened at the crater. He was only told they had found an empty crater near the area. That's what the official ISTF recorded.

GCHQ remained in two minds, something Jack intended to change.

"Jack, Nash? How could we ever have a normal life while operative technologies and artifacts are still at large? We saved the world," she whispered, almost to herself.

"We did," Nash said again. "But at what cost?"

"I don't know," she said, her voice rising louder this time. "We'll always be plagued by guilt. That crater was supposed to be something good."

"I know, but not in the wrong hands," Nash replied, his voice cracking with emotion for the first time. "I just wish there was a way out of this."

"There's no way out of this," she said. "We have to live with it."

"Then we do it together," Nash said. "Always."

In the days that followed, they instructed ISTF to spread the rumor that they had moved the artifacts to other locations. And if questioned, they would shrug and tell the questioner that they just heard it from someone else.

It was a rumor.

It was impossible to know for sure.
It might have happened.
It might not have happened.
Calla looked at the men. "This is it, then."

EPILOGUE

A Week Later
Scorpion Tide Yacht, Off the English Coast

NASH WALKED to the deck of the yacht, where he found Stan sitting in a chair. Stan's penetrating gaze met Nash's.

"Nash, I need your help," Stan said.

Nash took a sip of the amber liquid in his glass. The smoky flavor of the scotch lingered on his tongue as it glided down his throat.

"What can I do for you, Stan?" Nash asked.

"I'm taking over the leadership of the Blackhorse Group," Stan said.

Nash was surprised. The Blackhorse Group was still an international syndicate with a lot of power in cities worldwide. The group had a public leader, but he also knew that the real power lay with those who operated in the shadows.

"I don't understand," Nash said, uncertain.

"Paxton is getting too close to finding out Calla's real weakness. And I don't like it," Stan said.

Nash felt a knot form in his stomach. "This is a shock," he

said quietly.

"Yeah, I'm well aware of that. But this is going to happen, anyway," Stan replied calmly.

Nash took another sip of his scotch. "Well, know that you have the KJ20-Ops behind you. We may have resurrected old wounds, but for the better."

Stan nodded. "Everything I've worked for is for my family, and I want you to know you are safe under my watch."

Nash took a moment to process what he was hearing. "So, does that mean you'll let me know whenever another operative artifact is on the radar that could hurt my wife? Or my kids, if we ever have any?"

"Absolutely. My forefathers formed the Blackhorse Group to protect the operatives and their secrets, made up of historians and explorers funding artifacts and history-related exploration. It's the only defense that can safely work alongside the operatives and help take on Laskfell and what he may throw at us next. There's still so much we don't know in the six hundred years since the Divide. Today we can continue to be a highly secretive undercover organization that only lives in the digital world through whispered rumor."

"Add the new KJ20-Ops to that. Okay," Nash said. "I'm in."

"Good. So, you're taking over?" Stan asked. "That Rodney Cook will not be amused."

"He shouldn't be. Yes, but like you, we will operate below the radar. They may have trained me as an assassin, but..." Nash trailed off.

"That's all I need to know," Stan said with a smile. "I'm so proud of you."

Nash reflected on the fact that his father-in-law was now taking over a powerful organization that had been secretly developing for centuries. With Stan leading the Blackhorse Group, he and Calla might have a chance.

JOIN THE ADVENTURE

SHORT REVIEW

Thank you for joining Calla, Nash, and Jack on this adventure!

As an author, I highly appreciate the feedback I get from my readers. It helps others to make an informed decision before buying.

It only takes a few minutes. If you enjoyed **The Decrypter and the Atlantis of the Sands,** please consider leaving a short review where you bought the book or by going here:

www.rosesandy.com

BE THE FIRST TO KNOW

Be the first to learn about new releases and other news from Rose Sandy, by joining **the e-updates** newsletter. See you there by going here:

https://rosesandy.com/signup/

JOIN THE CONVERSATION

While you are at it, swing by the official Rose Sandy Facebook page (www.facebook.com/rosesandyauthor) to join a community of adventurers, history, and technology enthusiasts.

Finally, if you enjoy pictures of travels, book inspirations, historical mysteries, and science and technology thrills, check out my feed @rosesandyauthor on the Instagram app.

IN THE DECRYPTER SERIES

Book 1: The Decrypter: Secret of The Lost Manuscript
Book 2: The Decrypter and The Mind Hacker
Book 3: The Decrypter - Digital Eyes Only
Book 4: The Decrypter - The Storm's Eye
Book 5: The Decrypter - The Pythagoras Clause
Book 6: The Decrypter and the Beale Ciphers
Book 7: The Decrypter and the Atlantis of the Sands

She's a museum curator, a doubter, and a skeptic. It all changed when the British government asked her to decrypt a code written in an unbreakable script on an ancient manuscript whose origin was as debatable as the origin of life. Then there was the issue of her long-lost parents.

Using her knack for history and technology, she bands with two faithful friends and is thrown into a dangerous journey of cyber espionage investigating the criminal, the unexplained, the scientific, and the downright unthinkable.

More here: https://rosesandy.com/the-decrypter-series/

WHAT READERS ARE SAYING ABOUT THE DECRYPTER SERIES

"Takes you on a ride and refuses to let you off until you reach the very end."

"A brilliant read! I recommend this to anyone who enjoys mystery, suspense, thrillers, or action novels. The detail is astounding! The historic references, location descriptions, references to technology, cryptography…. this author really knows her stuff."

"An action-packed adventure, technothriller across several continents like a Jason Bourne or James Bond movie, but with an actual storyline!"

"Brilliantly written. I loved the very descriptive side, which was a good way of visualizing and getting to terms with each new place, as the action takes place in several different countries."

"The description is so rich, so immensely detailed that it just draws you in completely to its world."

"There is great tension and chemistry between the two main characters, Calla and Nash, that has you begging for more."

"The historical references, location descriptions, references to technology, cryptography…. this author really knows her stuff."

There is great tension and chemistry between the two main characters, Calla and Nash, that has you begging for more."

IN THE SHADOW FILES THRILLERS

A CROSSFIRE BETWEEN TECHNOLOGY, SCIENCE, AND INTERNATIONAL CORPORATE ESPIONAGE

Book 1: Breaking the Code
Book 2: The Kohinoor Conspiracy

A series about intelligent women caught in the crossfire between technology, science, politics, international espionage, and the men who drag them there.

Guaranteed action adventure in each book, you'll fill the need for thrills, and savor satisfying cliffhangers as you follow a secret organization, **The Shadow Files,** and two of its former agents around the globe.

Sworn enemies, one is on a mission to safeguard the globe from economic corruption, and one swears he'll protect the victims.

Each book can be read as a stand-alone story. More here: https://rosesandy.com/the-shadow-files-series-2/

ABOUT THE AUTHOR

Rose Sandy never set out to be a writer. She set out to be a communicator with whatever landed in her hands, but soon the keyboard became her best friend. Rose writes suspense and intelligence thrillers where technology and espionage meet history in pulse-racing action adventure. She dips into the mysteries of our world, the fascination of technology breakthroughs, the secrets of history and global intelligence to deliver thrillers that weave suspense, conspiracy and a dash of romantic thrill.

A globe trotter, her thrillers span cities and continents. Rose's writing approach is to hit hard with a good dose of tension and humor. Her characters zip in and out of intelligence and government agencies, dodge enemies in world heritage sites, navigate technology markets and always land in deep trouble.

When not tapping away on a smartphone writing app, Rose is usually found in the British Library scrutinizing the Magna Carta, trolling Churchill's War Rooms or sampling a new gadget. Most times she's in deep conversations with ex-military and secret service intelligence officers, Foreign Service staff or engrossed in a TED talk with a box of popcorn. Hm... she might just learn something that'll be useful.

For more books and updates.

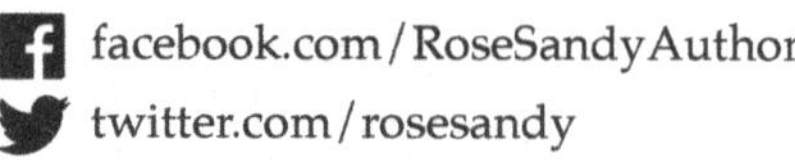

www.ingramcontent.com/pod-product-compliance
Lightning Source LLC
Chambersburg PA
CBHW011027190726
48290CB00011B/2742